New Year's Resolution:

FAMILY

ABOUT THE AUTHORS

Award-winning author **Anne McAllister** says she never makes New Year's resolutions. Promising something for a whole year seems to her to be asking for trouble. In "Never Say Never," her story for this collection, she thought Holt and Lucy would benefit from learning this bit of wisdom. She hopes, too, that they have learned what she already knows—that families, even when they're exasperatingly nosy and relentlessly helpful—are really pretty great.

Barbara Bretton spends her days sunning on Caribbean beaches and her nights dancing with Liam, Mel and Sean. Her good twin stays home in New Jersey and writes books! And Barbara has written many. With over eight million copies of her books in print worldwide, she enjoys a warm place in the hearts of romance readers everywhere. After thirty contemporary and historical novels, this bestselling author is listed in the prestigious *Foremost Women in the Twentieth Century*.

A writer since childhood, **Leandra Logan** was thrilled to sell her first young adult novel in 1986. Since that time she has written many books for both teenage and adult audiences. She is recognized as a bestselling author, her books frequently making the B. Dalton and Waldenbooks lists, and she has been nominated for numerous industry awards. A lifelong resident of Minnesota, she lives in the St. Paul area with her husband, Gene, and teenage children, Cindy and Tom.

New Year's Resolution:

FAMILY

Anne McAllister
Barbara Bretton
Leandra Logan

Harlequin Books

TORONTO • NEW YORK • LONDON
AMSTERDAM • PARIS • SYDNEY • HAMBURG
STOCKHOLM • ATHENS • TOKYO • MILAN
MADRID • WARSAW • BUDAPEST • AUCKLAND

HARLEQUIN BOOKS
225 Duncan Mill Road, Don Mills,
Ontario, Canada M3B 3K9

ISBN 0-373-83332-6

NEW YEAR'S RESOLUTION: FAMILY

The publisher acknowledges the copyright holders
of the individual works as follows:

NEVER SAY NEVER
Copyright © 1998 by Barbara Schenck
3,2,1...BABY!
Copyright © 1998 by Barbara Bretton
MOTHER FIGURE
Copyright © 1998 by Mary Schultz

Printed in U.S.A.

CONTENTS

Anne McAllister

NEVER SAY NEVER

CHAPTER ONE

"BAH—*AH-AH-AH-CHOO*—humbug!"

Holt Braxton flicked off the radio before the announcer even finished giving the weather report he didn't need, and scowled out the window of his tenth-floor apartment at the snow swirling past.

Swell. Just what he needed. A white Christmas.

He glanced at his watch, tapped his foot on the parquet floor, and drummed his fingers on the window ledge. Below him the traffic was already beginning to snarl on Central Park West.

It was three days before Christmas and everyone in New York City—Holt excepted—was determined to go home for the holidays. Holt *was* home for the holidays; but if he weren't, he wouldn't be going.

He liked holidays all right; no one called and bothered him so he could get more work done. It was home that was highly overrated.

It was a damn shame that his secretary, Lucy, didn't feel the same way.

Lucy had said she was leaving the office an hour ago. She'd promised to stop by on her way out of town en route to Vermont. He gritted his teeth now at the memory of her cheerful words.

How the hell long did it take to get from the mid-

Fifties on the East Side to the lower Seventies on the West Side, anyway?

Too long.

Holt's fingers kept drumming on the window ledge until he felt another sneeze coming on. Then he groped for a tissue and muttered to himself as he blew his nose. He'd had the cold for almost a week. It should have been over by now. He could be patient with these things just so long.

Maybe he could coerce Lucy into making a little of that homemade chicken soup she'd put together the last time he was sick.

So what if it was outside the normal scope of secretarial duties? Lucy wasn't your average, run-of-the-mill secretary. Not a late-twentieth-century one, anyway.

Lucy made coffee without complaining that it wasn't in her job description. She sewed on buttons and got gravy stains out of his ties. She remembered his nieces' birthdays and kept track of his mother's whereabouts *besides* being able to do typical secretarial things, like typing one hundred words a minute and taking shorthand faster than he could think. She was better than a computer. She not only corrected his spelling and cleaned up his grammar, but also wrote polite conciliatory little notes on his behalf to all the people he managed to offend on a day-to-day basis.

And she made the world's best chicken soup.

Not that he'd ever told her so. Gravy stains and buttons and conciliatory notes were one thing. Chicken soup fell way outside even *his* definition of a secretary. It was, well...more the sort of thing a wife would do.

Holt didn't want Lucy thinking about becoming his wife.

He didn't want *any* woman thinking about becoming his wife!

Holt Braxton was a confirmed, determined bachelor. When he was twenty-one years old, he'd made a resolution never to marry. He was thirty-four now, and he'd never found a single reason to change his mind.

But he wouldn't mind a bowl of Lucy's chicken soup.

The last time he'd been sick, she'd come to his apartment with some papers for him to sign, and while she was there, he'd sneezed and coughed and complained about the lack of remedies for the common cold.

"My grandmother makes chicken soup," Lucy had said matter-of-factly. "It always works."

"Chicken soup?"

The way he'd said it would have challenged any woman. And Lucy was never one to back away from a challenge. She'd told him to get out of the kitchen and she would prove it.

"Go for it," he remembered saying derisively,

and he'd gone back into the living room. There he looked over the contracts, while in the kitchen Lucy diced and chopped. While she took dictation for a dozen letters, the chicken stewed in a pot. While he signed the letters and scanned the mail, she boned the chicken, added the vegetables and seasonings, and put it back on the stove.

Then she'd gathered up the contracts, the letters, the mail he'd wanted answered at once, and had headed for the door.

"Let it simmer another four or five hours. Then eat it. You'll feel better," she'd promised. Then, giving him one of her bright smiles, she'd left.

Holt had intended to let her chicken soup simmer right down to the bottom of the pot. He didn't need any woman fussing over him, he'd thought indignantly.

But then, Lucy wasn't fussing. She was gone.

And throughout the day the smell from the kitchen had penetrated the stuffiness in his head. It made his mouth water. He chewed a cough drop. It made his stomach growl.

By evening, he was weak with hunger. He went out to the kitchen and dished up a bowlful. Just so he could tell her it didn't work when she nagged at him about eating it, he assured himself.

He forgot that Lucy never nagged.

The soup was passable, he'd thought, taking one

sip, then another. He would finish the bowl. That would make her happy.

He finished one, then another.

Lucy never knew. She never asked.

She seemed to take it for granted that her remedy had worked. And he'd never had to admit that before he went to bed that night he'd finished off the pot.

He still hadn't told her.

He thought he might—as a Christmas present—*if* she ever got here!

His fingers tapped a staccato beat on the window ledge again. He craned his neck and studied the ever-increasing traffic snarl. He sighed at the sight of the snow-white blanket accumulating in the park below.

The buzzer blared.

In three strides he was across the room. "Send her up," he barked into the intercom.

When his doorbell rang a few moments later he jerked the door open. His jaw dropped. "Roz?"

A ravishing blonde stood there beaming at him. "Surprise!"

It was that, all right.

Expecting efficient, bustling little Lucy, Holt was astonished to find tall, blond, decorative-but-definitely-not-efficient Rosalind Keating batting her eyelashes in the doorway.

It was like going to the coop for a hen and finding a peacock in its place.

"What in hell are you doing here?" he demanded as she sashayed past him into the room. "The doorman didn't say you were—"

"You didn't give him a chance." Roz, the daughter of Holt's closest business associate, twirled around and beamed at him. "You just said, 'Send her up!' I thought you knew." Her beaming smile segued into a first-rate pout. "I thought you saw me coming."

"From ten stories up?" Never mind that he'd been trying to see Lucy. He raked a hand through his hair.

The last person he wanted in his apartment right now was Rosalind Keating. She was one of those women who already had plenty of ideas about his need for a wife. As Den Keating's only child and, therefore, the light of his life, Roz had recently been trying to become a fixture in Holt's life.

She was more than passably pretty and knew it. She would look good on any man's arm. And she had made it perfectly plain that she was willing to serve as his hostess whenever and wherever he chose. That, at least, she could do. Having grown up at Den's knee, she knew how to work a room.

But she also knew how to insinuate herself into Holt's life.

He had always done his best to keep a proper distance from her. When he took her to a play or a film, he always declined the invitation to coffee in her apartment afterward. The one time he'd found himself boxed into a corner and forced to ask her to be hostess, he certainly hadn't presumed that it meant she should spend the night.

And the one time she *had* spent the night—because she'd had a bit too much to drink and had fallen asleep before he could take her home—he'd slept on the sofa like a perfect gentleman, and had made sure Den knew it the next day. He hadn't taken advantage of her sleepwalking tendencies, either.

Now his eyes widened as she set down a suitcase beside the sofa. "What are you doing?"

"Why, coming to stay with you." She batted her lashes.

"What?"

"Daddy's not home. He's flown off to Paris. There's a meeting he can't miss, he says." Her pout was world-class now. "So there won't be anyone home for the holiday. There's nothing for me to do there anyway," she added. "And Daddy doesn't like me driving in the snow. So I thought—" and now the pout vanished and her eyes began to sparkle "—I'll just stay here. There's so much to do in the city!"

The way she was looking at him made Holt feel pretty sure she didn't mean plays and films and concerts.

Like a deer caught in a hunter's sights, he stared

at her. His face, he hoped, looked blank. His mind was whirling a million miles an hour.

Both he—and Roz—knew that Den Keating was a stickler for propriety. He liked to call himself a nineties man. But Holt knew his business associate was more 1890s than 1990s. He looked askance at unmarried couples who lived together, who even traveled together. And the minute Den learned that his daughter had spent a week—*a week!*—unchaperoned with Holt in his apartment, he would be demanding their marriage.

And the minute Holt declined, he would be kissing his business with Den goodbye. Damn.

He sneezed.

"Oh, poor dear!" Roz was all fluttery concern. "Are you sick? You should be in bed. Here, let me help you." She backed him toward the door of his bedroom at the same time that she started to attack the buttons on his shirt.

"I'm fine. Really. I just—"

The buzzer sounded again. *Thank God.*

He pushed past Roz. "Is it Lucy?" he demanded into the intercom this time. Then, "Send her right up."

Roz frowned. "Lucy? Your secretary? What's Lucy coming here for?" Roz was sounding irritable now. Holt could feel her breathing down his neck as he fumbled to rebutton his shirt. He yanked open the front door.

"It's about time," he said, grabbing Lucy's arm and hauling her in.

Lucy's eyes, practically the only part of her face visible between her bright blue hat and scarf, widened. "It's a mess down there in case you haven't noticed." She had a suitcase in one hand and a manila envelope in the other, which she handed to Holt.

He tossed it on the table, caught a glimpse of Roz's hungry stare and did the only thing that occurred to him. He pulled Lucy into his arms and kissed her hard!

If he'd thought Lucy's eyes were wide a moment before, it was nothing compared to the way they looked now!

She went stiff, then stunned, in his arms. In the brief instant he bothered to consider the kiss himself, he thought it was pretty stunning, too.

Then he heard Roz's exclamation. "Holt!"

He broke the kiss and stared down into Lucy's astonished face.

"What are you—?" she began.

"Waiting for?" he finished before she could. "You. It's about time. I'll just grab my bag. Come on—" he took her hand and hauled her with him when he saw she was about to speak again "—you can help me."

He towed her into his bedroom and shut the door as Roz exclaimed, "Holt!" once again.

"What on earth!" Lucy stood, her back to the door, gaping at him.

Holt didn't even glance at her. He went to his closet and jerked it open, pulled out a suitcase and flung it on the bed. "Where are we going?"

Lucy gaped at him. "*I* am going to Vermont," she said. "You're—"

"Coming with you."

It was—the more Holt thought about it—the solution to all his problems. He could avoid spending the week with Roz, and thus avoid the marriage trap and preserve his good standing with Den. Plus he wouldn't be here in case his older sister made her annual swoop through the city. He had no use for Tamara. She rarely had any for him. This would just make avoiding her that much easier so neither of them had to pretend to a hypocritical display of sibling affection.

And if he went with Lucy, they could get the work done he needed her help to do. He hadn't wanted her to leave. She'd insisted she had to be home for Christmas.

So, fine, he would go, too.

"Jeans?" he asked her, yanking open a drawer to his dresser. "Do I need jeans? What about a suit?"

"A shrink, I should think," Lucy said tartly, astonishment giving way to annoyance. "You're certifiable, you know that? You're *not* coming with me!"

"Oh, but I am, sweet Lucy," Holt said. He tossed undershirts and shorts in on top of the jeans, added a sweater and a couple of shirts. "That ought to do it."

"Nothing will do it! You're not coming. Nothing you can say will make me take you!" She looked frantic. Not like the usual unflappable Lucy Potter at all.

Holt smiled serenely. "No?"

"No."

"I always thought you liked your job."

You could have heard a snowflake fall in Central Park. You actually could hear Roz pacing on the wall-to-wall carpet in the hall next door.

Lucy stared at him with those huge brown eyes.

Holt stared back implacably. He hadn't got to be the corporate wheeler-dealer he was by backing down. He never bluffed. Or if he did, no one ever knew it.

The panic seemed to flicker in Lucy's eyes. Then slowly it faded and her expression grew curiously blank. Was there another emotion there?

Holt wasn't sure.

He didn't care because he got what he wanted when she gave a small, grudging nod of her head. He smiled, satisfied. He clicked the suitcase shut.

"Right. Come along, now. And smile. You're supposed to be enjoying this." He took Lucy's arm and steered her back into the living room where Roz was still pacing. She looked at him, confused and accusing.

"You're welcome to stay in the apartment, of course," he said, steering Lucy toward the door. He grabbed the contracts from the table, stuffed them in the outside pocket of his briefcase, then shrugged into his jacket. "But I'm afraid I won't be here."

Roz stared. "But I thought—"

Holt shook his head regretfully. "I'm going home for Christmas."

"With your secretary?" Roz's expression wavered been outrage and disbelief.

Holt gave her a bland smile. "With my fiancée," he said.

"YOUR *FIANCÉE?* How dare you?" Lucy was fuming as the elevator door shut. She had to fume. If she didn't, she would faint.

What did he mean, commandeering her, steering her out the door and down the hall like he owned her? And that kiss!

She wouldn't even let herself think about that kiss!

She glared at her boss indignantly in an effort to make him uncomfortable. As usual, she had no success.

In the eleven months Lucy had worked for corporate wheeler-dealer Holt Braxton, she had never managed to disconcert him once. She had, in fact, never seen anything disconcert him at all—until today.

Ordinarily Holt was aplomb personified. She remembered once telling her grandmother that he was impervious to shock, that nothing ever rattled him. It was like having Gibraltar for a boss, she'd said.

And so she had thought—until a few minutes ago.

Then, for just an instant, faced with Roz and her suitcase, Lucy had seen him rattled. And then he'd grabbed her. And kissed her.

And lied!

And now, wouldn't you know, all his unease was over. He was leaning against the elevator wall, riffling through the contracts in his hand, completely unconcerned by the kiss and by the flagrant lie he'd told.

"Why would you tell her such a thing?" Lucy demanded.

He glanced up finally, then shrugged. "I had to say something," he said patiently. "What should I have said? That I was going home with my secretary so we could work over the holiday? You think she'd believe that?"

"Of course not," Lucy muttered. "No one ever believes the truth."

A grin slashed across Holt's face.

She wished it hadn't. She hated seeing Holt Braxton's grin. It was so disarming. So wicked and so tantalizing at the same time.

Holt Braxton should come with a warning tattooed on his forehead that read: THIS MAN IS DANGEROUS TO YOUR EMOTIONAL HEALTH.

Lucy, fortunately, was under no illusions about that. She knew all about disarming masculine grins. She was A Woman Of Experience. Bad experience.

"You're not coming home with me," Lucy insisted, looking down at the suitcase by his feet.

Holt didn't reply. He went on reading the contracts, scribbling in the margins, running his tongue over his lips, muttering to himself.

Lucy wanted to kick him. "Listen to me. You're not coming. You don't even have to come down with me! Didn't you hear her? Your Ms. Keating said she would go to stay with another friend since you weren't going to be there. You'd be safe—" her mouth twisted on the word; it was hard to believe Holt ever thought himself vulnerable to anything, even a predatory female "—if you went back now."

"She is not *my* Ms. Keating, which is the reason I said what I did. But besides that," he went on in his damnably logical tone, still not looking up, "going with you is a perfect solution."

"To what?"

"To everything," he said simply. "To Roz, of course. But not just to Roz. To getting this work done. You know you were leaving me in the lurch."

He gave her an accusing look. "These Dynabot contracts are far from finished."

Of course she knew that. He'd been alternately ranting about, then haggling with Davis Russell, the Dynabot CEO, for days. But that didn't mean she had to stay and work over Christmas just because they hadn't come to their senses until seven o'clock last night.

"I have a right to holidays," she reminded him.

A sardonic brow lifted. "Surely even you can't celebrate all the time."

Even you... Like she was some party animal.

Hardly. And surely he knew she wasn't. After all, he'd made a point of telling her when he hired her that he was a no-nonsense boss, that he believed in business first, last and always.

"So do I," she'd assured him fervently. She had put the rest of her life behind her when she'd left Boone's Corner, Vermont, the week before, and she had been quite willing to fling herself wholeheartedly into Braxton Enterprises. It was dependable. It was predictable. It didn't raise her hopes and give her false expectations the way Timothy had.

Dr. Timothy Neal was the reason she'd left Boone's Corner in the first place. If Timothy hadn't discovered that he loved Whitney Fields, Lucy would be Mrs. Timothy Neal now, and she would still be living near Boone's Corner and working as the secretary/receptionist/medical-records-transcriptionist in her husband's office.

Instead she was living in a studio apartment in New York City and working sixty hours a week for Holt Braxton. She hadn't been back to Boone's Corner since she'd left in January.

And she was only going now because she couldn't stay away. She missed her family too much.

Though her own parents had died when she was three, her father's parents had stepped right in, taking Lucy and her sisters, Augusta and Chloe, to live with them at their Vermont dairy farm. There they had created such a loving environment that Lucy, despite having lost her parents, had always considered herself blessed.

Life at the Potter farm in particular and in Boone's Corner in general was everything any of the girls had ever wanted. In fact when Augie had married Jake, an agricultural engineer, eleven years ago, they had only moved to the next farm over; and besides working for the university extension, Jake had helped Grandpa with the dairy farm. Their three kids were in and out of the Potters' house as if it were their own. And they would be there now because Jake had taken Augie with him to Korea on an assignment.

Chloe, a nurse, worked ten miles away at the hospital in the next town and still lived at home. Her fiancé was staying there, too, at the moment, while they built a house in town.

The farmhouse was crowded, noisy, bustling, full of life. Full of family. Exactly the way her grandparents liked it. Family was their great joy in life.

It had always been Lucy's, too. She had hated to leave, but she knew she couldn't live every day in Boone's Corner with Whitney living the life she'd planned as her own. And so she'd gone to New York.

But she couldn't stay away for the holidays. She'd always loved holidays and family and home. There was no place else on earth she would rather be. Besides, if she didn't come home to spend Christmas with everyone else, they would think it was because she hadn't got over Timothy.

She *had* got over Timothy. Lucy was sure of it.

"I'm glad," her grandmother had said cheerfully when Lucy had called at Thanksgiving. "I'll line up some new men."

That was something Lucy hadn't considered. "I don't want any new men," she'd protested.

"Oh, dear." Her grandmother's tone said that it was obvious Lucy hadn't got over Tim at all.

"I don't need help finding a man, Gram."

But Grandma was not dissuaded. Over the next three weeks she had come up with no less than five potential suitors for Lucy.

"The new vet in Gaithersburg," she said, ticking

them off. "And Brent, that nice young plumber. And Rose Ellen's cousin, John Patrick from Boston, is coming for Christmas. And Lew Cline. Remember him? He was a friend of Frances Neillands's. And Ernie's nephew, Hank. Not bad, eh?" Lucy could envision her grandmother rubbing her hands together.

"It's not necessary," Lucy had said again. And again.

But it hadn't helped until she'd told that one little white lie that had made her grandmother stop. The lie she wasn't going to think about. The lie that made it absolutely imperative that she get rid of Holt.

"My train leaves in half an hour," she said to Holt now as the elevator doors opened and she rushed out through the walnut-paneled entry, past the doorman and the gold-plated wall sconces.

"I'll drive you."

"It'll be faster to take the subway."

"Not all the way to Vermont."

She stopped dead and stared at him.

"I don't want to ride a train to Vermont," he said patiently.

"I wasn't taking the train to Vermont! I was taking it to Boston. I was getting a bus to Vermont." It took hours and hours. Even more than usual at holiday time, but it was the only option. "And you're not coming with me!"

He wasn't. *He couldn't!*

"I am," he said implacably, taking her arm. "And we're driving."

HE COULD HAVE STAYED in his apartment. His kissing Lucy and calling her his fiancée had, in fact, routed Roz, sending her and her suitcase and her marital aspirations off to someone else's apartment with soulful eyes and recriminating stares.

So the question was: Why hadn't he stayed?

Holt pondered the question as they sat stalled in traffic on the Triborough Bridge. It wasn't as if he really wanted to spend Christmas in Vermont, God knew.

The very thought was schmaltzy. There would be pine trees and snow-covered fields and little New England clapboard houses with snowmen in front of them. The next thing you knew, Danny Kaye and Bing Crosby would dance past, singing "White Christmas." Not his cup of tea at all.

Then why?

The traffic inched forward.

He flexed his hands on the steering wheel.

Why? He could hear the unspoken question from the woman sitting next to him in the passenger seat. She was staring straight ahead, her hands folded in her lap, her hair neatly anchored at the nape of her neck, like she was someone's very proper secretary or maiden aunt.

She *was* someone's proper secretary—*his* proper secretary. And he imagined she was probably someone else's maiden aunt. He'd seen pictures of children on her desk, but he'd never inquired who they were. He didn't care.

She was his secretary. That was all.

But she sure as hell hadn't kissed like a secretary! At least, no secretary Holt had ever kissed. Not that he made a habit of kissing secretaries.

She had kissed like a woman who enjoyed it, who reveled in it, who would do it again—and more—if given half a chance.

Was that what he was doing? Giving her half a chance?

Of course not. He was coming along because he wanted to get these contracts finished, because he had a meeting with Davis Russell in Dallas the day after Christmas and working with Lucy to get the contracts in shape now was the sensible thing to do, because—he sneezed—maybe he could still talk her into making some more chicken soup.

Or maybe, he thought as the traffic moved forward another ten feet, he could get her to kiss him once more—and make him better.

SHE COULD GET RID of him.

She was sure she could get rid of him. She *had* to get rid of him. That was all there was to it. There was no way she could turn up at her grandparents' house with Holt Braxton in tow.

She glanced at the man in the driver's seat now—the man who for the past five hours had been threading his way through snarled city traffic, jammed bridge traffic, and congested interstate traffic with the same steady relentlessness she saw every day.

The traffic was thinning now, though the increasingly heavy snowfall still made things difficult, but Holt drove on. And she knew, because she knew her boss, that he would keep driving all the way to Boone's Corner unless she did something to stop him.

"What were you planning for the holidays?" she asked. It was the first thing she'd said in three hours and seemed to startle him.

He blinked, hesitated a moment, then said, "Nothing."

"Nothing?" She looked at him closely, surprised. She knew that the main focus of his life was his work. But even workaholics took Christmas off. Didn't they?

"What about your family?" In the six months she had worked for him, Holt Braxton had never mentioned a family. He was a very private man, of course. But even private men had relatives.

"What about them?"

"Won't they...be expecting you?"

"No."

"No?"

"*N-o.* Which letter didn't you understand, Ms. Potter?" he asked acidly.

Lucy hunched her shoulders inside her parka. "Sorry. It's none of my business."

"No, it isn't." His tone was gruff, brooking no argument.

"But as your fiancée..." she dared to venture because she was desperate.

He gave her a sharp glance, then his jaw tightened. "My father's in California. My mother's in Switzerland. They've been divorced for years. My sister is descending on the city after Christmas, but she only wants to use the apartment. She doesn't give a damn if I'm in it. In fact, she'd prefer that I wasn't. We are not the Cleavers. We never had a happy holiday the whole time I was growing up, and as soon as I could stop being a part of them, I did. Satisfied?"

Lucy had to consciously close her mouth. "Um," she said faintly. She ventured a quick look at his hard face. "I'm sorry."

"I'm not. It's a pile of crap, all this holiday nonsense! Family feeling, good tidings, peace to all. Ha. Christmas is a battleground more often than not! An occasion to fight, to feel slighted. It makes good business sense if you're in retail, but that's all!"

Lucy blew out a breath. "Well," she said mildly, "at least you're not indifferent."

He blinked, clearly startled. Then that wicked grin slashed across his face once more and he laughed. A hard laugh, more bitter than mirthful. And then he said quite grimly, "You're right, there, Lucy Potter. Indifferent I'm not."

"Well, you won't like my family, then. They love Christmas."

"I won't be bothering your family, and they won't be bothering me. I'll drop you off, then find a hotel and—"

"Boone's Corner doesn't have a hotel."

"A motel, then."

"Or a motel."

"People sleep in the streets, do they?"

"Street," Lucy corrected. "There is only one. Main one, that is. We, um, don't get a lot of tourists. There's an inn in Gaithersburg, of course, about ten miles away."

"No bed-and-breakfasts? I thought Vermont had bed-and-breakfasts around every bend."

"There's, um, one." But she didn't want him staying there. Her grandmother was far too friendly with the nuns who ran it, Sister Ernestine and Sister Bertha. "I don't think they're open over the holiday."

"I'm sure I can convince them."

Lucy was sure he could, too. Holt could charm

birds out of trees. He could probably charm the habits off nuns. Getting them to give him a room would be child's play. She didn't say so.

"We'll check," Holt said.

No, they wouldn't. She was going to ditch Holt before they got anywhere near Boone's Corner.

When they stopped for a meal near the Vermont border, Lucy called her grandmother. "Tell Grandpa not to meet the bus."

"You're not coming?" Grandma sounded crushed.

"Of course, I'm coming. I just didn't take the bus. I...got a ride."

"A ride? With who?"

"A...friend. He...*I'll*—" Lucy corrected herself "—be dropped off. Later. Don't wait up."

"Of course I'll wait up."

"We'll be very late," Lucy said hastily. "You should just go to sleep and get some rest. You know you're going to have a houseful of people."

"I already have a houseful of people," her grandmother said tartly. "And I won't rest until you're one of them. I'll be waiting."

Lucy knew it was pointless to argue. All she could hope was that her grandmother fell asleep before Holt dropped her off.

It was almost three in the morning when they reached Boone's Corner.

"It's there." She pointed to the farmhouse on top

of the hill. "The drive is just beyond that tree. I'll walk up. No sense trying to drive. The car would get stuck." And Grandma would doubtless be awakened.

"If it hasn't got stuck before, it won't get stuck now," Holt said grimly.

"But—"

But Holt turned in at the unplowed drive and churned up the hill. "I said I would bring you home. I'm not leaving you in the middle of a deserted road."

Lucy gritted her teeth. *Please, God, let them be asleep,* she prayed.

The answer was no.

The door flew open as they drove up, and her grandparents came out onto the porch.

"Stop here! You can turn around and—"

Wasted breath. Holt didn't stop until the car was next to the house. "Door-to-door delivery, Ms. Potter," he drawled. "Never let it be said that I don't take good care of my secretary."

Lucy gave him a tight smile as she started to open the door. "Thank you. I won't keep you."

Her grandfather seized the door handle and pulled it the rest of the way open. "Ah, Lucy!" He hauled her out, gave her a bone-crushing hug, then passed her on to her grandmother who did the same.

"I'm so glad you made it!" Her grandmother squeezed her and gave her a smacking kiss. "This terrible snow. I wanted to tell you to wait. But I wanted to see you so badly! You have to tell me all about him. I wish you could have brought him. Who *did* you bring?'' She tried to peer past Lucy into the interior of the car.

Lucy stood in her way. "Just click the trunk latch and I'll get my suitcase," she said to Holt. "You don't have to get out."

But he already was. He lifted out her suitcase; she practically snatched it out of his grasp. "Thank you very much. I appreciate the ride. I—"

"I'm Tom Potter." Lucy's grandfather came around and stuck out his hand to shake Holt's. "I want to thank you for bringing our Lucy."

Holt smiled. "No problem. I need to keep her close. She and I—"

"Are really tired," Lucy cut in desperately. "We've had a long drive and he needs to get back to Gaithersburg."

"You're from Gaithersburg?" Her grandmother came down the steps to peer at Holt more closely. "I'm Dorothy, by the way." She, too, shook Holt's hand. "Who's your family?"

"No family," Holt said. "I'm just staying there."

Lucy's grandparents looked at each other, then at Holt. "No family?" Dorothy said, dismayed.

"No family?" Tom echoed. "What'd you say your name was, son?" he asked, as if knowing it would help him conjure up some relatives.

Oh, God, thought Lucy.

"I'm Holt Braxton, Lucy's—"

"Fiancé!" Dorothy finished for him, her face breaking into a delighted smile.

Lucy shut her eyes. But not before she saw her grandmother haul Holt into her arms and give him an official welcome-to-the-Potter-family hug.

CHAPTER TWO

"I CAN EXPLAIN," LUCY said under her breath as her grandparents hustled them into the house.

There was no sending him off to Gaithersburg now, and Lucy knew it. Grandpa took Holt's suitcase as well as Lucy's, while Grandma herself dragged Holt into the living room.

Stay somewhere else? They were horrified.

How could Holt think such a thing? How could Lucy have agreed to it? No fiancé of any granddaughter of theirs was going to stay in some impersonal inn over the holidays or any other time, for that matter! What kind of a family would Holt think Lucy came from?

A crazy one, Lucy answered silently. She shot a glance at Holt as her grandfather poured him a shot of whiskey and thrust it into his hands. "I see you have a bit of a cold. Best thing for a cold," he said.

At the same time her grandmother tugged Holt's jacket from his shoulders. "Got to warm you up, my dear." She gave her granddaughter a disapproving look. "For goodness' sake, Lucy, you shouldn't have let your man drive all this way, sick as he is."

He's not my man, Lucy wanted to protest at the top of her lungs. But she couldn't.

Because as far as her grandparents knew, he was.

So much for little white lies that didn't hurt anyone.

Holt, God bless him, hadn't said a word.

He looked poleaxed. He stood by the fireplace, whiskey glass in hand, his face pale, his eyes wary, while her grandfather put another log on the fire and her grandmother fussed over him.

"You must be starved after that long drive. I'll make sandwiches. Roast beef with horseradish. I make my own," Grandma said. She started toward the kitchen. "Or I can make pancakes if you'd prefer. Or waffles. And I do have some leftover chicken soup."

"Soup," Holt said, as if he were grabbing a lifeline. "I'll have soup."

It was the first thing he'd said since he'd told them his name, and he sounded more frantic than she'd ever heard him. His gaze kept darting around as if he wasn't sure where the attack was going to come from next.

Neither was Lucy. Except she had a sneaking suspicion it might come from him.

Grandma beamed. "Soup, it is. Come along, Holt. You don't mind my calling you Holt, do you? I know we just met, but if you're going to marry our Lucy—"

"Grandma!"

Grandma scowled at her. "I can't be calling my

grandson-in-law-to-be Mr. Braxton, now can I?"
She took Holt by the arm and steered him toward
the kitchen. "Thomas, you take Holt's bag up. He
can share the chicken room, I think. With Eldon."

Holt's eyes widened. Lucy could almost see his
mind computing that. Chicken room? Eldon?

"I can explain," she mouthed again.

"Wish we had more room," Grandma was saying. "But the family gets bigger and the house never
seems to. I hope you won't mind crowded. But it's
all family. We're so happy you're going to be a part
of it." And with that, Grandma switched back to her
new favorite topic. "It was a surprise, of course,
hearing you'd got engaged. But I must say we're
thrilled. We were so worried about her, you see."

"Grandma!"

"Worried?" Holt prompted, ignoring Lucy's protest the same way her grandmother had.

"It was such a shock," Grandma went on. "Timothy taking up with that Fields girl that way." She
made a tsking sound and shook her head in dismay.

"Timothy?" Holt's eyebrows hiked up. He
looked over his shoulder at Lucy. She glared at him.
She could explain about Eldon and the chicken
room. She didn't want to explain about Tim.

"Hasn't she told you about Timothy?" At Holt's
negative response, Grandma gave Lucy a disap-
pointed look. "You weren't intending to keep it a
secret, were you, dear?"

"No, but—"

"He and Lucy had been a couple for so long," Grandma said, apparently having decided that Lucy's protest was pretty feeble. She led Holt through the kitchen door, confiding, "We were afraid she'd pine."

Holt's brows went even higher. "Lucy? Pine?"

Lucy gritted her teeth. "I think perhaps Holt should just go to bed, Gram," she suggested. "He's feverish. He needs rest."

"And so he will get it...after he gets a bowl of my chicken soup." Grandma was rummaging in the refrigerator as she spoke. "Sit down, Holt."

Holt pulled out one of the old oak straight-backed chairs and sat. It wasn't the sort of casual-yet-controlled posture Lucy usually saw him take. Now he sat on the edge of his seat, like a tiger waiting to pounce.

Lucy watched him warily, wondering when he would spring—on her.

Grandma put the soup in a pot and set it on the stove. "I'm so glad you found the time to come. We were hoping you would, but Lucy said you were too busy. That you had to go to Dallas."

"I do have to go the day after Christmas."

"But in the meantime, you can be here. I'm glad you realize it's important. I was afraid you might not. But I should have realized that Lucy would never pick a man who was too busy to spend his holidays with family. Of course, I suppose you could be spending them with *your* family,'' she reflected as she stirred the soup.

"No," Holt said firmly. Then, after a beat during which Grandma looked at him in astonishment, he added hastily, "I'd much rather be here. I need Lucy," he said with a fervency that only Lucy seemed to hear the irony in.

Her grandmother beamed at him.

Lucy's cheeks burned. "He doesn't mean it that way," she said hastily.

But Grandma thought he did. "I don't mind knowing that he's feeling territorial. He wouldn't want you here when he wasn't, would you, Holt?"

Holt considered that. "Definitely not," he drawled. The way he looked at her made her feel like she was a rabbit caught in headlights.

Lucy gave him a weak smile.

He patted the chair next to him. "Come and sit down and have some soup with me."

"Thank you, but I'm not hungry."

"Keep your man company, Lucy," Grandma said. "He's just said he needs you."

"Only to work," Lucy said.

"Not so," Holt retorted. He seemed to be enjoying himself, damn it. "Lucy keeps my whole life in order. She sews on my buttons, makes my appointments, types my letters, and incidentally makes wonderful chicken soup, too." Holt smiled at her grandmother. Then he held out a hand to Lucy once more and looked at her expectantly.

Lucy knew he would hold it there until hell froze over—or until she sat beside him.

She sat down. He took her hand in his. She tried to pull away. He held her fast and smiled at her. She thought his teeth looked like fangs.

Her grandmother beamed. "Ah, young love."

Lucy groaned.

HE WAS DRIVING HER NUTS.

All the time he sat in the kitchen and ate his stupid bowl of chicken soup, she waited for the other shoe to drop. Waited for him to announce that he was *not* her fiancé, that she'd made up the whole thing.

He never did.

He held her hand. And watched her from beneath those ridiculously long dark eyelashes of his. And answered her grandmother's questions about his cold and his cough, and let her give him some sort of herbal concoction that her friend Annabel MacKenzie had made last winter that helped clear her head. And he never said Lucy had lied at all.

Not even after he'd eaten two bowls of the soup and drunk the herbal tea and swallowed some other home remedy Grandma had pressed on him and then said, "You'll be right as rain in the morning. You just need a good night's sleep. Show him to the chicken room, Lucy.''

And everyone looked at her expectantly. Even Holt.

He took her hand while she led him up the stairs to the chicken room. "What are you doing?" she hissed at him.

"Acting territorial," Holt said pleasantly through his teeth as they climbed the stairs. "It seems to be expected."

"*I* don't expect it."

"Really? I thought we were engaged."

She turned back and glared at him. He was at eye level as long as she stood a stair above him. "I only said—"

"You jumped down my throat when I said the same thing to Roz," he reminded her.

"That was different."

"How?"

"It just was! I never— I never *kissed* you!"

"Kiss me now." He was grinning at her again—that awful, tempting Holt Braxton grin.

"I will not!"

"Then show me to the chicken room," he said, and she heard sudden weariness in his voice. "I'm about to drop."

A close look, even in the dim light of the stairway, showed her that he was telling the truth. "You do look awful."

"Thank you." They stared at each other.

Their faces were very close together. Their lips were very close together. Too close. Remembering that kiss, Lucy backed up a step. "Come on."

He came. Breathing down her neck, it seemed to Lucy.

"What happened with Tim?"

"We were engaged. Now we aren't."

"He broke it off. For some hussy known only as 'the Fields girl.'"

She turned to see a corner of his mouth quirk. It wasn't even a question, but Lucy felt compelled to nod. "It was a surprise. Tim and I were engaged for five years and—"

"Five years?"

"We'd known each other all our lives," she defended herself. "It was no whirlwind, love-at-first-sight sort of courtship. It was…understood. I thought," she added lamely. Then, at his raised brows she added, "Well, it was more than my imagination. I had a ring." Her bare finger still felt naked sometimes without the ring she'd worn for so long.

"But *five years?*"

"He had to finish school. Med school," Lucy explained, but it sounded weak even to her. "He thought we shouldn't get married until he finished. And then, well…instead of marrying me, he married Whitney."

"Whitney?" Holt said the name with disbelief.

"Some people are named Whitney."

"Only in books."

"She's very lovely. And her father was a surgeon at the hospital where Tim did his residency. I don't blame him."

"You ought to," Holt replied darkly. "What kind of jerk strings a woman along for *five years* and then dumps her?"

"Not you, certainly. You're definitely not Mr. Long-term Commitment!" Lucy retorted, angry now.

"I never got engaged to anybody!"

"Yes, you did. To me."

Which brought them right back to where she'd come in at his apartment hours ago.

Holt seemed to realize it, too. He blinked. Then he raked a hand through his hair. "Right."

They stared at each other again.

"I only used your name because my grandmother was trying to line up a dozen potential Tim replacements for me while I was home."

"And you didn't want any? Why? Are you still 'pining' for Tim?" His sarcasm annoyed her.

"No, I am not 'pining' for Tim. I just didn't want to be bothered with a lot of uninteresting men."

"How do you know they wouldn't be interesting?"

"They wouldn't be interesting to *me*."

"Why not?"

She ground her teeth. "Because I'm not in the mood to get involved again. I don't want to get involved again. And she wouldn't stop coming up with men, so I...I just said I was engaged."

"To me."

"Yours was the first name that popped into my head."

"Lucky me."

"Ditto," Lucy said, annoyed. "What about Roz?"

"What I told Roz was nothing more than a small white lie born of desperation."

"Exactly like mine."

Impasse. They stared at each other.

He scowled. "We were out of there in five minutes."

"But Roz still thinks it."

"It's not the same."

"It's exactly the same. And you invited yourself along to Vermont. That's worse."

His scowl deepened. "To work. Not to play fiancé. You used me."

"And you used me," she countered. "We're even."

He didn't look convinced.

"Look, I know you're annoyed. I'm sorry. I shouldn't have done it, but I did. And you never would have known if you hadn't come along. But you did, and you brought me all the way to the door.

And you've eaten Grandma's chicken soup under false pretenses, so you're stuck.''

"Stuck?"

"Stuck. How's it going to look if all of a sudden you say we're not engaged? They'll wonder why you didn't say so in the first place, and then I'll be forced to tell Roz you were having her on and—''

He was looking at her as if he'd never seen her before. "You conniving little—''

"I'm only doing what I have to do. What I learned from you in every corporate deal you ever did—Put on just as much pressure as you need to in order to get things done.''

"Legally.''

"I don't think what I did was illegal. No more than what you did in front of Roz. This is not a big deal,'' she went on. "It's a Christmas holiday. You said you weren't going home anyway, and—''

"I wasn't going home. Not to anyone's home.''

"Well, you did. And I can't tell them now. Grandma has been really worried that I'm not over Tim. She's fretted for months. And this is just three more days.''

"You only had to pretend for three minutes.''

She had no answer to that, so she just met his gaze hopefully, waited, counted on his sense of fair play.

He sighed. "You want to pretend we're madly in love?''

"Of course not! I'd never fall in love with a self-centered, arrogant jerk like— Oops."

A corner of Holt's mouth lifted. "That's what I like about you, Lucy, my love. You have this unflinching willingness to tear a strip off me whenever you feel it's necessary."

"I'm not your love," Lucy retorted, her control snapping, and, damn it, it *was* necessary *right now*. She had reached the end of her rope, but she wasn't going to beg. "You've just finished telling me that! Oh, go to hell!" She turned and started back down the stairs. "I'll tell them."

Holt grabbed her arm and hauled her up short. "No."

"It's what you want."

"I've changed my mind."

"Why?"

He shrugged, his expression unreadable. "Because I want to."

"Why do you want to?" Lucy looked at him suspiciously. "What are you getting out of it?"

"What makes you think I'm getting something out of it?"

"You wouldn't do it otherwise. So, what? Besides the contracts." She knew it wouldn't just be for the contracts. He would get them anyway, and he knew it.

"So I'd have another chance to do this," he said,

and before she realized it, she had been pulled hard against his chest.

And then he was kissing her again.

The first kiss, Lucy had assured herself, had been a fluke. It had caused her mind to spin and her knees to weaken because it was so completely out of character, so wholly unexpected. It had left her shaken—and shaking—because she hadn't seen it coming.

This one, she saw coming.

She took a step back, she turned her head. She closed her mouth. It didn't help.

Nothing helped.

Nothing could keep his lips from hers, could keep her heart from skipping over, could keep her body from pressing close. It was every bit as devastating as the last time he had kissed her.

More.

Because this time she couldn't say she didn't know what to expect. She couldn't pretend she'd been taken off guard. She'd been warned.

And she succumbed anyway.

She didn't know how long it took her to gather her wits, to muster a shred of common sense, to pull away and stand, shaking—shaken—her back against the wall.

Holt looked unnerved, too. Slowly he gave a small shake of his head, as if trying to clear it. He blinked. He didn't say a word.

Lucy ran her tongue over her lips, then realized that he might think she wanted a repeat performance, and snapped her mouth shut. She cleared her throat and tried to move purposefully past him and put her hand on a door. "This is where—" she was forced, damn it, to clear her throat again "—you'll be sleeping."

"The chicken room?" His voice had a ragged edge. He was still looking at her as if he'd never seen her before.

"It's because of the wallpaper." Her own voice still wavered, but her knees weren't trembling quite so much. She was getting control. Thank God.

"The wallpaper." He sounded like an echo.

"Look, this was probably a bad idea." No. No "probably" about it. It *was* a bad idea. "I'll go down now and tell them I lied."

"No."

"But—"

"No," he said more firmly. And then he eased around her and went into the chicken room and shut the door.

HE WAS OUT OF HIS MIND.

Why else would he be lying on his back in a narrow bed in something called "the chicken room" listening to a stranger named Eldon snore?

He couldn't see the chickens on the wallpaper yet. He would, he was sure, at first light.

He didn't know who Eldon was, either. Lucy's brother? Uncle? Cousin? Whoever he was, he needed his adenoids removed. Holt had heard freight trains that made less noise.

He folded his arms under his head and wondered what the hell he was doing here.

Impulsiveness wasn't in his nature. He was a risk taker, true enough. But they were always calculated risks. Yet today, in a move that was wholly out of character, he'd grabbed Lucy and passed her off as his fiancée, then allowed—no, even encouraged— her to pass him off as hers!

The first move had been the result of sheer necessity.

And the second?

He was rescuing her from her folly, he assured himself. One glimpse at her grandparents' enthusiastic welcome and she'd looked so desperate, what else could he have done?

He hadn't wanted to make her life harder, to ruin her holiday by subjecting her to her family's scrutiny—and subsequent pity. He had more compassion than that.

He did? Since when?

Holt shrugged uncomfortably against the sheets.

In the other bed Eldon whuffled and snorted and rolled over. Holt did his best to ignore him. He hadn't shared a bedroom with another man since his college days. Women were far preferable. They were warm and soft and they cuddled against him.

Would Lucy cuddle against him?

No, he told himself sharply. He did not want Lucy cuddling against him! He didn't!

Lucy was his secretary. And, for the space of a few days only, his fiancée. Because she needed him. She relied on him. That was all.

Other than the way she kissed.

Unconsciously Holt rubbed the back of his hand against his mouth. To erase, he told himself. Not to remember. But even when he tried to erase it, there was still the faint but persistent memory of the feel of Lucy Potter's lips under his.

The first kiss had been enough of a shock. A spur-of-the-moment way to convince Roz he was really not interested in her, he'd done it with no mind to Lucy at all.

But it had sure as hell awakened his awareness of her as something more than the woman he dictated letters to. He'd had no idea that her lips would be so soft, so yielding, so memorable. He'd had no notion that he would want to do more than simply touch his lips to hers. He *hadn't wanted* to do more than touch his lips to hers—then.

And what about the second kiss?

Well, that was to prove the first one had been a fluke. To assure himself that he'd been hallucinating, that Lucy wasn't really that desirable.

And now?

Holt rolled over and punched his pillow. Hard.

Eldon snorted, jerked, then went back to his nasal rumblings.

Holt went back to thinking about Lucy.

He wanted to kiss her again. He wanted to unpin her hair and run his fingers through it. And see if there was lacy underwear beneath those sensible little dresses or skirts and blouses she wore. And see what was under that underwear. Touch her. Love—

No! He didn't want to make love to her. He didn't!

He didn't need that kind of complication in his life. Hell, if he thought Roz was a complication, it was nothing to what having an affair with his secretary would be. He twisted onto his side and punched his pillow into submission. He thought about what Lucy Potter's hair would be like, spread out against just such a pillow.

He groaned.

He. Did. Not. Want. An. Affair. With. Her.

Much.

A HERD OF BUFFALO trampled over his head. The hounds of hell were baying in his ears. Holt sat bolt upright and found himself surrounded by two-dimensional chickens.

A moment of complete disorientation was followed by the realization that he was in Vermont, in

Lucy Potter's grandparents' house, in "the chicken room," and that he was destined to spend the holidays in the bosom of the Potter family, pretending to be engaged to his secretary.

In the clear light of day, last night's gallantry, if that was indeed what it had been, seemed excessive.

No, not excessive, he thought as the hounds kept woofing and the buffalo came running back. Insane.

He didn't do families. Or buffalo. Or hounds. Or, for that matter, chickens. He did work. He bought and sold corporations. He fine-tuned a company's management, streamlined its operations, then put it on the market again.

He didn't know how to manage anything here.

The buffalo pounded down the stairs and along the length of the hallway. The hounds of hell followed them, barking.

"Truffles!" he heard Lucy exclaim.

As a swearword, it left a lot to be desired. Holt shook his head. It hurt a little, but it felt clearer.

He frowned, then swallowed. His throat wasn't sore. He drew a conscious breath. His nose wasn't stuffy as it had been the day before, either.

Was he getting better as a natural course of events, or had Lucy's grandmother's chicken soup had the same healing power that Lucy's had?

The buffalo receded into the distance. The hounds stopped barking. Holt glanced over at the other bed in the room, the one that had held Eldon the Snorer. It was empty, neatly made. He glanced at his watch. 9:30. 9:30?

It couldn't be! He *never* slept past 7:00! Usually he was up at 5:00, making transatlantic calls, reading the papers, jotting memos, keeping an eye on his empire. How could he have—?

He got up and pulled on the jeans he'd brought and a brand-new sweater his nieces had given him last Christmas. He didn't usually wear jeans or sweaters. His life was conducted in suits and since prep school he'd never gone through a day without a tie choking his neck. He felt a little naked without one, though he doubted that Lucy's family would notice.

The thought of Lucy's family made his mouth dry.

He contemplated just staying in his room and going over the contracts. He could say he was still sick.

There was a light knock on the door. It cracked open. Lucy smiled tentatively at him. "Oh, good, you're up."

She met his gaze for only a moment. Then her eyes dropped and she seemed to be looking at his mouth. He thought she was probably thinking about the kiss, for her head jerked away suddenly, and she looked out the window instead.

He finished making his bed. "I'm up," he concurred.

"Breakfast is still on the table. Most of us have eaten, but—"

"I don't need anything," Holt said hastily. "Just a cup of coffee. Then I can get to work."

"Work," Lucy echoed doubtfully.

"It's what I'm here for." Holt tried to sound as businesslike as possible. It would never to do to stand here staring at her mouth and remembering what it felt like under his.

"I know that. But, well, Grandma won't be happy unless you have a good breakfast." Lucy shrugged. "It's the way she is. She'll be up here fussing over you if you don't come down. She's worried about your cold, you see, and—"

"My cold is fine. Much better." So much for lying and staying in his room. If Grandma was going to come fussing, he would be better off downstairs. "I'll be down," Holt said, defeated, "as soon as I've shaved."

HE WENT DOWN. He was overrun by dogs. Dozens.

"Two." Lucy introduced them. "Truffles and Brummel."

Children. Hundreds.

"Three," Lucy said. "My nephews, Luke and Joe. My niece, Holly."

Aunts and nuns. Hordes of them.

"This is Aunt Bea. This is Aunt Grace. This is Aunt Josie. And these are Sisters Ernestine and Bertha.'' Lucy presented him to a roomful of curious little old ladies. "They've come to bake for the soup kitchen's Christmas dinner. This is Holt Braxton, my boss.''

"And fiancé,'' her grandmother added cheerfully, setting a plate of eggs, bacon and pancakes in front of Holt.

His stomach growled. Even despite being the center of attraction, he was glad he'd come down. She placed a steaming cup of coffee next to the plate and poured him a glass of orange juice. He smiled at her. "Thank you.''

She ruffled his hair. "How did you sleep, my dear?''

Holt jerked up straight. She'd ruffled his hair?

He couldn't ever remember anyone—not even his parents—ruffling his hair. He fastened onto the coffee cup, his anchor in this whole new world. "I slept fine, thank you,'' he managed, his voice sounding a little rusty, even to him.

"Cold better?''

"Yes, thanks.'' He tried giving her a polite, distancing smile.

But Lucy's grandma did not seem to believe in distancing smiles. She beamed at him. "I knew it. I'm so glad. You'll be well enough to go for the tree, then.''

Holt blinked. "Tree?''

"Christmas tree,'' Dorothy explained. "When

Tom gets back from town you can all go cut the tree. The children can hardly wait." She looked as if she was giving him a treat.

"I've got a lot of work to do. Lucy and I—"

"Oh, Lucy's going, too," Grandma said. "She never misses."

Holt's gaze swiveled to find Lucy somewhere in the midst of the milling children, hoping she would back him up.

She gave him a smile and a helpless shrug. "It won't take long."

"I'll go over the contracts, then, while you're gone."

The entire roomful of noise seemed to stop. The children stopped wrestling with the dogs. The dogs stopped growling and throwing each other on the floor. The aunts stopped stirring. The nuns stopped chopping and dicing. Everyone looked uniformly dismayed, aghast, appalled.

"You don't want to go with them?" Grandma was astonished. The look she gave Lucy was halfway between censorious and pitying.

Holt sighed heavily, feeling the mantle of doom settle on his shoulders. "I'll go with them to get the tree."

Immediately the room burst into life once more. The children wrestled, the dogs rolled, the aunts and nuns buzzed and chattered as they sifted and stirred and chopped and peeled.

"More bacon, Holt?" Grandma asked, her relief apparent. "More pancakes?"

He hesitated. But they were the best pancakes he'd ever eaten in his life and his stomach was feeling much happier even if his mind wasn't. Might as well make part of himself happy. And he would need strength to deal with Lucy's family and their infernal Christmas tree.

He held out his plate, feeling rather like Tiny Tim. "Please."

CHAPTER THREE

HOLT FELT AS IF HE'D been thrown to the wolves.

Just as he'd been finishing the biggest and best breakfast he'd ever eaten in his life, studiously ignoring the three-ring circus that was the Potters' kitchen, Lucy's grandfather came stumping in to announce that he was ready to go.

"Yippee!" shouted both boys.

"Hooray!" shouted the girl.

And there ensued a general flurry of mittens and mufflers, jackets and ear bands and boots. Then they headed for the door, followed by both dogs.

"Don't forget the galoshes!" Lucy called.

"Galoshes?" Holt echoed. They all looked like they were wearing boots to him.

But then one of the boys hauled the big black-and-brown-and-white dog—the one incongruously called Truffles—onto his lap and proceeded to put bright red fabric galoshes on her.

Holt stared. He felt like he was Alice falling down the rabbit hole. "Why," he asked carefully, "is that dog wearing boots?"

"She needs them," Lucy said matter-of-factly. "She got frostbitten paws when she was a pup. They're very sensitive to cold and she can't go out unless she wears them. She hates being cooped up inside, so I made her some.''

When she said it, it sounded perfectly plausible, as if it were commonplace for every dog to wear galoshes—or as if every family would make them for one who needed them. Holt decided he would have to think about that.

"Come on, Luce! What're you waiting for?" the little girl, Holly, said. She looked at Holt, still sitting at the table. "Aren'tcha coming?"

He came.

But the moment he walked out onto the porch, he stopped, one hand gripping the pillar like the life preserver he knew it wasn't.

He could not do this. Children? Dogs? Galoshes? Grandfathers? Christmas trees?

No. Not even for Lucy. He opened his mouth to tell her so.

"Think of them as a rowdy board of directors of a hostile corporation," she suggested before he could.

He shot her a quick glance. She seemed serious.

"It's only a Christmas tree," she told him soothingly.

"I don't do Christmas trees. I never have."

She looked shocked. "Never?"

He shook his head.

"Then you need to," she said with determination. "Come on." She took his arm.

"But—"

"It won't hurt. And I promise we'll do the contracts this afternoon." She sounded like she was holding out a treat to a child.

Holt gave her a desperate look.

She gave him a smile in return. Then she tugged him down the steps and into the yard.

He felt like he was jumping out of an airplane without a parachute.

LUCY HAD SEEN HER BOSS in boardroom confrontations with some of the biggest sharks in the business. She'd seen him go nose-to-corporate-nose with men who had a reputation for eating other CEOs alive. She'd seen him work countless rooms, schmooze with everyone from the chambermaid to the president of multinational corporations.

And she'd never seen him at a loss for words. She'd never seen him cowed. She'd never even seen him nervous. He was in his element there.

She'd always assumed that he would be in his element anywhere, that there was nothing Holt Braxton couldn't do.

She'd been wrong.

He couldn't do this.

Not easily, anyway. He'd sat in the middle of the kitchen like a soldier in an enemy minefield, never showing a sign of the easy charm that stood him in good stead in boardrooms across the country. Instead he'd retreated into distant politeness with her grandmother and aunts and the nuns.

She'd thought perhaps all the women intimidated him, and that he would be more comfortable with the children. But he hadn't been exactly thrilled at the prospect of joining them, either.

When Lucy had said, "They don't bite, you know," he'd looked positively relieved, as if her comment hadn't been a joke.

He was no more relaxed now as they sat three abreast in the front of her grandfather's pickup truck. She and Holt were jammed shoulder to shoulder, but not by his choice. He was practically pushing against the passenger-side door as if he couldn't get far enough away from her.

Well, that was fine with her. She was far too susceptible to him already. The kiss he'd given her last night had kept her awake until dawn. She'd debated getting up and confessing all to her grandmother, and she'd told herself that if she felt the same way in the morning, she would.

In the morning, though, faced with her grandmother's obvious relief at her engagement, and her saying over and over how glad she was that Lucy was over Tim and that she could see now that life did go on, there was no way Lucy could say she'd made the whole thing up.

Still, seeing Holt as uncomfortable as he clearly

was, made her wonder if she shouldn't have, for his sake if not for hers.

On the other hand, she thought this might actually be good for him. He was too good a man not to learn to enjoy a family. And if any family was worth enjoying, it was hers.

She'd hoped he would make some small talk with her grandfather as he did with his business associates, even his adversaries. She'd seen him do it a hundred times. But apparently he wasn't comfortable with her grandfather, either.

When they got in the truck, Grandpa had asked him how his cold was.

"Better," Holt had said.

Then silence reigned.

As they went over the hill, Grandpa commented on the amount of snow that had fallen overnight.

"A foot at least," Lucy said. "Don't you think?" She turned to Holt.

"Yes," Holt agreed.

And the silence began again.

Grandpa talked about the price of milk. Lucy offered her opinion. Holt didn't reply at all. Grandpa bemoaned the state of the roads and grumbled about the salt killing the trees. Lucy seconded his opinion. Holt didn't say a word. All the while his hands were curled into fists against the tops of his thighs. His knuckles were white.

Lucy was torn between wanting to comfort him and wanting to kick him.

Finally when Grandpa pulled up into a narrow drive and Joe bounded out of the back to open the gate, the old man glanced their way. "Don't feel like you got to keep your hands off her entirely."

"Huh?" Holt's head jerked up.

"Go ahead an' put your arm around her," Grandpa said with a wink. "I'm not going to get out my shotgun for that. Besides, you're engaged, aren'tcha? We already know you're going to make an honest woman of her."

Holt swallowed. "Er, yes."

"Well, then..." Grandpa smiled and cocked his head, looking at them, waiting. Expectantly.

"Grandpa, he doesn't need to—" Lucy began.

But just then Holt seemed to realize what it was the old man was waiting for. He straightened and Lucy saw him loosen and flex his fingers. "Er, right," he said. He slipped his arm around her and drew her hard against him.

Now it was Lucy's turn to go rigid in the warmth of his embrace. "Holt!" She could feel his breath stirring the tendrils of her hair. She could smell a hint of his very expensive aftershave. She could almost brush her cheek against his jaw. She turned her head away.

Even so, he breathed, "Hmm?" into her ear.

She shivered.

Her grandfather made a tsking sound. "Never used to be that shy, Lucy," he chided.

No, she hadn't. But that had been with Tim. Of course she'd never been shy with Tim. She had known Tim forever. He'd been her boyfriend since they were small. She knew him better than she'd ever known anyone.

Or, she reflected, she'd thought she did.

Apparently she hadn't really known Tim at all.

"Relax," Holt said sotto voce into her ear. "If he won't shoot me, he won't shoot you."

When she turned her head, the intensity in his blue eyes startled her. Despite his earlier tension, now he seemed very definitely the Holt she knew, the Holt from the office, the Holt firmly in control of his destiny.

And hers.

All the more reason not to relax, Lucy thought despairingly, trying to sit up straight.

But try as she would, Lucy couldn't seem to hold herself away from him. Gravity was against her, and so was her grandfather, so was Holt. And so, for that matter, was her own body. Before they'd gone more than halfway up the next hill, she found herself settling into Holt's encircling arm. It was easy to do. Too easy.

Holt's arm tightened as she shivered. "Cold?"

"I'm fine." She struggled to sit up straighter, not

to lean into him. "You don't have to smother me," she added tartly.

But the words were wasted. He didn't let go. In fact he hugged her close all the rest of the way up the hill to the patch of family woods where every year the Potters cut their Christmas tree.

Even when they got out of the truck, he kept his arm around her.

"You don't have to hang on to me!" she protested.

But he didn't let go. "I do, Lucy," he said, sounding oddly serious. "I do."

And there was something in his voice that made Lucy cease her objections. Besides, it was rather nice having his arm there as long as she remembered he wasn't serious about her.

"Fine," she muttered. "Come on, then."

Looking for a Christmas tree, Potter-style, was always a hectic experience. The theory was generally that the more opinions voiced, the better the end product; the more disagreement, the more likely the tree eventually selected would be The Best Tree In The World.

Holly and the twins contributed their part. Truffles certainly contributed hers! Even little Brummel, a Scottish terrier whose main interest in trees seemed to be lifting his leg on them, showed definite preferences. Grandpa threw in his two cents' worth. Lucy couldn't help arguing for "the undertree," as

Joe called it—the scraggly, half-bald tree that would stand for centuries before someone chose to take it home.

But through it all, Holt didn't say a word.

At first Lucy thought he was staying silent just because he hadn't seen the definitive tree yet. Then she thought he was doing it out of strategy, holding back his opinion until they'd worn themselves out arguing, at which time he would point out his choice, and it would—as Holt Braxton's choices always were—the obvious best.

But he didn't say a word.

They trudged for miles, studying tree after tree. Arguing, disputing, laughing, teasing, recalling other wonderful trees—and other completely disastrous ones, usually Lucy's. The twins brought up the time their Aunt Chloe had climbed her favorite and then had fallen out and broken her arm. Grandpa and Lucy recalled when Augie, the children's mother, had been so pregnant with the twins that she'd had to be towed through the woods on a sled. And then they had to retell of the time right after Holly was born, when Augie and her husband, Jake, had packed her on their backs, determined not to miss the annual tree-cutting.

"Wish they were here now," Luke grumbled.

"They'll be here in the morning," Lucy consoled him. "And you know they wish it, too." She gave his shoulders a squeeze. She knew the kids were eagerly awaiting their parents' return tomorrow. She also knew they were lucky to have a great-grandmother and grandfather so ready and willing to have them move in at any time. It was the biggest blessing of her family, she'd always thought, that even though they tended to scatter all over the globe at times, they still were there for one another no matter what.

She wished for Holt's sake that he had a family like that. Then he might have felt more comfortable today. The only time he ventured a comment was when he was asked point-blank by one of the twins which tree he thought they ought to take home.

"I'd take the one Lucy picked."

Both boys had stared at him, horrified. Lucy was equally astonished.

"That runt?" Luke demanded.

Joe howled, "It's a lopsided tree with two tops and a hole in one side!"

"It needs Christmas and love just like all of us do," Lucy maintained stoutly when she found her voice.

The boys groaned. Holly said, "Are you sure, Aunt Lucy? I mean…it is pretty little." She cast a doubtful look in the direction of Lucy's choice.

Lucy expected that Holt, having praised her choice, would then deflect their attention to a better one. She'd seen him do that sort of thing in business meetings time and time again. But he didn't. He didn't say another word.

"I kinda like this big ol' full one myself," Grandpa said, pointing to reveal the one he was standing in front of.

Next to Lucy's choice it looked like the perfect tree.

"Now *that's* a tree," Luke agreed, eyes shining.

"Let's take that one," Joe said.

"Is that okay, Aunt Lucy?" Holly wanted everyone to be satisfied.

Lucy smiled and gave the little girl a hug. "It's wonderful. And anyway, I think maybe my tree needs a little more time to grow up. Don't you?" she asked Holt.

He looked nonplussed, then nodded. "I guess."

"Will you help us cut it?" Joe asked him.

Holt looked even more startled at that request. But then he nodded and took the saw Luke handed him. He bent to the task, taking turns with Joe and Luke when they got tired of sawing.

Grandpa looked at her over the crouched tree-cutters and smiled, then said quietly, "He'll do."

GIVE HIM A JUICY boardroom confrontation any day. Give him a wheeling, dealing businessman or a financial wizard trying to steal his last dime or anyone but children, dogs and old men with expectations.

It was one thing to bluff his way through a business transaction. It was entirely something else to fit into a family like the Potters.

Holt had been raised on boardroom confrontations. He'd watched his father slice through boardroom shenanigans like a knife through soft butter. He'd barely got out of college when he tried it himself. He'd taken to it like a duck to water. It was in the genes, he thought. In his bones.

Cutting Christmas trees wasn't. Laughing and arguing and fighting over things that would have made his sister slip a stiletto between his ribs made him nervous as hell. The only thing that was remotely easy to do was when Lucy's grandfather had bullied him into slipping his arm around Lucy and hauling her close.

That hadn't been hard at all.

He'd relished the warmth of her body pressed against his. He'd savored the fresh-flower smell of her shiny brown hair.

He'd wanted to kiss her again right there.

He didn't because, despite what her grandfather had said, Holt figured the old man probably *would* shoot him when he found out their engagement wasn't real. And there were other things to do. Other things to think about.

Like the family dynamics going on in front of him.

All his experience with family matters had been bad. Wrangling was bitter, not jovial. Disagreements led to shouting and slamming doors, not tussles in the snow and laughter all around. He didn't know how to respond to any of what went on among the Potters, so he'd kept his mouth shut.

It was safer.

And it was lonely.

Seeing them interact, watching them argue and joke and tell stories had made him wistful, had made him wish—

He'd never wished for, had never wanted a family! Still didn't.

But something about Lucy's fresh-flower scent and the brush of her hair against his cheek, something about her grandfather's easy inclusion of him in the conversation, something about the boys' inviting him to help them cut the tree made him think...just for a moment...

It was insane. Wrong. It would never work. He needed to get things back on a professional footing.

At once.

"Now we can decorate," Holly cheered as they got out of the truck and carried the tree toward the house. "Are you gonna do the lights?" she asked Holt. "My daddy always does the lights, but he's not here." She looked at him hopefully.

Holt shook his head. "Some of us have work to do."

Holly looked at Lucy, crestfallen. Lucy didn't look all that happy, either, and Holt felt a stab of contrition, then dismissed it. She'd suckered him into this, and she'd agreed to work on the contracts, so they could just damned well do it now. He gave her a steady, unblinking look.

Finally she nodded her head. "I have to," she told the little girl. "It's important."

"As important as the tree?" Holly asked doubtfully.

"Not to you—and not to me. But to Holt it is. We'll be along shortly," her aunt promised.

They wouldn't, Holt wanted to say. He had every intention of keeping her working for the rest of the afternoon. No more fiancé nonsense. No more thinking about kisses. Just work.

Lucy poked her head into the kitchen where her grandmother and the flock of aunts and nuns were still baking. "Holt and I are going into the study to get some work done."

"Work?" Holt heard her grandmother say dubiously. There was a second's silence, then more brightly she said, "Oh. Of course, dear. Whatever you want."

Holt heard a general murmur of assent behind her and someone sang out, "Enjoy yourselves."

Another voice admonished, "Ernie!"

"Well, don't you think they will?" a voice that must have been Ernie's countered.

"I would," another voice said.

"Bert!" exclaimed Lucy's grandmother, scandalized.

The delighted murmur grew. Holt heard a chuckle. He frowned.

"Oh, for heaven's sake," Lucy muttered under her breath.

"What?" He was baffled.

She hunched her shoulders. "They don't think we're going to be working."

"They don't? What do they think we're going to be doing?"

Lucy's cheeks went crimson. "Guess."

"Oh." The penny dropped at last. Somehow he found the notion as embarrassing as Lucy obviously did. At the same time, it played havoc with his intent to get their relationship back on a professional basis.

"We could, you know," he suggested casually as he followed after her down the hall. A good businessman always had to reevaluate conditions.

Lucy gave him a long, silent, over-the-shoulder look.

"For, um, practice?" he added hopefully.

She whirled around. "I am not practicing any such thing with you!"

Holt took a quick step back and held up his hands defensively. "Right, Lucy. Far be it from me to suggest any such thing, Lucy. Besides—" he grinned "—you don't really need much practice, Lucy."

Lucy made a furious sound somewhere deep in

her throat and her face got even redder. Her fingers balled into fists. She took a step toward him.

"It was a compliment," he swore, stepping back. "A compliment. I was merely intimating that you're a very good kisser."

"And you would know, of course!" she spat. "Perhaps you'd like to stamp your endorsement on my forehead in gold letters. The Holt Braxton seal of approval."

He cocked his head consideringly. "Well, I'd have to do a little more research before I could give you that."

"Oh!" Lucy's mouth clamped shut in a tight, furious line. "Get the contracts, Mr. Braxton. I'll meet you in Grandpa's study." And she turned and stomped up the stairs.

"I LIKE HOLT," GRANDMA said that evening as she was washing the dishes after supper. "But he seems a little shy."

"A little," Chloe agreed as she dried a glass. She slanted a glance in Lucy's direction. "Quieter than Tim, anyway. But don't they say still waters run deep?" She made goo-goo eyes and laughed, and Lucy strangled her own damp dish towel.

"He's reserved, that's all," she said. "Besides, he's still recovering from his cold."

What else could she say? She didn't think he would thank her for explaining his discomfort around families. They would fuss over him, if they knew, and that would only make things worse. As far as she was concerned, his not talking had distinct advantages. It made the chance of him saying something she would regret that much less. And if she worked at it, she could be sanguine enough to pass off comments like Chloe's with aplomb.

After all, nothing had happened between them in the study, though he'd kept her there working all afternoon. He'd brought in the contracts and set to work as if his references to her kissing ability had never occurred.

"Of course, he's recovering," Chloe said. "Especially with you to take care of him all afternoon!" She laughed again.

"I helped him work on some contracts he needed to finish," Lucy said firmly.

"Right. Like I was just handing wrenches to Eldon when I went with him last week to Mr. Macgruder's to help with the plumbing."

Lucy goggled at her. "You—Eldon? On Mr. Macgruder's floor?"

Even Grandma stared at Chloe, shocked.

Chloe heaved a long-suffering sigh. "We did not do anything on Mr. Macgruder's floor."

"You used his bed?" Lucy was aghast.

Chloe looked murderous. "We did not use his bed! We just...fooled around a little." She made a small huffing sound. "Stop it. This is getting out of hand!"

Lucy grinned. "You're just miffed because I managed to turn the tables, for once."

Chloe was the flirt among the Potter sisters. Augie had met and married Jake within three months. Lucy had—foolishly, it turned out—committed herself to Tim from second grade. But Chloe had, in her own words, "shopped around." She'd dated actors and archaeologists, skiers and skaters, businessmen and bank VPs. For a while she'd even dated an astronaut, always looking for the perfect man, convinced she would find one among the many who passed through Vermont, never looking close to home.

She didn't look at local boys. So it was disconcerting, to say the least, when six months ago, the plumber working on the new bathroom fixtures turned out to be Eldon Crocker, a boy she'd gone to high school with. It was even more disconcerting when she found him attractive. And astonishing beyond all telling when she fell in love with him.

But after a week of being astonished, Chloe had settled in to being totally pleased with herself, and went right back to being the one who had opinions about everyone else's love life. Lucy loved her sister dearly, but sometimes she wanted to throttle her.

"I'm not miffed," Chloe said now. "But Tim ought to be. Holt's a hunk compared to him."

Lucy couldn't deny it. Not when she was claiming

to be engaged to him. "He is pretty good-looking," she allowed.

"Good-looking? He'd stop traffic."

"Well, don't tell him that!" Lucy said, horrified at the very real possibility that the outspoken Chloe might. "He's not used to being around a whole houseful of raving lunatics."

"He'd better get used to it," Chloe said. She stood on her tiptoes and lined up the glasses she'd just dried on the top shelf.

"He will," Grandma said. She turned and leveled her gaze on Lucy. "He may be a little quiet and reserved, but he's a good man. Steady. Principled. Honest. A grandmother can tell these things."

Lucy felt coals being heaped upon her head.

"He'll take part when he's ready," Grandma said. She cocked her head, listening. "There. See? Isn't that him talking to Tom and Eldon now?"

Lucy listened. It was Holt, all right. But he wasn't talking. He was arguing. And so were Eldon and her grandfather. She could hear them now, their voices raised and getting louder by the minute.

"Guess he's taking part," Chloe said, giggling.

"That's the damnedest thing I ever heard," they heard Eldon say.

And Holt replied, "It's the honest-to-God truth. Just ask her if you don't believe me!"

And then her grandfather's voice rose above them all. "Lucy!" Then, "You just wait'll I get my shotgun!"

CHAPTER FOUR

"DON'T, GRANDPA! It's not his faul—" Lucy raced in and stopped dead in the doorway to see all three men standing beside the fireplace, staring at the old musket hanging above it. Their mouths were wide open.

"Lucy?" her grandfather said.

She gulped. She looked wildly from her grandfather to Holt and back again. She was sure they'd been arguing. She was sure she'd heard Holt say that something was the honest-to-God truth, that she would corroborate it. That their engagement was a sham, she'd thought he was saying.

What else would have inspired Grandpa to go looking for his shotgun?

But whatever it had been, they didn't look like they were in the midst of a struggle to the death. In fact they looked astonished at her bursting into the room, shouting at them.

"You called me. I—I thought..." But she could hardly say what she had thought, could she? "Weren't you...arguing?"

"I noticed that old musket above the fireplace," Holt said, "and I was telling them about that auction at the armory that we went to a few months back.

Remember when we were taking old Cedric Harrington-Smythe around?"

Lucy remembered. It had been an Early American antique sale and Cedric Harrington-Smythe, the president of a company Holt was thinking of buying, had bought a rusty old gun for several thousand dollars. It had looked like garage-sale material to Lucy, but she'd never claimed to know her antiques.

Now she said faintly, "What about the... shotgun?"

"Holt was saying he reckoned that old musket was worth twice what his buddy paid for that gun he bought," her grandfather explained. "And I'm not planning on selling the musket, but I thought maybe I'd have him take a look at that old shotgun Uncle Jack left me. Might be worth something, and—" he grinned "—now I'm getting all you girls settled, I won't be needing it anymore."

"Oh," Lucy said faintly. "Um," she said. "What a good idea," she said. "You do that."

"I've got a better idea." Eldon spoke up. He grinned his devilish grin, the one that had disarmed the very particular Chloe. "If you ladies are finished in the kitchen," he added. "I wouldn't want to distract you...."

"Eldon," Lucy warned, having seen that grin before.

It widened perceptibly. "Well, I've offered to

help often enough, but your grandma always chases me out."

Grandma was like that. She wanted no men in her kitchen while dishes were being done. Lucy and Chloe were more enlightened, but it was Grandma's kitchen.

"So what's your idea?" She was ready to latch on to anything to distract from her mistaken burst into the living room, which she could see was still puzzling her grandfather.

"I bought Chloe a present when I was in town today," Eldon said. "But I'm willing to share." He looked at the other men and winked. Then he went to the hall tree where his jacket was hanging, fished in its pocket and pulled out a sprig of greenery. He grinned and held it up. "How about it?"

Lucy gaped. "Mistletoe!"

Eldon beamed. The twins groaned. Grandpa smiled indulgently. Lucy looked at Holt. He looked at her. There was nothing professional in his gaze. It was so hot she jerked her eyes away and started backing toward the kitchen.

"We're not really quite finished with the dishes," she said hastily, only to have her words immediately contradicted by Chloe and Grandma who were coming into the room just behind her.

"Mistletoe?" Chloe said. She looked at Eldon and beamed just like he was.

"Is that the kissing bush?" Holly wanted to know.

"Yeah," Luke said, making a gagging sound.

"You're not kissin' me!" Holly shrieked and ran to hide behind one of the chairs.

"You don't kiss your sister," Joe told her scornfully. "You kiss your girlfriend." He breathed a sigh of relief. "We don't gotta kiss anyone," he assured his brother. They looked at each other with identical expressions of relief.

Lucy could have used some similar relief. She felt as if someone had a noose around her neck and was tightening it by the minute.

Eldon centered the mistletoe over the opening between the living room and the dining room, and hammered a tack through the branch, then stepped back to survey his handiwork. "Looks good to me."

"Let's see if it works," Chloe said, wrapping her arms around him.

"Oh, yeah, let's," Eldon agreed. It was a very thorough, very official-looking kiss. Lucy watched, uncomfortably aware of how intense it was. Chloe had always danced away from her many boyfriends, making them try to catch her, giggling and squirming whenever they had. She didn't giggle when Eldon kissed her. She didn't squirm. She kissed him as eagerly and as thoroughly as he kissed her.

Neither one of them seemed to hear Joe say, "Oh, gross!" and Luke say, "Enough. Enough!"

They might have kept kissing into eternity, Lucy thought, if Grandpa hadn't cleared his throat and said, "Don't you go using up all the magic, now. We've got to have a turn."

Breathless and blushing, but not really letting go of each other, Eldon and Chloe stepped back. Grandpa swept Grandma into his arms and drew her under the mistletoe.

There was more than a little enthusiasm in their kiss, too. For a couple who had been married almost sixty years, Lucy thought her grandparents had quite a lot of passion left. She'd always admired their devotion. It was something she'd always hoped to emulate in her own life, in her own love. But seeing it with Holt...

She couldn't even look at him.

She looked at the twins instead. She expectedly groaned again. But the twins only stared, awed, not groaning at all. They both looked thoughtful as the kiss ended and their great-grandparents stepped apart and looked into each other's eyes and smiled.

Lucy held her breath, waiting for the inevitable, steeling herself.

"Kiss me, Grandpa," Holly said, and Lucy breathed a sigh of relief. The day was saved!

Her great-grandfather bent down and drew the little girl up into his arms and carried her under the mistletoe. He rubbed his nose against hers while she giggled, and then he gave her a smacking kiss and handed her to her grandmother who did the same. "Anyone else?" he asked.

And as one, everybody turned to look at Lucy and Holt.

"I don't—" Lucy began, then stopped. *I don't want to,* she'd been going to say. *I don't!* But when she looked at Holt, she knew, in spite of herself, that it wasn't true. She did.

She *wanted* his kiss. She wanted to kiss *him.* Even though it had been like setting fire to a pile of dry tinder both times she'd brushed her lips against his, even though it was sure to be a mistake, she couldn't help it. She wanted to do it again.

"I don't know what we're waiting for," Holt finished for her, a raspy edge to his voice. And then he pulled her into his arms and drew her under the mistletoe.

This time it was different. Not as volatile. Not as jolting.

Or, maybe *more* jolting—because it felt right. So right.

When Lucy's lips met his, the wrongness vanished, the mistake melted. She felt as if she was coming home. There was warmth and there was welcome and there was eagerness and, yes, a hint of passion. But it was, thank God, passion controlled. She could feel it in him—the control, the tension, the rein under which he held himself. And that was good.

At the same time she could feel the need, the desire in him—and in herself. And that was bad.

What was she going to do?

Stop.

What else could she do?

She had to *stop!* She jerked back, out of Holt's embrace, but she couldn't keep from looking at him. And she didn't know if she was comforted or not, to see that he was as shaken as she was.

"Pretty powerful stuff, mistletoe," Eldon said a little too heartily.

"Indeed," Grandma said. She sounded a little trembly herself. She smoothed her hair and gave herself a little shake. "Now, then, what about that Christmas tree?" she said briskly. "Don't you think it's time we decorated it?"

They had put it off from the afternoon so that Holt and Lucy could participate. Holt had rolled his eyes. Lucy had been grateful. Now the twins and Holly cheered and Lucy felt like cheering herself.

And if Holt seemed to withdraw, well, as far as she was concerned, too bad. She wasn't going to let herself worry about him. Not when he kissed her like that!

"Chloe, bring out the Christmas cookies. Lucy, you get the cider," Grandma directed. "Eldon, you and the boys get the ornament boxes down from the attic. Holt, go with them."

He opened his mouth to protest. "I don't know anything about—"

"Our traditions? Of course not, but you will. And you'll need to know where everything is for next year." Grandma brushed right over that. "Come along, Holly, you and I will pop some corn and get the cranberries."

They all scattered. The children were eager, the adults definitely in need of something other than mistletoe to keep them on the straight and narrow. Lucy cast one quick glance over her shoulder at Holt, and saw him being led away by Eldon and the boys.

Good, she told herself. He didn't look pleased.

HE WASN'T EXACTLY unhappy, either. A fact that surprised him as much as it would have surprised Lucy, had she known.

Somehow, after his awkwardness in the morning and his determined attempt to keep things on a professional level with Lucy all afternoon, Holt had found himself anticipating their reentry into Lucy's boisterous family.

Not, he assured himself, because the stress of working with her all afternoon and not thinking about kissing her had been getting to him! Nothing of the sort. He had, of course, thought about it. A little bit. And thinking about it was...well, distracting. So he was in the mood to be distracted.

Why not follow Eldon and the twins to the attic? They didn't seem disinclined to have him. He'd done his share of cutting the tree and dragging it down to the truck. They'd started to talk to him then. Knowing he was from New York, they'd asked him about the Rangers and the Knicks and the Yankees. He had season tickets to the Rangers. The boys were agog. They'd found common ground.

He found it with Eldon, too, discussing, of all things, bathroom fixtures. Holt had bought a Midwestern company a year ago that made period reproduction bathtubs and commodes. It had been badly run and was floundering when he'd picked it up for a fraction of its worth. He'd debated gutting it and, because he'd found the fixtures attractive, had changed his mind.

Eldon told him it was one of the smartest things he'd ever done. "Lotta call for that sort of stuff these days. People restoring and renovating, they like everything to match, right down to the toilet. But it's gotta be well made. Those are the best on the market—when you can get 'em."

Delivery, Holt assured him, was no longer a problem.

"Then you'll make a mint," Eldon said and clapped him on the back. "Good man."

Just how good a man, Holt was called on to prove by Lucy's grandfather. "I was wondering," he said as Holt and Eldon carried boxes of ornaments downstairs, "if you'd like to help with the milking in the morning."

"Milking?" Holt repeated, nonplused.

"Just a notion. I was recalling how you were saying earlier that a fella ought to know his business from the ground up. Reckoned since you're marrying into the farm, that you might want to know the milk business—from the teat down, so to speak." Tom's eyes twinkled.

Caught—and intrigued—Holt found himself agreeing.

"I'll knock on your door when I pass, then," Tom said. "Be about four."

In the morning? Holt wanted to ask. But of course he knew the answer to that. And yes, when they'd been talking after supper he'd said something about always wanting to know thoroughly any businesses he was involved with.

"Like dairy farming," Tom had said, deadpan.

"Why not?" Holt remembered saying blithely. Well, fair enough. It might be interesting. Lucy's grandfather was an interesting old man. Careful. Meticulous. Shrewd. With a sly sense of humor that tended to catch Holt off guard.

He'd never given a lot of thought to dairy farmers before. He'd never met one, nor had any desire to. If he had thought about them at all, which he wasn't sure he ever had, they certainly hadn't seemed very interesting.

But Tom Potter was. In his dry, understated Vermont way he embodied the virtues Holt valued, like plain speaking, reliability, consistency, the ability to weather the storms of life.

Holt figured there were plenty of boardroom execs who could learn a thing or two from Tom Potter.

He figured *he* could learn a thing or two from Tom Potter.

Tom patted him on the shoulder now. "You don't have to come if you don't want to. You're on vacation, after all," he said, offering Holt an out.

But Holt shook his head. "I'll come."

Tom smiled. "Lucy said you're a good man." Holt had the feeling that Lucy's word carried a lot of weight with her grandfather.

He was glad she thought so. He felt his chest expand, as if he were breathing better, deeper. He looked toward the doorway where Lucy was just coming through carrying mugs of hot cider. He found himself smiling at her and, tentatively, it seemed to him, she smiled back.

Something odd and decidedly foreign stirred inside him. Awakening. Unfurling. Causing yearnings in Holt that he'd never felt before. He didn't understand them. But as he sat there by the fireplace and dutifully strung the popcorn and cranberries that Holly and her great-grandmother provided, he felt himself settling in. He felt his muscles easing, his body relaxing.

There was soft music on the stereo. Cellos and flutes and gentle Christmas melodies that he'd heard a million times on the radio in New York, and which had done little more in his mind than mark the month as December.

Now they wove in and out of his mind, hauntingly familiar and at the same time surprisingly new. He heard in their instrumental tones the words of songs he'd ceased listening to years ago.

He listened now.

He heard words of hope, of love, of family, of searching, of finding. As he watched Lucy and Chloe and Eldon string the lights on the tree, he settled back into the armchair by the fire and let the music and the mood flow over him. Holly and the boys were putting hooks on the ornaments, and Grandma was pushing a needle and thread through gingerbread Christmas cookies.

It seemed all very Norman Rockwell-ish, the sort of Christmas he'd always heard about and read about, so far from his own experience that he had scoffed at it.

He wondered if there had been something in that coffee Dorothy Potter had served after dinner that lulled his resistance and made him nostalgic for Christmases he had never known. His own had been bitter affairs at which one or the other of his parents invariably didn't appear, his sister resented his presence, and he resented hers.

No one seemed to resent anyone here.

It was perfect. Too perfect, he told himself.

He tried to pull himself together, to tell himself that, if the coffee was just coffee, there must have been something in the cough medicine he was taking that was muddling his mind.

But he hadn't taken any cough medicine today. He'd eaten Dorothy's chicken soup and he'd listened to Eldon snore and he'd slept in an old feather bed that seemed to wrap him in softness—and today he'd been fine, more than fine—cured. And happy, too.

Holt Braxton? Happy in a Norman Rockwell Christmas?

He *was* hallucinating.

He needed to go to bed.

He hauled himself to his feet. "I'm going to turn in," he said abruptly.

All eyes in the room swiveled to look at him. The adults' expressions—Lucy's excepted—were unreadable; the kids' were uniformly astonished.

"Without helping us decorate?" Holly demanded, aghast.

"How come?" one of the twins wanted to know.

"Are you sick?" the other one asked.

"Maybe." Holt raked a hand through his hair distractedly. "I just need to...call it a day."

He didn't look at Lucy. She'd think he was bailing out on her. A real fiancé wouldn't be hiding out in his room, and he knew it. But he couldn't help it.

Who knew what he'd do if he stayed? He'd already cut a Christmas tree today. And kissed under the mistletoe. And strung popcorn and cranberries.

Next thing you knew he'd be writing a letter to Santa.

And asking for what?

He looked at the family assembled before him— a family who squabbled and argued and laughed and worked and played together—the sort of family he didn't believe in.

No, he told himself firmly. Even if there *was* a Santa Claus, he wasn't asking for that!

LUCY WAS ALMOST asleep. Or she tried to tell herself she was almost asleep. It was after midnight. She'd thrown herself with abandon into the family antics once Holt had gone to bed, determined not to think about him and to be her old self. And it had exhausted her.

She was sure she would sleep if Chloe would just shut up and let her. But her sister tossed and turned on the other side of the bed, babbling about Eldon and the house they were building and debating whether or not they ought to get married on Valentine's Day.

And Lucy mumbled and hmmmed and considered putting the pillow over her head—or smothering Chloe with it. "It's late," she said finally. "Very late. Everyone's asleep but us."

"Not everyone," Chloe said with a giggle.

"No, any minute now Grandpa will be getting up to do the milking. Be quiet so we can sleep."

"I don't want to sleep," Chloe said.

"Well, I do."

"You won't."

"What?"

But Chloe didn't answer, because just then there was a light tap on the bedroom door. Chloe bounded out of bed and grabbed her robe.

"See you in the morning," she said.

"What? Chloe!"

But her sister opened the door, slipped out—and let someone else in.

Lucy stared into the darkness at the figure standing there. *"Holt?"*

CHAPTER FIVE

IT WAS INDEED HOLT.

He stood in a pair of sweatpants, bare-chested, his back pressed against the door, his palms up and facing her. "This was not my idea."

Lucy drew her knees up against her chest under the blanket, then wrapped her arms around them tightly. "What do you mean? What are you doing here? Where did Chloe go?"

"Where the hell do you think she went?"

Lucy thought about that. "Oh," she said after a long moment. Then, "You *let* her?"

"How the hell was I supposed to stop her?"

"You didn't have to come here! If you hadn't come here—!"

"Would you have liked me to explain to Eldon exactly why I was so puritanical that I was declining to trade bedrooms and spend the night with my fiancée? I didn't see that I had any choice when Eldon suggested it!"

"*Eldon* suggested it?"

"You think *I* did?"

"Well, no. Of course not," Lucy said hastily. "I just... I didn't think... Chloe would never..."

But obviously Chloe would. More to the point, Chloe *had.*

And now she and Eldon were together in each other's arms in the chicken room.

And Holt was here with her.

Lucy looked around desperately. "There's only one bed," she said faintly.

Holt seemed to have just noticed that, too. He said a rude word under his breath. "So that's why Eldon thought he was doing me a big favor when he said I could come here."

"You'll just have to go back," Lucy said.

"And say what? 'Lucy threw me out'? 'Excuse me, but I don't want to spend the night with my fiancée, after all. You won't mind going back to the other room, will you, Chloe? What? Oh, of course I'll wait until you get dressed.'"

Lucy's face burned at his sarcasm, and only partly on her sister's behalf. Mostly on her own. "This is awful! I never meant—"

"Obviously," Holt cut in. "But it's happened."

Lucy pressed her forehead against her knees. "You're right. Poor Chloe. It would be so embarrassing to Chloe."

"Not to mention me," Holt said dryly.

At his tone, Lucy lifted her head to look at him. He really was being an incredibly good sport about this. "I'm really sorry. I didn't expect this to happen."

"Obviously."

"You can fire me when we get back to New York," she offered.

"Thank you very much." His tone was even drier.

She felt her cheeks warm. "I know you hate all this."

"I don't, actually." He shoved himself away from the wall and came to stand a little closer to the bed.

Lucy looked up. "You don't?"

He shook his head. "Oddly enough, no. I...like your grandparents."

She smiled slightly. "I'm—glad."

Then, afraid that that might sound as if she was hoping he might like them as future in-laws, she added quickly, "I like them, too. Love them. They raised me and my sisters after our parents were killed," she explained.

"They're wonderful people. And they've obviously done a good job on you. A very good job," he added quietly. "Looks like they're doing an equally good job with the boys and Holly."

"They try. Augie and Jake are home most of the time. It's just that Jake had to go to Korea to an ag seminar, and he wanted Augie to come along. Augie wasn't sure she should, it being so close to Christmas, but Grandma and Grandpa said they ought to go—to make a second honeymoon out of it."

"Sounds like a good idea."

"They like having the kids here," Lucy said, aware that she was beginning to babble. He was looming over her now. She had to tip her head back to look up at him. If she didn't, she would have to stare at his hard flat belly and hair-roughened chest. "They say it keeps them young." She ran her tongue over her lips.

Even in the dimness of the moonlit room his chest was a pretty eye-catching sight. After letting her gaze drop once, Lucy kept it glued on his face. "Why are you, er...?"

"I was wondering if maybe you'd let me sit down?"

"Oh, well, of course. I just—" She scooted over, trying to scrunch herself up into a very tiny space on one side of the bed. The bed had seemed plenty big enough when she and Chloe were sharing it. It had shrunk drastically since her sister had left the room.

Holt sat and swung his feet up on the bed, then leaned back against the headboard so they were sitting next to each other. Neither spoke.

From the next room there was the soft sound of squeaking bedsprings. *Oh, God*, Lucy thought.

"I really like the Christmas tree we cut today," she said quickly, doing her best to paper over the noise.

"Do you? I thought you had your eye on another

one." Holt seemed to be doing his best to talk over the sounds coming from the other room, too.

"Well, yes. But I knew I wasn't going to get it. Everyone else likes perfect trees. I have a soft spot for the less-than."

"You've got a kind heart."

"I'm a soft touch," Lucy agreed.

"It's more than that," Holt said. He reached out and picked up her hand and began playing with her fingers.

Lucy stiffened momentarily. She heard the bed-springs quickening. But she couldn't seem to say anything. Her mouth felt dry. She knew she ought to pull her hand away, but there was something about his touch that made her let him continue.

She liked it. It made her feel connected to him. She didn't pull away.

"Are these the fingers that are going to milk old Bess?" she asked after a moment, tangling hers with his.

"They are," he said gravely. Then he shook his head. "Never thought I'd milk a cow."

"You don't have to," Lucy said quickly. "He won't care." Her grandfather, she meant.

"He will care," Holt said. He folded his fingers around hers. "It's a test."

"Test?"

"Whether or not I'm too much of a city boy to get my feet dirty in the barn, first of all. And whether or not I'm willing to make a fool of myself. And whether or not I'm worthy of you."

"But you're not my fiancé!"

"But he doesn't know that."

"You don't have to do it for me!"

"I'm not. I'm doing it for me."

There was something firm and implacable in Holt's voice. And she knew he was committed to this.

"But why?" She couldn't help it. She had to ask.

He lifted his shoulders slightly in a vague shrug. "Because I respect him. He's worked hard his whole life for something he believes in. I find that admirable. And I watched him with the boys all day. He lets them work, but he also lets them make mistakes. That's the best way to learn. So when he asked me if I'd like to take a turn, well, I thought maybe he'd be the same with me." He slanted a smile in Lucy's direction.

It was quiet now; the bedsprings had stopped. She could hear the combined sounds of their breathing.

"Yes," she agreed quietly. "He will be." Her grandfather was a man of infinite patience if he thought you were trying. He had always given A's for effort. He was slow to judge and quick to praise.

"You'll do fine," she said. And she believed wholeheartedly that it was true. "And I appreciate your doing it."

"My pleasure," Holt said. And he didn't sound

as if he were lying to her. They sat in companionable silence for a long time.

Then Lucy asked, "What were your grandfathers like?"

"I never knew either of them. They died before I was born."

"That's too bad." Lucy's fingers curled around his, giving a gentle squeeze of sympathy.

"I got by," he said gruffly. "What you don't have, you don't miss."

"Don't you?" Lucy said softly, turning her gaze toward him. "I wonder."

He gave her a sharp look.

"I barely knew my parents," she said. "They died when I was three. But I've always missed them."

"I'm sorry." The gruffness was still in his voice, but the edge on it had softened a little. Then he added in a quiet but firm voice, "I wouldn't have missed mine."

Lucy looked at him closely, convinced at first that she hadn't heard right. He was holding himself absolutely still. He barely even seemed to be breathing. But the unblinking way he met her gaze in the moonlight told her that she'd heard him right enough.

"Will you...tell me about them?" She shifted her gaze from his face to their linked fingers, almost able to feel the tension vibrating through them.

"Not much to tell," he said dismissively. "They had their own lives. I had mine."

"Nothing like my family," Lucy guessed.

"Nothing."

"They made you nervous." It wasn't a guess any longer.

"I didn't know how to handle it, if that's what you mean. I don't do families. I don't know how. I never have."

"You did mine just fine. They like you a lot. Chloe told me so."

"Chloe just wanted to trade bedrooms with me."

"Not just that," Lucy said firmly. "She liked Tim. She likes you better."

The moment she said it, she wondered if she shouldn't have. It made it sound as if she was angling to keep him on as a real fiancé. "But she'll understand. She'll get over it when we break things off," she added hastily.

Holt dropped her hand. "Right."

They sat there then, next to each other, not touching now. Together. And yet alone.

The bedsprings in the next room began again. Louder.

Lucy's fists clenched. She swallowed a lump in her throat. "I'm sorry," she whispered. "I never should have got you into this."

"My fault as much as yours."

They lapsed into silence. The bedsprings didn't.

"I can't believe they're doing this!" Lucy said, her control snapping. "How could they! In Grandma's house!"

"Wouldn't you?" Holt asked. "If you were in love?"

"No! Of course not!" Lucy protested, furious, wanting to put her hands over her ears, wanting to shut it all out.

"Liar," Holt said, and his tone made her look at him sharply. He looked amused. Then, quite suddenly, he slipped an arm around her and hauled her close, at the same time sliding down into the bed so that they lay tight together.

Lucy stiffened. She struggled.

"Don't," Holt said against her ear. "I'm not going to do anything. *We're* not going to do anything—but sleep."

Sleep? Lucy almost groaned. How on earth could he even think about sleeping under the circumstances?

"Shh." His breath was warm against her cheek.

Lucy tried to resist, tried to stay away. But she couldn't. She sighed; she settled. She nestled even closer.

Now it was Holt who seemed to groan.

She turned her head to glance at him. "Something wrong?"

"Oh, no," he said, his voice ragged. "Why would you think that?"

There was a muffled moan from the other room. Gradually the bedsprings slowed. Stopped.

Neither Holt nor Lucy moved. They waited. They listened.

And then there was the faint soft sound of Eldon. Snoring.

Holt muttered an imprecation under his breath. Lucy laughed softly and, surprisingly, found that her tension was uncurling as she snuggled in his arms.

"Good night," she whispered. "I owe you."

"Good night," Holt whispered back. "You're damned right you do."

HE WAS UP AT 3:45 a.m. playing musical bedrooms with Chloe.

It wouldn't do, he told Lucy, for him to be coming out of the wrong bedroom when Tom got him up to milk the cows.

"You're sure you want to do this?" she asked when his movements awakened her. It was warm and deliciously comfortable lying spoon-fashion with Holt Braxton. She didn't want to stop.

"I know what I'd rather be doing," he said. "But I'm not going to get to do that, either, so I might as well."

Lucy flushed at his implication.

"Good night, sweet Lucy," he whispered and dropped a kiss on her cheek. "Get some more sleep." And then he was gone out the door.

Lucy huddled down on her side of the bed, feeling lost and bereft and knowing she shouldn't be feeling anything of the sort. Then the door opened and Chloe slipped in.

"He's conscientious, your Holt," she grumbled as she climbed into the bed. "Tearing me out of Eldon's arms that way."

"More conscientious than you are, that's for sure," Lucy groused. "Grandpa and Grandma would be shocked."

"Do you think so?" Chloe said. "I don't. You saw the way they were kissing."

"Still..." Lucy argued.

"Go to sleep," Chloe said, snuggling down into the feather mattress. There was a moment of silence. Then she giggled.

"What?" Lucy demanded.

Another Chloe giggle. "I was just going to ask if it was as good for you as it was for me."

Lucy thumped her over the head with the pillow.

IT WAS A MATTER OF PRIDE.

Why else would he stagger out of bed at 4:00 a.m to clump through snow to a drafty old barn and fumble with frozen fingers to help Lucy's grandfather with a bunch of discontented cows?

He supposed they weren't really discontented—at least not until *he* started trying to get them hooked up to the milking machine. But his blundering efforts made them restless and impatient. He got impatient with himself and tried harder—with worse results.

Fumbling and cursing, he tried again. The cow sidestepped again. Finally he felt a hand on his shoulder. He turned and saw Tom Potter smiling at him sympathetically.

"They aren't fond of a man with cold hands." He winked. "And you might want to sweet-talk 'em a little. And take it easy. I'm not grading you. You're here. That's what counts." And then he gave Holt's shoulder a squeeze and went back to what he was doing.

Holt stood there for a long moment, still feeling the light pressure of Tom Potter's hand on his shoulder. He thought about how right it felt; about how he'd never felt anything like it, not even as a boy when he'd longed for just such a gesture from his own father.

He'd told himself eventually that it didn't matter, that his father's interest and approbation were unnecessary, that he could—*would*—get along fine without them. And so he had.

But now, with the touch of Tom's hand on his shoulder, Holt felt something inside him ease, uncurl. A knot he hadn't even known was there seemed to loosen. He rubbed his hands together, then said to the cow, "We can do this. We're going to do this. You and me."

The cow looked at him quizzically, then went back to chewing. Holt bent his head, crouched and got back to work. It was easier this time.

Life seemed easier, too.

BUT NO LESS COMPLICATED.

There was still the charade with Lucy to be carried forth. There was still the gauntlet of her relatives to endure.

He came in from doing the milking to find Lucy's grandmother in the kitchen, fixing his eggs just the way he liked them, then tousling his hair—again— when she set his plate in front of him. "Eat up," she told him. "And there's plenty more where that came from."

He discovered that yesterday's wonderful breakfast was not a one-off. Today's was mouthwateringly good, too. And sitting there at the table with Lucy's grandparents, letting their conversation wash over him, was pleasant. Warm. Comfortable.

Later, while they were waiting for their parents to arrive home, Joe and Luke invited him to play a new video game with them. If his knowledge of the Rangers had gone a long way toward making him an acceptable family member, his ability to make it to level twelve when they couldn't get past six made him a star attraction.

Augie and Jake, arriving just after noon, exhausted from their flight and jet lag, still took time from hugging their kids to look him over and then hug him, too.

"Welcome to the family," Augie said. "We're so happy to have you."

And Jake said with a smile, "Grandpa says you'll do," which was clearly high praise.

Holt found himself smiling, too.

His smile must have made him seem approachable, because Holly asked if he'd help roll the balls to make her snowman. They were big snowballs. Her father was jet-lagged. Eldon was fixing a leak for the nuns. She needed a strong man. He couldn't let her do it alone.

Then Chloe needed his advice about a sweater she wanted to buy for Eldon. "It's a little flashy. Maybe not his type. But sometimes he needs a challenge, you know? It's just at a shop in Gaithersburg. Please? Surely Lucy can spare you that long. After all, you had all night together," she added with a wink and a grin.

He'd never been asked his opinion on a gift for someone else before. He wondered if maybe he could get a little advice from her.

When he came back from Gaithersburg Jake and Eldon said, "We're cutting firewood. Come on."

Holt had never cut firewood in his life, and he was pretty sure he'd look like a fool in front of them. He debated coming up with an excuse. The contracts, after all, were still undone. But he didn't because he realized that they really didn't need his help, they were simply being friendly, making an effort to include him. They didn't know he had no right to be included.

He wasn't going to tell them.

He went along, daring to admit even as he did so, "I've never been much with an ax."

"No time like the present to learn," Jake said cheerfully. "I'm so sleepy I'd cut my foot off, but I think I can boss you around."

He could. He did. And he was a good teacher. Holt had a sense of satisfaction as he swung the ax and heard it bite into the wood. And as he worked, his muscles bunching and stretching, he felt he was part of an almost-primal rhythm. Slowly—very slowly—the wood stacked up. Jake applauded. Eldon said, "Not bad."

Holt was pleased.

"Appreciate it," Grandpa said when he came past. He looked toward the barn. "But time to get to the milking again."

Holt glanced at his watch and groaned.

"Time flies when you're having fun," Grandpa said with a grin. "Jake's here now. He can do it."

But Holt said, "I don't mind."

He was better at the milking this time. He found a rhythm in the work. The second time around meant he began to know some of the cows—which ones were easier to deal with, which ones tried to sidestep away.

"Nice try," he said to one particularly determined bovine after she danced away from him several times before he succeeded in getting the milker attached. "Gotcha." He grinned.

She gave him a baleful over-the-shoulder stare, then switched her tail in his face.

"Take that," said a voice behind him.

He jumped, and turned to see Lucy standing there. She smiled at him and his heart did an equally jumpy thing in his chest.

It was practically the first time he'd seen her all day, the first time he'd been close to her since he'd held her in his arms. While he had been playing video games and making snowmen and going into Gaithersburg with Chloe, Lucy had been helping her grandmother, wrapping presents and making cranberry sauce and baking pumpkin bread. He'd caught glimpses of her, but there had never been time to talk, to touch.

And he wanted to do both.

Just for now. Just for a little while. It wouldn't be permanent. But if he was going to play fiancé, he thought he ought to get a few of the benefits.

"I just came to tell you that supper's almost ready," she said. There was more color than usual in her face. She glanced at him and then turned her gaze on her grandfather. "And to see how close you were to finished."

"That's why you came, eh?" her grandfather said with a knowing look that moved from her to Holt and back again. Her blush deepened.

"Right. Well, you and Holt finish up, then," Tom said, rubbing his hands down the sides of his overalls. "I'll just go on up to the house. Don't be too long," he added with an arch look, but he gave Holt a nod of approval on his way out.

They watched as he walked across the snowy yard. Beside Holt, the milking machine continued to pump. Around them the animals munched and rustled about and muttered, then went right on being cows. And Holt became aware that even in a barn with forty cows, it was possible for a couple to be alone.

He shot a sideways glance at Lucy.

She ran her tongue over her lips, then said, "Right, um. Let's get to work."

"That's not why he left us."

She shook her head. "He's a romantic. We can ignore him."

"I don't want to." He turned her to face him.

"There's no one here now," she said. "You don't have to keep up the charade."

"Yes, I do." He put a finger under her chin and tipped it up so she had to look at him.

"Why?" she asked desperately.

"Because you have to go in for dinner looking thoroughly kissed."

"Of course I don't! He'll understand. He'll know we were working. He'll admire your restraint."

"He'll have my head examined." He drew her closer.

"Holt!" She lifted her face and looked right at him. She pressed her hands against his chest, but she didn't push him away—not even when he bent his head.

Then— "Oof!"

Their mouths were crushed together as he slammed right into her. A large wet, very unexpected tongue caressed the back of his neck. "Hey!"

Lucy pulled away, stumbled and glanced wildly around. "Truffles!"

The dog backed off Holt, grinning madly and wagging her bushy tail.

"Oh, wow! Oops, sorry." The twins appeared in the doorway to the barn.

"We were playin' tag in the yard and she musta seen Lucy," Joe said.

"Maybe she thought you were attackin' her," Luke suggested.

"Maybe she thought she was helping." Joe grinned.

"She got galoshes prints on your back," Luke told Holt. The boys both thought that was hysterically funny. Lucy, turning him around and examining his back, began laughing, too.

Holt met her gaze, torn between annoyance and resignation. He shouldn't have been surprised, he told himself. A cow's tail across the face. A dog's galoshes on his back. Lucy laughing at him. But her laughter wasn't mean. It was contagious. It asked to be shared.

He laughed, too.

Then he grabbed her and hauled her into his arms and kissed her.

Her eyes flew open. She stared, astonished, into his. "What *are* you doing?"

He grinned. "What any good red-blooded fiancé would do."

Or any man who had a terminal case of frustration and knew this was as close as he was likely to get to assuaging it.

"Wow," he heard one of the twins say.

And the other one said, awestruck, as Holt kept right on kissing Lucy, "And there isn't even any mistletoe."

IT WAS ALL AN ACT. A very good act. But still, an act.

Lucy knew that. The same way she knew that Holt had spent the night with her because he had to.

She shouldn't have gloried in it. She certainly shouldn't have allowed herself to enjoy it so much.

But she had.

She'd tried to stop him, hadn't she? she asked herself righteously. She hadn't kissed him back this time, had she?

Well, no. But she hadn't closed her lips tightly and resisted his tongue's teasing entry. She had put her hands on his chest, but her fingers had tightened on his jacket, holding him close, not pushing him away.

She couldn't help it.

Just as she couldn't help the twins pushing her tight against Holt later that evening when they all crowded into the pew for Christmas Eve services at church.

She knew it was wrong, too, to stand beside him as they sang carols and let him fold his hand around hers. But Tim was there with his new wife, looking at her with interest and concern, and she needed Holt just then. Didn't she?

"That's Tim," she'd said under her breath to Holt. And his fingers had tightened and he'd turned and leaned over and brushed a kiss across her ear—right there in the middle of the service.

It was only because of Tim, she told herself. Only because of Tim that he'd done it.

And only because of Tim that she'd let him.

It wasn't until she slipped into bed next to Chloe late that night that she admitted to herself what a liar she was. She liked Holt holding her hand. She liked him kissing her. She liked—

"Your turn," Chloe murmured, rolling over and propping her head up on one hand.

"Huh?"

"To trade places," Chloe said, exasperated. "I went last night."

Lucy's eyes nearly popped. "Trade places?" Her voice was almost a squeak. She felt her whole body heat at the prospect. "Go to…Holt, you mean?"

"Unless you've stashed some other fiancé you'd rather spend the night with," Chloe said dryly.

Lucy didn't say anything at all. Her throat felt suddenly tight. Her heart kicked into overdrive. Her body seemed almost to quiver.

Spend another night with Holt? Curl in the warmth of his embrace? Feel his breath on her cheek? His lips against her hair?

"Lucy, it's Christmas Eve. The kids are going to be up before Grandpa, for heaven's sake. We literally have not got all night! Get going."

"But," Lucy said.

"Um," Lucy said.

"Well," Lucy said.

Before she could say anything else, there was a noise at the door. It opened and Eldon slipped in. His grin flashed white in the darkness. "I didn't think the place was ever going to settle down." He glanced at Lucy. "Holt's waiting."

IT WAS MAYBE HALF-a-dozen steps down the hall to the room where Lucy and Chloe were sharing that big feather bed. It would have taken Eldon maybe five seconds to get from one room to the other—if he walked slow—which it didn't look as if he would. It would take Lucy another five to come this way.

Holt had already counted to sixty.

She hadn't come.

He gave her another thirty seconds. Sixty.

He waited. And waited.

He drummed his fingers on the mattress. He twisted the sheet in his hand.

She wasn't going to *stay* there with them, was she?

And do what—have a ménage à trois with Eldon and Chloe?

The thought made him sit up straight in bed, brows drawn down. Of course she wasn't!

Then where the hell was she?

It would be just like Lucy to decide that last night was tempting fate enough. She had been on the other end of that kiss in the barn this afternoon. She knew what was happening in his body. She had to know another night of celibate cuddling was not in the works.

So, was she on the sofa? Had she decided slipping into Holly's room was a better bet? Or was she going to spend the night in the hall?

His patience shot, Holt vaulted out of bed and jerked open the door to look.

Lucy, standing like a wraith in her nightgown on the other side, let out a little squeak.

"What the—!" He grabbed her hand and hauled her into the room—into his arms. "Where the hell have you been?"

"Been?" Another squeak. "Just...out there."

"Standing in the hall? Why?"

"Because. I—" She stopped. "I didn't think you'd want— I wasn't sure—"

"I am." He'd never been more sure of anything in his life.

He wanted her. All day long he'd wanted her. All last night he'd wanted her.

"Holt!"

"Lucy." And then his lips found hers, touched hers, plundered hers. She was every bit as sweet as he remembered.

He picked her up and carried her to his bed.

CHAPTER SIX

SHE LOVED HIM.

And why not? She wasn't asking for "forever." Only for tonight.

It wasn't much. Hardly anything. One night. That was all. And didn't she deserve some closeness? Some intimacy? Some love?

So what if he didn't love her? She knew that.

And anyway, after what had happened with Tim, how much more could she possibly be hurt?

That, at least, was her rationale for giving in, for letting Holt lay her on the bed, for letting him settle himself astride her, for kissing him as eagerly as he kissed her.

Not that she spent a lot of time rationalizing. Thinking of any sort was not high on her list of priorities just then. She only had one priority: Holt.

He was more than enough.

She'd felt the warmth of his bare chest the night before when he'd wrapped his arms around her and pulled her close. But she hadn't reached out a hand and deliberately touched him before.

She did now. She brushed her hand lightly down the middle of his chest once, then again. He made a soft sound deep in his throat as he straddled her and looked down. She couldn't see the expression on his face in the darkness. But she could feel his intensity in the faint tremor in his fingers as they touched her.

Neither of them spoke.

To speak would be to break the spell. It would remind them of who they were, of what they were doing here. Lucy didn't want to remember that it was a sham; that when Christmas was over, her engagement would be, too.

It didn't matter.

The only thing that mattered was Holt.

Holt, the man, not the boss. The Holt who had protested that he didn't do families—and then did hers. The Holt who had never milked a cow or chopped a log or strung a strand of popcorn-and-cranberries or made a snowman or, she was willing to bet, spent an entire celibate night holding a woman in his arms.

That Holt mattered. Her boss, she liked; but the man inside him—*that* Holt—she loved.

She ran her hands up his arms, across his shoulders. She touched his jaw, she tangled her fingers at the back of his neck and drew him down into her arms.

And he came to her eagerly, impatiently, and at the same time gently. There was no doubt that he wanted her every bit as much as she wanted him. She could feel the desire in him at the same time she could appreciate his willingness to take it slow, to accommodate her, to make it last.

Lucy desperately wanted it to last. Not just for tonight. Forever.

But she knew better than that.

And so she concentrated on the moment, concentrated on the man. "Yes," she said when he touched her. And, "Do you like that?" she asked, touching him.

The hiss of breath she got as a reply told her the answer was yes. She smiled and touched again. She felt him shudder, and felt a similar shudder run through her at the soft, gentle touch of his fingers stroking her, teasing her, readying her.

And she was ready. So very ready. "Now, Holt," she urged him. "Now! Please!"

His grin flashed above her, white in the darkness. "I thought you'd never ask."

And then he came to her and made them one.

Lucy wrapped her arms around him, held him close, drew him in, and settled into the rhythm he chose. It was a rhythm so primal—and so perfectly attuned to hers—that however much she wanted them to, the feelings they were building couldn't last.

The explosion of his release triggered hers, and she felt herself soaring—but not alone. For however long she had—seconds, minutes, hours—they were together. She was as much a part of him as he was a part of her.

And when he finally slept, she hung on to as much of the dream as she could.

THERE WAS, OF COURSE, milking to be done.

"Cows don't know it's Christmas," Tom said as he and Holt and Jake stumped out to the barn. It was cold, it was dark, the wind blew down out of the north, rattling the bare trees. The moon cut a silvery swath across the icy yard. It was bleak and otherworldly to Holt. Tom and Jake seemed to take it in stride.

"You don't have to come," Tom said to Holt for the third time.

But he did.

He'd made himself get up even before Tom, trying not to wake Lucy as he slipped out into the cold early-morning darkness.

She'd been sleeping soundly, beautifully, and he was damned if he was going to wake her to chivy her back to her own room. If Eldon wanted to play musical beds later on, that was up to him. In the confusion of Christmas morning, Holt was fairly sure that no one would notice who came out of what bedroom—or care.

He cared. Too much.

About Lucy. About her family.

He didn't want to, God knew. This hadn't been

part of his game plan. His game plan was to go through life with as few strings as possible.

Loving Lucy all through the night hadn't changed that.

But it had made him feel guilty. He had taken advantage of a situation he had no right to. Even in business, he never did that. He might be a shark, but he was a fair shark. There was nothing fair about what he'd done last night.

And what was worse, he wanted to do it again. And again. He wanted to wake up next to Lucy every morning.

What kind of nonsense was that?

It was pure nonsense. Doubtless a product of his guilt. And if struggling out of bed at 4:00 a.m. to trudge out to a cold barn and wrestle with a bunch of bossy bovines was the only means he could see to assuage a little of that guilt, well, so be it.

He made up his mind to get out of this land of hope and dreams and make-believe—and back to real life—as soon as he could.

IT WASN'T QUITE that easy.

There was Christmas to be got through first. Things were pretty much the way he expected them to be by the time they came in from milking, which was to say noisy and hectic and just a little wild. Also, as he'd figured, no one had noticed where Lucy or Eldon had spent the night.

Everyone was gathered in the living room, opening presents and oohing and aahing and laughing and congratulating each other on their perceptive choices. He slid down to sit on the floor next to the twins, let Grandma press a cup of coffee into his hands, and sat back, content just to watch the chaos, to be where he belonged—on the outside, looking in.

But then Lucy began to open the present he'd got her.

It wasn't much—a small ring of inlaid turquoise that seemed to go with a necklace he'd seen her wear a lot. He'd had no intention of giving her anything beyond a substantial Christmas bonus—until he went shopping with Chloe yesterday afternoon.

Chloe's enthusiasm had been infectious, and her eagerness to please Eldon made Holt realize that it was what a real fiancé must feel. And so he'd begun to keep an eye out for something for Lucy. After all, he told himself, everyone would certainly doubt their engagement if he didn't even get her a gift.

It ought to be easy to find a gift, he'd assured himself. What did women like?

It didn't take him long to realize that it didn't matter what ''women'' liked. It was what Lucy would like that was important. He'd prowled the shops of Gaithersburg from one end to the other, rejecting this and that and beginning to despair.

And then he'd found the ring. It wasn't an expensive one. It had, in fact, quite a simple setting and the tiny stones were just that—tiny. But it looked like Lucy. He could see her wearing it. And so he'd bought it. An "engagement" ring.

She'd open it and appreciate the joke.

But now, as she was carefully undoing his clumsy wrapping job, he wondered if he hadn't made a big mistake.

Her fingers stopped moving when she held the bare box in her hand. It was small and square and functional and could hold only one thing.

"What is it?" Holly demanded.

"Let's see," said Joe.

"Show us," said Luke.

Slowly Lucy lifted her gaze to Holt at the same time she drew the ring from the box. She didn't smile. She looked stricken.

He felt oddly stricken, too. "I know it's not much," he said quickly, "but I thought...that necklace you sometimes wear is turquoise...and I saw this and, well..." He forced the words through his lips, aware suddenly of how presumptuous it was, how very wrong he must have been. Hell, with his luck, the necklace might have been a gift from Tim.

Lucy still didn't say anything. Slowly she took the ring out of the box and turned it around with her fingers.

Chloe bent to look at the narrow sterling-silver

band with the finely cut turquoise inlay and exclaimed, "Oh, Lucy, it's perfect!"

"Let's see!" Augie demanded, then said, "Oh, Lucy, how marvelous. He really knows you!" And she turned her gaze on Holt, her smile and her approval reaching her eyes.

Grandma and Grandpa demanded a look. So did Holly and the twins and Eldon and Jake. They all thought it was wonderful, perfect, the ideal ring for Lucy.

"And you didn't have a ring," Grandma said, smiling from one to the other of them. "We wondered, but...well, you know...sometimes we don't understand these modern relationships and we didn't want to ask."

Holt barely heard any of them, except to wince inwardly at the "modern relationship" comment. He was still looking at Lucy's white face.

He hadn't wanted to hurt her! That was the last thing he wanted to do. It had just seemed like the right thing—the perfect thing—a tiny joke between the two of them, and something she would like anyway. Something he could say—when this was all over—that he meant for her to have.

To remember our engagement by, he'd been intending to say jokingly.

It didn't seem very funny right now.

"If you don't like it..." he began again.

"I like it." She spoke the words so softly he

could barely hear them. She ducked her head, her eyes blinking rapidly. Then, as he watched, she ran her tongue over her lips, then splayed the fingers of her left hand and tried to slide the ring on.

It fit. Perfectly.

HE KEPT SAYING, "If you don't like it..."

But she loved it. That was the problem.

How had he known? How had he chosen a ring she would have chosen for herself? It was so perfect—and so perfectly unexpected.

Of course, it was meant as a joke. She understood that. Sometime in the far-distant future—in another galaxy, perhaps—she might even be able to smile about it.

Now she put it on and curled her fingers into a fist, letting them memorize the feel of it. The moment she put it on, she knew she would hate to take it off, just as she knew that in not very many hours she would have to.

They were leaving for the city after dinner. Holt had to fly to Dallas in the morning. The family wasn't happy about that, but they understood.

"At least you got here," Grandpa said.

"And you'll be coming back," added Grandma.

But Holt wouldn't be. Once they had left, the charade would be over, the ring would be returned. It would be up to Lucy to break the news to them. A broken engagement—one that *she* broke, this time. She could manage that.

Couldn't she?

Of course.

She could tell Holt thank you. She could tell him she appreciated his efforts on her behalf. She could tell him he'd done a wonderful job. And he had— so wonderful that she'd fallen in love with him for real.

But she couldn't tell him that.

She knew—had always known—that Holt Braxton had no use for women who had more than a fling on their minds. It was why he'd turned his back on the glamorous Roz, wasn't it? She'd been fun as long as she'd known her place in his life, but the moment she'd changed the agenda, he'd turned his back.

Just as he would turn his back on Lucy once they were out the door. It was no big surprise.

The surprise was discovering how much it was going to hurt.

Don't think about it! Lucy told herself, curling into the rocking chair and letting the holiday cheer of her family wash over her. They were all delighted. Happy for themselves, happy for her. Was it so wrong to pretend to be happy herself for just a little while longer?

Go ahead, she permitted herself. *Just for a little while longer, go ahead and pretend.*

So she let herself smile at him. She let herself brush elbows with him at the dinner table. She even let herself share a kiss with him under the mistletoe right before they had to leave that afternoon.

She tried not to let herself remember what it had been like to make love with him. She tried not to think about having to take the ring off and give it back to him.

Oh, God, why had she fallen in love with him?

It served her right, she supposed. It was some sort of divine comeuppance, an almighty chiding for having lied about having a fiancé in the first place. *Please, God, just a few minutes more.*

And she got a few minutes more.

But then, inevitably, it was time to go.

"It was so good to see you," Grandma said, hugging her tightly as they stood beside the car. "I've worried about you down there in that big city. I was afraid you wouldn't be happy. I'm so glad you are—and that you've got Holt." She gave Lucy an extra squeeze. "He's everything I ever hoped for you."

He was, Lucy thought. It was just too bad it wasn't true. She smiled wanly and tried to swallow the growing lump in her throat as she returned her grandmother's hug. "I'm glad I came, too."

Her grandfather gave her a hug then, and said with a nod of approval, "He's a good man. I like him."

"Yes," Lucy said. "I do, too."

Her sisters and brother-in-law said the same. Luke and Joe thought he was a good guy and that maybe, if he had a couple of extra Rangers tickets... And Holly wanted to know if this time she was really going to get to be a bridesmaid.

"'Cause last time I didn't, y'know," she added pointedly.

"I...hope so," Lucy said faintly. She hoped Holt hadn't heard that. He was crushed in her sisters' embraces, and she imagined he was hearing enough that he didn't want to hear. "We really need to get going," she said a little desperately. "It's a long drive back to the city."

"Right," Holt said, extracting himself from Chloe's hug. Was there desperation in his tone, too? "Thanks for everything," he said to her grandparents.

"Thank *you*," Grandma said, wrapping her arms around him, "for making our Lucy so happy."

Her grandfather clapped him on the back. "Glad t'have you in the family, son."

Holt's smile was strained to the breaking point. He looked away. "I appreciate that, sir."

"None of that sir, stuff. We're your grandpa and grandma, too."

"Gotta go. Bye, all," Lucy said quickly, hopping into the car.

Holt got in and started the engine. His movements

were jerky and he almost gunned the engine as they headed away from Lucy's family who stood, waving madly after them.

Lucy turned back and gave one last wave of her hand. Then Holt turned out onto the highway and they left Boone's Corner behind.

BACK TO THE REAL WORLD.

The world of business worries and impersonal demands, of quarrelsome managing directors and blockheaded CEOs. Those, he could handle.

He couldn't handle any more Potters. He wanted no more hugs, no more smiles, no more warm welcomes. He should have been immune to them. He was annoyed with himself that he wasn't.

He'd had years to develop his resistance, after all.

He slanted a glance in Lucy's direction. She was staring straight ahead. She looked miserable. Of course she was miserable. She was leaving her family whom she loved—her family who loved *her*—and going back to New York, back to anonymity, to work.

It must be horrible for her. She was such a warm person, so caring, so giving. So...responsive.

God, yes, she was responsive! He should know.

He supposed she was regretting having slept with him. He wasn't going to ask. He didn't want to know it if she was. *He* wasn't regretting it. Feeling guilty, yes, but not regretting it. Not for his own sake, at least. No matter what else he might come to regret in his life, he was never going to regret that.

He'd never made love with a woman like her. Even now, just a glance at her could make him want her.

He didn't dare let himself think about it.

"You don't need to go in to the office early tomorrow." They were the first words he had spoken in two hours. He said them as they crossed the bridge into Manhattan, as the real world loomed all around them. He said them in order to put the two of them on safe footing again. "You don't actually have to go in at all. It's a paid holiday, and I know it. But if you do, I'd appreciate it if you'd e-mail me copies of the changes we made when you put them in the contracts. And keep Robertson off my back."

For a moment he didn't think she was going to respond, but then she said tonelessly, "I'll go in."

"Where do you live?"

Her head jerked up. "What?"

"I'm taking you home. I need to know where you live."

"Oh. Right." The tonelessness was back again. "In the Village." She gave him the address, then added, "You don't have to. I can get a cab from your place."

"Nonsense. Of course I'll take you. It's the least I can do."

Which is why you're doing it, he said silently on her behalf. She didn't say it. She didn't say anything. Her hands were knotted in her lap. She was twisting the ring he'd given her.

The streets of Manhattan were almost empty. Early Christmas evening was obviously the time to get through the city in record time. He was pulling up in front of her building before he knew it, before he was ready for it—and it was time to say goodbye.

He started to park, but Lucy said, "Don't bother. I'll just jump out here." She tugged her coat around her and did just that. "Pop the trunk latch and I'll grab my stuff."

But he wasn't going to do that. He got out and opened the trunk, piled her arms with gifts her family had given her, then took a load himself and managed a smile. "Lead on."

She hesitated for a second, then shrugged and led him up the front steps and into the building. He followed her up two flights of stairs, then waited while she opened the door to her apartment.

It was the Potter farmhouse transplanted to New York City. He stood inside the door and felt a wave of something—nostalgia? homesickness? longing?—wash over him. No, of course he didn't feel any of those things. It was surprise, that was all. But there they were—the same hooked rugs, the same homey furniture, the same mismatched crockery, the same pile of crocheted afghans by the rocking chair.

He set down the load of gifts and her suitcase, then straightened to look around and savor it, only to have Lucy thrust something at him. "Here."

Automatically he took it, then looked down. It was the ring. He frowned. "What are you doing? This is your Christmas present."

"It's your fiancée's Christmas present," Lucy contradicted. "I'm not your fiancée anymore—not that I ever really was—so I'm returning it."

"I gave it to you," Holt said firmly. He thrust it back at her. "Take it."

She wrapped her arms across her chest. "No."

"Damn it, Lucy, take it! I bought it for you. I want *you* to have it."

"I don't want it!"

He felt as if she'd punched him in the gut.

She stepped around him, opened the door, lifted her chin, and waited. "I appreciate your help," she said stiffly. "It was kind of you."

"Kind?" he echoed. He couldn't ever remember being called "kind" in his life.

"Kind," Lucy repeated. "Goodbye, Holt. I'll send you the e-mail in the morning."

Still he didn't move. Still she waited.

For what?

What could he do? What could he say?

His fingers tightened around the ring so hard that

the edge of the turquoise cut into his palm. "I'll give you a call from Dallas."

SHE KEPT ROBERTSON off his back. She sent him the contract changes by e-mail. She took his call when it came the next afternoon and answered with her usual calm efficiency. He didn't have to know that she had red puffy eyes and was blowing her nose.

"You sound stuffy. Did you catch my cold?" he demanded.

"No."

She caught the office up on everything that needed to be done, was thoroughly and disgustingly efficient. She was a model secretary—and more miserable than she'd ever been in her life.

It was worse than with Tim.

When Tim had left her for another woman she'd felt outrage, she'd felt betrayed, she'd felt anger.

When Holt went to Dallas, she felt lost, as if the compass guiding her life had failed her, as if the light that lit her days had gone out.

It was stupid. It was insane. How could she feel lost without something—some*one*—she'd never had?

Rationally, she assured herself, she couldn't. But rational thought seemed to have nothing to do with what she felt. She missed him dreadfully. She wanted him to come home, and she knew it would be the worst thing in the world if he did.

He couldn't come home until she could get a grip on herself. He couldn't walk into the office and act like Holt Braxton—brisk and businesslike, yet pausing every so often to reminisce about milking Grandpa's cows—until she could get through a day without using half a box of tissue.

She made things worse by not telling her grandparents that they'd broken off the engagement.

She rang them as soon as she got to New York just to say they were back and safe, but she couldn't tell them then. It was too soon. They would know it couldn't be true. They'd probably want to come down and talk sense to her and Holt. There would be plenty of time to tell her family.

But she didn't tell them two days later when her sister Chloe called to say she and Eldon had decided on a February wedding. "Not Valentine's Day, though. The week after. You can be my bridesmaid," Chloe said.

"Of course," Lucy said.

"Holt can be an usher."

"Well, um...he...might be out of town."

How could she ruin her sister's joy by telling her that she and Holt had called if off then?

But when her grandmother called on New Year's Eve to wish her a Happy New Year, she could have—*should have*—said her engagement was at an end.

She didn't. She stared in blank misery at the four walls of her apartment and couldn't find the words. She knew how much they liked Holt, how happy they were for her. They were still talking about it.

"I am so glad your moving to the city worked out," Grandma said. "It seemed like a pretty extreme response to Tim's behavior, but obviously it was what you were meant to do. You'd never have met Holt if you hadn't, would you? It's wonderful to be young and in love. I'm so happy for you."

She couldn't say it was all a sham then, could she? She said, "Thank you," in a small voice.

"What's wrong, dear? You sound sad."

She was sad. But she couldn't explain that to her grandmother, either. "I'm missing him, that's all." That, at least, was the truth.

"Of course you are, dear," Grandma replied. "You love him."

And heaven help her, that was the truth, too. It wasn't just loving him for one night or a few days, or just pretending to be "in love" with him for her family's sake and her own pride.

It was the real thing.

"And he loves you," her grandmother went on quite firmly.

No, he didn't.

"He's a good man," her grandfather put in on the

extension. "He's got his values in order and his head screwed on straight."

It was the Tom Potter seal of approval. And Lucy couldn't deny it, either. "I know," she agreed in the same small voice.

"He'll be back soon, won't he?" Grandma said soothingly.

"The day after New Year's," Lucy said, past the lump in her throat. Not that it would do her any good.

"Only two days," her grandmother consoled. "Go to bed early tonight. Get up late tomorrow. Watch the Rose Parade and a couple of football games and he'll be home before you know it."

Lucy smiled at her grandmother's prescription for getting through the days. "Maybe I will," she said listlessly.

"And drink a nice glass of hot milk," her grandfather said. "Vermont milk."

Lucy laughed past the tears starting to dampen her eyes. "I will, Grandpa. Thanks for calling. I love you both."

"We love you, too, Lucy," her grandmother said. "And we couldn't be happier for you. I hope this coming year is as wonderful as the past. I'm sure it will be. A marriage is even more marvelous than an engagement. Happy New Year, my love."

"Happy New Year," Lucy echoed hollowly. She hung up.

SHE DRANK HER GLASS of hot milk. She went to bed early. She curled around her pillow and tried to go to sleep. The pillow tickled her nose. The room was too warm, then it was too cold. Outside she could hear revelers laughing and yelling and shooting off firecrackers, gearing up to celebrate the coming New Year. On with the new. Out with the old. They were putting the past behind them.

Exactly what she needed to do. Again.

God, she was useless. After the disaster of Tim, surely she should have learned something. Not to wear her heart on her sleeve, for example—or anywhere in her body, for that matter.

But she had. And now, here she was, in love with a man far less suitable than even Tim had been. A man who would never love her. A man who, by his own admission, didn't intend to love anyone. A man who—

She was interrupted by the sharp sound of her doorbell. She ignored it. The people on the first floor were having a party. Somebody had hit the wrong bell.

It rang again. Longer this time. More insistently.

"Go away," she said, rolled over and put the pillow over her head.

The next sound she heard, though muffled by the pillow, was a sharp rapping on her apartment door. She jerked the pillow off and sat up. What on earth?

The rapping came again. She scrambled out of

bed and padded to the door to peer through the peep-hole. Her eyes opened wide.

"*Holt?*"

He heard his name, even though she thought she'd barely breathed it. "Lucy? Open the door."

She put her hand to the top lock, then stopped. "W-wait." She backed away from the door, hugging herself and hurrying to pull on her robe. She ran her hands through her hair. It was hopeless. She blew her nose.

What was he doing here?

Hastily she tied the sash of her robe and set about opening the locks. When the last one was unlocked, the door shot open and Holt strode in. It was the way he walked into board conferences and takeover meetings—tall and powerful and competent. And with his head screwed on straight.

Or was it? His hair was tousled, his tie was askew. He looked pale and drawn and as if he hadn't slept in days. Surely the meetings with Davis Russell hadn't been that bad.

Or maybe they had. Maybe that was why he was here. To get things on track again. To work!

Suddenly she was incensed. "If you think I'm revising contracts or taking dictation tonight, you're out of your mind!"

"I don't think—"

"And if you want me to come down to the office

and find some stupid memo you've misplaced, the hell with you!"

"I—"

"And if you need me to sew on a button so you can go out to some business New Year's celebration with the glamorous Roz, you can go straight to hell!"

Oh, God, she shouldn't have said that! She shouldn't have said any of it! Lucy whirled away, and hugging her arms tightly across her breasts she retreated to the far side of the room.

"Go away," she muttered, keeping her back to him. "Just…go away."

"No."

But it wasn't a forceful *no*. Or a flat *no*. Or an omniscient *no*.

It was a quiet *no*.

She slanted a glance his way. He looked awful. Worse than she'd ever seen him. Had he lost the deal entirely? She tried to read his expression. It seemed to be a mixture of worry and consternation and something else. Hope?

No, of course not. He couldn't possibly hope he could change her mind and get her to work tonight. Not after that outburst.

"I didn't come to ask you to work tonight," he said quietly.

She turned her head and looked at him more closely. "You didn't?"

He shook his head. "No."

She traced a braid in the hooked rug with her toe. "Then why...?"

But she couldn't ask. There was no answer she wanted to hear. She shrugged and turned away again. Footsteps came up behind her. She edged away, but she was practically on the window ledge, as it was.

"I think I love you," he said.

Lucy was sure she hadn't heard those words. She went totally still. Didn't move. Didn't breathe. No. He couldn't have said that. Not to her. He wasn't ever going to say them to anyone.

But if he hadn't, then— "What?"

He was so close she heard him draw a breath. She listened as if her life depended on it. In fact, it did.

"I think I love you," he said again.

She turned then, looked up into his eyes, and saw the hope she'd thought she'd seen there. She saw something else, too, which she knew she'd never seen there before: fear.

"That's why you came back?" she asked softly, incredulously. "That's why you're here?"

He nodded once, then ran his tongue over his lips. "I told Russell I wasn't ready to think about the contracts. I *couldn't* think about them. All I could think about was you."

She stared in disbelief. "Holt Braxton, New York's most single-minded businessman?"

A corner of his mouth quirked. "I was single-minded, all right. I was missing you. I kept thinking about the farm, the kids, the family. About you. About making love to you—"

"Holt!"

"About how wonderful it had been. How real it seemed. More real than what I was doing in Dallas, that's for sure. I called your grandparents."

"You called them?" Lucy stared. "Why?"

"Because I was afraid to call you. And—" he shrugged "—I wanted to talk to them. I...missed them. I wanted to explain, to apologize. I thought you'd told them already—about the engagement, I mean. And I was hoping maybe they wouldn't hate me for lying to them. I didn't want them to. And then I discovered you hadn't told them."

"The time wasn't right. I couldn't—"

"Why? Why couldn't you?" There was an urgency in his voice she'd never heard before. Not in all the million-dollar deals. Not in the takeovers. Not in the nitty-gritty give-and-take of his corporate life.

Because, she realized, this wasn't the corporate Holt Braxton. This was the man inside him—the real man—the one no one else ever saw—except her.

"Because," she said, looking into his eyes and blinking back tears—of happiness, this time, "I love you, too."

EVERY MAN HAD DREAMS.

A fast car. A career he loved. A million dollars

by the time he was thirty. Holt had all those. He'd always thought they were enough.

Until Lucy.

He didn't know when he began to want more, when he began to want *her*.

Maybe it was the chicken soup that had started it. "Chicken soup. Good for what ails you," Lucy's grandma always said.

Holt had known it was good for his cold. He hadn't realized there was anything else ailing him.

There was.

He was alone. More than alone—he was lonely. Rootless. Wandering.

Seeking.

But until Lucy and her family came into his life, he hadn't known for what.

He knew now. He had it now—a home, a family. Lucy. Love.

Lucy and love were synonymous as far as he was concerned. He couldn't imagine life without her. He couldn't imagine life without her large, boisterous family—without the teasing and the squabbles and the cows and the prints from dog galoshes on the kitchen floor.

It was everything he didn't even know he'd wanted—until he'd had it and then had faced living without it. Marrying Lucy, he had it again. He was content. Complete.

Or thought he'd thought he was.

Until that May day four months later when Lucy had come into the bedroom and put her arms around him and said, "You're going to be a daddy."

He could still remember the numbness, then the stark terror that had followed.

He didn't want a family like the one he'd grown up in. He never again wanted to feel the coldness and the distance, the jealousy and the bitter resentment he'd experienced as a child.

Lucy must have seen all that in his face. She was incredibly good at reading him. He remembered the way she'd touched his cheek and then pressed her lips to his mouth. "Families are what you make them, Holt. Ours will be wonderful. I promise."

And now, as he stood at the foot of his wife's hospital bed on New Year's morning, watching her nurse their five-hour-old son, a look of blissful contentment on both of their faces, he began to believe it. He felt the knot that he'd carried inside him since that May day begin to loosen, and he came around the side of the bed and bent to kiss her. To kiss them both.

Families were what you made them.

He knew that he and Lucy would make theirs one of love and laughter, of joy and hope.

"He's a keeper," Grandpa said from the doorway where he and Grandma smiled at the three of them.

"Oh, yes," Holt managed, his voice surprisingly ragged.

"So are you," Lucy whispered in his ear. She looped an arm around him to draw him down onto the bed with her and tiny Thomas Potter Braxton. The baby's hand curled around Holt's finger and clung tightly.

He looked at their linked hands, then felt Lucy's come to join them, and he wrapped his hand around them both. A flashbulb popped.

Jake said, "Gotcha!"

Chloe said, "First picture of the new family."

The entire Potter extended-family beamed at them. Eldon carried in a sprig of mistletoe and held it over the bed.

With no urging at all, Holt kissed his wife again. "I love you," he said. Then he looked around. "I love you all."

He really was part of a family now—and he'd come home to stay.

Barbara Bretton

3,2,1...BABY!

CHAPTER ONE

New Year's Eve, 1971

"WILL YOU LOOK AT THEM." Mary Patricia O'Callaghan tapped gently on the nursery window and smiled at her pink-wrapped bundle of joy. "Aren't they too precious?"

Gina Antoinette Marino was partial to the bundle wrapped in blue that lay in the isolette next to Mary Pat's little one. "Who would've figured we'd deliver on the same day?"

Mary Pat linked her arm through her best friend's. "I think it's fate," she said. "Our fathers-in-law started a business together. Our husbands inherited it. And now here's the next generation."

Gina's eyes misted over with happy tears. "It's all so perfect," she said, wishing she had some tissues handy. "Like a fairy tale."

"Yes," said Mary Pat, wishing she had some tissues herself. "Oh, Gina, wouldn't it be wonderful if little Mary Katherine and Anthony Joseph grew up and fell in love one day, just like in *Sleeping Beauty?*"

"It could happen," Gina said, brushing a happy tear from her cheek as the nurses quietly celebrated the stroke of midnight with ginger ale and fruit punch. "We're like one big happy family as it is. They'll see each other all the time, just like we do. What's to keep them from falling in love?"

New Year's Eve, Five years later

"I won't!" Mary Katherine O'Callaghan screamed as Mary Pat tried to braid her thick coppery hair. "You can't make me!"

"I'm your mother, missy, and I certainly can make you go to Tony's birthday party." This one child was more work than her other three put together.

Kate burst into a Niagara of tears, accompanied by shrieking loud enough to wake the dead. "But it's my birthday, too!" she wailed. "Why can't I have my *own* party?"

Mary Pat stopped braiding and turned her daughter around to face her. "You know why, Kate. We're having the New Year's party here at our house tonight. Aunt Gina is having the birthday party at her house."

"But why is it Tony's turn to have the birthday party?" Kate demanded. "Why do I always have to do everything he does? I don't like him, Mommy. Why can't I just have a birthday with people I like?"

Mary Pat didn't have an answer for that.

Next door, Gina Marino wasn't doing much better.

"Now you stop that this minute, young man," she said sternly to her five-year-old son. "If you so much as look at Kate cross-eyed, you'll answer to me."

"She's dumb," Anthony Joseph Marino said, his dark eyes flashing with temper. "I don't want a dumb girl at my birthday party."

"Kate isn't dumb," Gina corrected him. "She's your best friend."

"Is not," Tony said. "Mikey's my best friend."

"Then Kate's your best little girlfriend."

"I hate girls," Tony said.

"You don't hate your sisters."

"Yes, I do," he said. "They're girls, too."

Gina smiled and ran a comb through her son's thick, unruly black hair. "You won't always feel this way about girls," she said, giving him a hug whether he wanted one or not. "One day you'll wake up and Kate O'Callaghan will look pretty darn good to you."

"Will not," Tony said, his lower lip protruding stubbornly.

His mother just smiled and crossed her fingers.

New Year's Eve, Thirteen years later

"JUST THIS ONCE," Mary Pat begged her daughter as the eighteen-year old girl glared at her from across the kitchen. "Go out with Tony one time and I'll never ask you again."

"I don't know why you all find it so hard to believe, but Tony Marino and I hate each other."

"Don't say that!" Mary Pat quickly crossed herself. "You two grew up together. You're best of friends."

"In your dreams we're best of friends, Ma, but in the real world we hate each other's guts."

"Such vulgar talk," Mary Pat said, wrinkling her nose. "Is that what they teach you in that fancy college?"

Kate laughed. "You don't want to know what they're teaching me in that fancy college, Ma. You might decide to pull me out and make me work for the family business."

"And would that be so terrible?" Mary Pat countered, a tad stung by her daughter's words. "I'd say the family business has been plenty good to you over the years."

Kate rolled her eyes. "Ma, I've heard all this before. You know I'm looking for something different."

"Don't let your father hear you say that. He has his heart set on having you join the company after you graduate."

"Daddy knows all about my plans, Ma. You're the only one who's having trouble with it."

"The only thing I'm having trouble with, young lady, is this stubborn attitude when it comes to Tony Marino. One date in eighteen years is hardly asking a lot of either one of you."

Kate arched a feathery auburn brow. "So Tony isn't too crazy about this idea, either?"

Mary Pat scowled at her beautiful young daughter. Kate looked much too happy for her taste. "That's right," she said, wishing they'd never let her go away to college. "His opinion of you is even lower than your opinion of him."

Spots of color flamed on Kate's cheeks. "What did he say?"

"Why don't you ask him yourself?" Mary Pat suggested. "At the party."

"This is New Year's Eve," Kate reminded. "What kind of mother forces her daughter to date someone she doesn't like on New Year's Eve?"

"A smart mother," Mary Pat retorted. "A *very* smart mother."

NEXT DOOR, GINA hammered on the bathroom door with her tightly clenched fist. It seemed as if both of her fists had been clenched since her son had come home on Christmas break.

"Anthony Joseph Marino, this is your last warning. If you don't come out of there by the time I count to ten, I'm going to ground you until you're old enough for social security."

Tony mumbled something and Gina had the feeling she was probably better off not knowing exactly what he said. Unfortunately, she was also his mother and mothers had to know everything; it came with the territory.

"I'm counting, Anthony," she said in her sternest voice. "Ten. Nine. Eight. Seven. Six. Five—" The door swung open and she bit back a triumphant smile. He usually managed to hold out until two and a half. She wondered if this was a sign of incipient maturity or desperation. Either way, she considered it to be one small battle won.

"Kate's too stuck-up," Tony said, looking down at her the way only her six-foot-tall firstborn could. "She's full of herself. Everybody knows it."

"Kate's a lovely girl," Gina said, "and you promised you'd take her to the company party."

"You didn't tell me I'd have to dance with her."

"She's beautiful!" Gina stared at her son in disbelief. "She has her pick of boyfriends."

"So let her get one of them to take her to the party and leave me alone."

"You're taking Kate, young man, and that's that. Now finish getting dressed so you can pick her up on time."

"THEY'VE BARELY SAID three words to each other all night," Mary Pat said as she and Gina watched their offspring stumble angrily around the dance floor.

"I know," Gina replied. "I think it's time we admit defeat."

Mary Pat's eyes glistened with tears. "They look so beautiful together, don't they? Tony's so dark and handsome."

Gina nodded. "And that fabulous auburn hair of Kate's. She could be on a magazine cover."

"Can you imagine what beautiful children they'd have?" Mary Pat sighed loudly.

"Little angels," Gina said, dabbing at her eyes with the corner of a tissue. "We'd be in grandma heaven."

"But it's not going to happen in this lifetime, is it?"

Gina met Mary Pat's eyes. "I don't think so."

"Come on," said Mary Pat, linking her arm through her best friend's. "Let's go drink ourselves under the table."

Just before midnight

"DO YOU THINK THEY suspect anything?" Kate asked as Tony parked his old blue Chevy behind the movie theater, far away from the glare of the streetlights.

Tony grinned at her, his teeth flashing white in

the darkness. "We did it, kid," he said, turning off the ignition. "They don't have a clue."

"I hate lying to them," Kate said. "I mean, they'd be so happy if they knew."

"Sure, they'd be happy," he said, "and they'd be all over us, Katie. I love them, too, but you know they wouldn't give us room to breathe."

"I know you're right, but they looked so sad tonight that I—"

"Think about it, Katie. They'd tell us where to live, what to eat for breakfast, when we should have our first kid. I'm not ready for that." He drew her into his arms and kissed her deeply. "I don't want to share us with anyone yet. Not even our families."

Kate looked down at the plain gold band on her left ring finger. "We'll have to tell them sometime. This isn't the kind of secret you keep forever."

He grinned at her and she couldn't help but smile back at him. Funny how the same wise-guy grin that made her want to kick him in the shins when they were kids could turn her heart into jelly now.

"I can keep it secret as long as you can," he said, touching her nose with his finger. "I want you all to myself."

"We have to be practical about this," she said, feeling anything but practical at the moment. "People talk, Tony. Our friends at school know we're married. What if someone mentions it to our parents?"

"You worry too much."

"And you don't worry enough."

"I don't have to," he said, still grinning at her. "You worry enough for everyone in the family."

"So I'm a worrier," she said, embarrassed. "Somebody has to think about these things." It was her lot in life to be the practical one.

"Why?" He leaned back against the cracked leather seat and met her gaze. The challenge in his glance was unmistakable.

"Because that's the way it is."

"Not much of an answer."

Her temper bristled. "If you have to ask such a stupid question, I'm not sure you deserve an answer."

"Life's too short to waste making up rules and regulations to live by. As it is, there are more than enough of those right now."

"I hate it when you talk like that," she said, torn between anger and a touch of fear. "If that's the way you feel, I'm surprised you got married."

"So am I."

Her eyes widened and she felt her stomach drop to her toes. She turned toward the window so he wouldn't see her eyes fill with hurt tears.

"You're not listening to me, Katie."

She drew in a steadying breath. "I heard every word you said. You're surprised you got married, too." Surprised and maybe regretful? That shouldn't surprise her. Tony was everything she wasn't: impulsive, adventurous, unwilling to settle for the easy when the difficult was just out of reach—not the kind of guy you would expect to settle down early with a wife.

"Damn right, I'm surprised." He was still looking at her with those sad dark eyes of his; those eyes she'd known from the day she was born. "I didn't count on falling in love with the girl next door."

She felt a smile tug at the corners of her mouth. "I wish you wouldn't say things like that when I'm trying to be mad at you."

"We're gonna be fine, kid." He pulled her into his arms and she pressed her nose against the side of his neck and inhaled. "I'll loosen you up and you'll keep me on the straight and narrow. Sounds like a good match to me."

"Say it again," she whispered, her lips brushing the warm skin of his throat. "I want to hear it one more time."

"We're a good match."

"Not that."

His chuckle rumbled beneath her ear. "You'll keep me on the straight and narrow."

"That's not it, either."

"I love you."

"That's it," she murmured. "That's what I wanted to hear."

They jumped at the sharp sound of an explosion

as fireworks rose up over the buildings at the eastern edge of town. The church bells rang out simultaneously and in the distance they could hear car horns honking and people shouting with excitement.

Kate angled her head so she could see Tony's watch. "Midnight," she said. "Our birthday is over."

"And the New Year's about to begin." He tilted her chin with his finger and kissed her in a way that sent shivers through her body. "Happy New Year, Mrs. Marino."

"Happy New Year to you, Mr. Marino."

"We're going to have a lot more happy new years, kid," Tony said. "A lifetime of them."

"Promise me," she said. "Tell me that we'll always be as happy as we are right this minute."

"Always," he said, and of course she believed him.

They were young and very much in love. Everything else would work itself out.

CHAPTER TWO

March—1997

"THIS FAMILY HAS TOO many celebrations," Kate O'Callaghan said as she tossed her suitcase down on the bed in her old room.

"Tell me about it," said her sister Erin. "I swear they wouldn't have postponed this thing if I was still in the delivery room having quintuplets." A beautiful two-week-old baby daughter nursed at Erin's breast.

"I thought we had the golden-anniversary celebration last year." Kate opened the suitcase and began transferring her clothes to the closet across the room.

"No, that was Sal Marino's seventy-fifth birthday party." Erin grinned as she moved Sarah from her left breast to her right. "His diamond jubilee."

Kate groaned and tossed her underwear in the top drawer. "Doesn't anyone ever just have a birthday anymore? The Marinos and the O'Callaghans could outparty Buckingham Palace."

"Kate." Erin's grin faded into something positively grim. "There's something I need to tell you."

A ripple of alarm slid up Kate's spine. She ignored it and continued unpacking. "Look at this, Erin! My black jacket didn't even wrinkle."

"He's going to be here, Kate. I heard Ma and Aunt Gina talking last night. For all I know, he's next door right now."

Kate sank down on the edge of the bed and buried her face in her hands. "I wish you hadn't told me that."

"I wish I didn't have to tell you, either, hon, but wouldn't it be worse if Tony surprised you?"

"I don't know," Kate mumbled. "This is pretty bad."

"At least they're not trying to set you up with him anymore. That'll make it a little easier."

"Nothing's going to make it easier, Erin," Kate snapped. "Not unless he suddenly decides to stay in Timbuktu or wherever he's living."

"He lives in Pakistan right now," Erin supplied.

"You heard Ma and Aunt Gina talking?"

Erin nodded.

"Pakistan." Kate sniffed. Wasn't that just like him. It was craziness like Pakistan and hang gliding and living out of a backpack that had doomed their marriage. Nice to know some things never changed. She fiddled with the pair of pajamas on her lap. "Is he bringing anyone with him?" Not that she cared. She just wanted to know so she wouldn't be surprised.

"I have no idea, honey."

She took a deep breath. Might as well go for broke. "Is he...married?"

"I don't know that either, honey."

"Doesn't matter," she said, tossing the pajamas into the dresser drawer on top of the underwear. "Just curious, that's all."

"You're talking to me, Kate." Erin met her gaze. "I was there."

"Ancient history," Kate said lightly. "Lots of teenage marriages fall by the wayside."

Erin was the only O'Callaghan who knew about Kate and Tony's failed college marriage. "I have to admit I always thought you two would beat the odds."

"So did I," Kate said with a small laugh. "Shows how smart we are, right?"

"Maybe if things had been different—"

"I think your hormones are talking," Kate said, smiling gently at her brand-new niece. "You never were the sentimental type before Sarah."

Erin glared at her sister. "Don't even start the hormone talk," she warned. "I've thought this for years, long before my hormones had opinions of their own."

"Erin, I—"

"No, listen to me, Katie. Don't you ever wonder what would have happened if you and Tony had given it a second chance? I mean, I think about old boyfriends sometimes and wonder 'What if...?' You can't tell me you never think about that.''

Think about it? Kate almost laughed out loud. Only about ten thousand times since their marriage was dissolved eight years ago. But she refused to let her sister know that. "I'm a realist, Erin. That's why I'm a researcher." She believed in what she could see and touch, not what her imagination conjured out of whole cloth—a fact that had put her and Tony at odds right from the start.

The boy she'd married had been a dreamer; the kind of guy who built castles in the air and actually believed they could set up housekeeping in them. He'd talked about the two of them backpacking their way around the world, weaving elaborate stories about the places they would see and the people they would meet, while all Kate could do was wonder how on earth they would be able to afford it.

There was no doubt about it: Practical people shouldn't be allowed to marry dreamers. Dreamers needed the space to let their imaginations run wild. Practical people loved to build fences. You didn't need a degree in psychology to understand why their marriage hadn't worked. The miracle was that it had lasted eight whole months.

"Well, at least you didn't have kids," Erin said. "Once you have a baby, you're tied together forever."

"Yes," Kate said, turning away. "A baby would have changed everything."

She made a show of looking out the window. "Look at that sky, Er. If I didn't know better, I'd say we had a spring snowstorm coming...."

IN THE HOUSE NEXT DOOR, Tony Marino pushed back his chair and raised his hands in surrender. "Enough already, Ma! How many calzones do you think one man can eat, anyway?"

"You're too skinny," Gina said, hovering over him. "I don't know what they feed you in the jungle."

"Leave the boy alone," Sal Marino said to his wife. "He's not too skinny. We're too fat."

Tony laughed at the dirty look his mother aimed his father's way. "I ate four of these things, Ma. If I fell in the swimming pool, I'd sink like a rock."

Gina swatted him with the hem of her apron. "Mind your manners," she said. "No matter how old you get, I'm still your mother."

Tony grinned at her. "I wouldn't mind another bottle of beer," he said.

"Coming up," said his old man.

"So," said Tony in his most casual tone of voice, "who's coming to the big party tonight?"

"The usual suspects," Sal replied, handing him a bottle of Bud. No fancy imported stuff for the Marinos. "The entire O'Callaghan clan. Hey, you haven't met the newest member yet. Erin had a baby girl.''

"Great," said Tony. Erin was a good kid. Easy to get along with, unlike her older sister. "How about Kate? Is she coming down from Boston?"

His father shrugged. "Beats me."

"She's coming," his mother said. "Mary Pat said she might bring the banker she's been dating."

"Banker, huh?" Tony took a pull of brew. "Sounds about right."

"Mary Pat says Kate's doing quite well up there in Boston," his mother said, oblivious of the edge in his voice. "Nice apartment. Nice friends."

"Nice doormat," Tony muttered under his breath.

"What was that?" His mother never missed a trick. "What did you say about a doormat?"

"I was wondering if she had a nice doormat for that nice apartment of hers."

"You don't fool me," his mother said. "You're talking about her banker."

Tony started to say he didn't give a damn about her banker but caught himself. In his mother's eyes, that would be a declaration of love. Better to wait and see what she had to say about things.

"You should be as grounded and mature as Kate," his mother went on. "Maybe if you'd stop running all over the world tilting at windmills, you'd manage to find someone you could settle down with."

"Maybe that's why I run all over the world, Mom," he said. "Because I'm not ready to settle down."

"You'll be thirty before you know it," his mother reminded him. "Of course you're ready to settle down."

"Leave him alone, Gina," Sal interrupted. "He'll settle down when he's ready to settle down."

"I want grandchildren."

Tony laughed out loud. "You *have* grandchildren," he reminded her. "Four of them." His younger siblings took their procreative responsibilities very seriously.

"I want grandchildren from *you.*"

"Then you'll have to wait."

Gina mumbled something and was about to launch into a full frontal assault on Tony's devotion to the family when his father said, "I think there's too much salt in the calzones," which precipitated a whole new line of discussion.

I owe you one, Pop. Tony lifted his bottle of Bud in his father's direction and caught the quick flash of a grin on his old man's weathered face. There were times when men had to stick together. He let his parents' good-natured banter flow over him, letting it wash away his jet lag and culture shock. It was nice to know some things never changed. He usually moved between time zones and hemispheres as easily as he crossed boundaries between countries. This time, however, he'd been knocked for a loop. The second he'd landed in town, he felt as if he'd been hit by a one-two punch Muhammad Ali in his prime would have envied.

And he knew why.

Kate.

His beautiful, practical Kate. The only woman who had ever made him think that there might be something to white picket fences and ''happily ever after.'' The last time he'd seen her was the afternoon they'd signed their divorce papers in that little store-front legal-aid office on campus. The next day he'd transferred to Northwestern, half a continent away.

Love hadn't been enough to bridge the differences between them. Hell, the Golden Gate Bridge couldn't have done that. She'd liked order. He'd liked chaos. She'd believed in goal setting and time management. He still didn't believe in any of those things.

They'd known all about their differences before they'd run off and gotten married in a tumbledown courthouse in North Carolina. Or was it South Carolina? He'd never been one for details. What did it matter? They'd vowed to honor and cherish each other and they'd somehow believed their love would be strong enough to see them through the tough times that were sure to come.

He tried to push the memories from his mind but they wouldn't go. He saw her as she slept, her slen-

der body curled around her pillow. He heard the
sound of her laughter. He felt her skin, warm and
moist from the bath. Their eight-month marriage
seemed more real to him in some ways than the
eight years of living since. It sounded damn stupid,
but he'd been aware of her nearness from the moment his plane landed. Nobody had needed to tell
him she was home, because he felt her presence
deep in his gut.

There was nothing unusual about that, he told
himself as he grabbed another beer for him and his
old man. She'd been part of his life from the day
they were born. They'd grown up next door to each
other, gone through school together, been forced to
endure family vacations together, and for almost a
year they'd lived together as husband and wife.

Sometimes when he was alone in a strange city,
surrounded by cultures he didn't understand, listening to languages he had yet to learn, he thought of
Kate and wished things could have been different.

TINY WHITE LIGHTS twinkled from the branches of
the bare trees surrounding Tavern on the Green.

"You're really going all-out tonight," Kate said
to her father as the chauffeur opened the passenger
door. "Limousines, Tavern on the Green. What's
next, Pop? A full orchestra?"

Matt O'Callaghan patted her hand. "Only cost a
few hundred more than a string quartet."

It took five limousines to transport the entire O'Callaghan family from Princeton across the Hudson River to Manhattan. Matt O'Callaghan believed in living large. Birthdays, anniversaries, christenings—whatever the occasion, Kate's father celebrated in style. Tavern on the Green, however, was extravagant even for him. She did a quick profit-and-loss in her mind and came up with none of the former and plenty of the latter. This wasn't even a tax write-off since it was a family affair.

But no matter. Kate had promised herself she would put her practical self aside for the evening and just enjoy the party, and, from the lush sound of the music floating toward her from their private room, that might not be too hard to do.

"Do you see Tony?" Erin stage-whispered into Kate's right ear as they stood in the entrance to the room.

"I haven't looked," Kate lied. It had only taken her a split second to scan the room and determine he wasn't there.

"I didn't see him in the lobby, either."

"Maybe he's not coming."

"He has to come," Erin said, sounding too determined for Kate's taste. "Do you really think Aunt Gina would let him stay home?"

"He's a grown man," Kate reminded. "He can do whatever he wants."

"Not when it comes to family parties, he can't."

"It's our family party," Kate said, as she caught sight of a dark-haired man stepping out of the shadows on the other side of the room.

Erin threw back her head and laughed out loud. "Right," she said. "The only way you can tell a Marino from an O'Callaghan is with a scorecard or—" Erin stopped. "What is it, Kate?"

"He's here." She turned her back to the rest of the room. "By the window."

Erin whistled low. *"Mamma mia,"* she said. "The boy's looking awfully good."

A wave of cowardice almost knocked Kate to her knees. "I can't do this, Erin. I absolutely can't."

Erin's eyes were fixed on a point over Kate's left shoulder.

"Honey, I don't think you have any choice."

"Tell me he's not coming this way."

"He's coming this way."

"I'm leaving," Kate said, her voice fierce. "Get out of my way."

"It's too late. He already saw you. He's—"

"It's been a long time, Katie."

His voice was exactly the way she remembered it: a deep, smoky rumble that made her feel lightheaded, as if she'd had too much champagne. She met her sister's gaze, then took a deep breath and turned around.

"Hello, Tony. It has been a long time."

Time had been kind to him. Very kind. The cute

boy she'd fallen in love with at college had been replaced by the man who stood in front of her—a stranger of the most intimate sort.

"You're looking good, Katie."

She inclined her head. "Thank you. So are you."

He patted his lean belly with the palm of his right hand. "Jungle living tends to keep you in shape."

Erin coughed theatrically and stepped forward. "And hello to you, too, stranger."

Tony's expression changed instantly. The guarded look in his eyes was replaced by delight. "Squirt!"

He opened his arms and Erin threw herself into his embrace, then leaped back, laughing. "Sorry," she said. "Nursing mothers aren't too huggable."

"So where is the heir apparent?" Tony asked. "I'm not going to believe you're a mom until I see the evidence."

"Oh, I'm a mom, all right," Erin said. "Ten hours' sleep, total, since we brought her home. The circles under my eyes should be evidence enough."

Kate cleared her throat. "Listen," she said, keeping her tone light and breezy, "I'll let you two catch up on old times. I should go see if Mom needs any help." She forced herself to meet Tony's gaze. "It was good to see you again, Tony."

If he was the slightest bit sorry to see her go, he didn't let on.

"Same here, Katie."

Katie. Damn him for doing that. Katie was what

he'd called her after they made love, back in those
long-ago days when nothing else mattered but the
feel of skin against skin. *Get a grip,* she told herself.
So what if he called her Katie or Kat or Queen of
the Universe. It didn't mean anything. He probably
didn't even remember the days when it had mattered
very much.

And that was when she made her big mistake. She
let herself look at him—really look at him—for the
first time since they'd said goodbye.

Her heart seemed to fill her chest when for a split
second she saw a glimpse of the boy she'd once
loved, hidden behind the slightly dangerous exterior
of the man he'd become. What she should have done
was turn and walk away from him—away from the
memories and the regrets—as fast as her legs could
carry her. She was a practical, levelheaded woman
who had never had trouble making the safe and logical choice—until that moment when she met his
eyes and the ice around her heart started to melt.

NOTHING HAD CHANGED.

All Tony had to do was look at Kate to know her
feelings toward him were the same as they'd been
the day they got their divorce. Redheads were supposed to be at the mercy of their emotions, but not
the ever-cool and practical Kate O'Callaghan. She'd
managed to obliterate any evidence of human feeling and was looking at him now as if they'd met for

the first time just two minutes ago. You would never know by looking at her that they'd shared so much as a cup of coffee.

Hell, two could play that game.

"I hear you've caught yourself a banker."

She didn't so much as bat an eye. "Are you talking about John?"

"I don't know," he said. "Am I? Ma called him The Banker."

For a moment he thought he saw a flash of something resembling human emotion flicker across her face but she quickly covered it up with a bland social smile.

"His name is John Griffin and he's an assistant vice president for Global Interbank." She lifted her chin slightly, just enough for an ex-husband to notice. "He would have been here but he had a big meeting in London."

"He wouldn't postpone it?"

"I didn't ask him to."

"He could have volunteered."

"It was an important meeting," she said, her cheeks flushed a pale pink. "Besides, I think I'm capable of attending a family party unescorted."

"I never said you weren't."

"Then what exactly were you saying, Tony?"

He thought for a second. "I'm saying—" He stopped in mid-sentence as the absurdity of the entire situation hit him. "Damned if I know, Katie."

And then an amazing thing happened. Kate's eyes crinkled, her mouth began to twitch, and suddenly the full-bodied, womanly sound of her laughter broke through and he felt the way he'd felt the first time he'd made love to her.

"C'mere," he said, opening his arms wide. "It's been one hell of a long time."

KATE'S HEART MELTED as she stepped into his embrace. It felt so right, being there in his arms. So perfect. The last eight years seemed to fall away from her and she was that hopeful, happy girl she'd been at eighteen when the world had seemed theirs for the taking.

He pulled her close and she wrapped her arms around him. "You've been working out," she said, with a soft laugh. "I thought you said you'd never become one of those gym rats."

"I haven't," he said, his voice a delicious rumble in her right ear. "Try lugging sixty pounds of gear through the jungle every day. You'd bulk up, too."

She wanted to tell him that she liked it, that he felt solid and real beneath her hands, that the feel of his chest against her breasts was doing more for her libido than her banker's most ardent kisses ever had. But of course, she didn't. You couldn't say something like that to your ex-husband, no matter how much you longed to run your hands through his thick dark hair or breathe in the smell of his skin.

Sometimes Kate thought she'd fallen in love with him because of the smell of his skin. All those years she hadn't given him a second look, then one day she'd found herself in his arms at a high-school dance and everything had changed. Soap and spice and something else that was his alone.

His hands slid down to her waist. "You've lost weight."

"A few pounds."

"More than a few. You're getting too skinny."

"I can't be that skinny if Ma hasn't noticed yet."

"She doesn't know you the way I know you."

The warning bells started going off inside her head, telling her to put an end to this before it went any further. Too bad she wasn't listening. She was high on the smell of his skin, as close to being drunk as she'd ever been on champagne. Her banker never made her feel this way. That was one of the things she'd told herself she liked about him. This kind of chemistry made for great sex but it didn't translate into real life. She'd made that mistake once and she wasn't likely to make it again.

So why not give in to the moment and just enjoy it for what it was?

"Oh, Tony," she said on a sigh. "It's good to see you again."

ON THE OTHER SIDE OF the room, Mary Pat O'Callaghan and Gina Marino watched in disbelief as Kate threw herself into Tony's arms and stayed there.

"Catch me, Gina," Mary Pat said. "I'm going to faint."

"Don't you dare," Gina warned. "We've waited almost thirty years for this moment. You're not about to miss it now."

"I wish I had the video camera."

"Sal brought his." Gina glanced quickly around the room. "Where *is* that man when you need him?"

"They're still hugging," Mary Pat said in a tone of wonder. "Do you think she fainted?"

Gina gave her friend a sharp poke in the ribs. "My boy Tony's a hunk. Why wouldn't she want to hug him?"

"He's been a hunk since the day he was born," Mary Pat declared. "And until this second, she didn't even want to shake his hand."

"Our prayers have been answered," Gina said, linking her arm through Mary Pat's. "Mark my words, we'll be planning a wedding before this year is out."

"Don't count your grandchildren until they're diapered," Mary Pat warned. "There's still a long way to go."

CHAPTER THREE

"THEY'RE TALKING ABOUT US," Kate said as Tony waltzed her across the shimmering dance floor.

"Let them," he said, sweeping her into a turn. "They're jealous."

Kate laughed out loud. "They're not jealous," she said. "They're in shock."

"Because we're dancing?"

"Because we're not fighting. We did too good a job over the years, Tony. They never knew how we really felt about each other, did they?"

"Not a clue," Tony said as he maneuvered her closer to the French doors at the far corner of the room.

Her eyes filled with tears and she ducked her head against his shoulder.

"Katie?" His voice was soft and low with concern. "What's wrong?"

"Too much champagne," she said, trying to convince herself that was the reason for her tears. She wasn't a weepy, emotional type of woman at all. She didn't even like that kind of woman.

"You need some fresh air."

"We're in Manhattan," she said. "They don't have fresh air in Manhattan."

"Prepare to be surprised, Katie-mine."

Katie-mine? Her knees turned to melted butter. If they hadn't been dancing indecently close, she would have puddled to the floor. The nuns at Saint Brendan's High School would have been scandalized by the way she was dancing with Tony. "Leave room for the Holy Ghost," they used to say as they separated the boys and girls on the dance floor. Not only wasn't there room for the Holy Ghost, there wasn't room to breathe.

And Kate liked it. She more than liked it. If she hadn't been enjoying herself so much, she might have been a little worried about exactly how exciting it was to be in her ex-husband's arms. In fact, he didn't feel like an ex-husband at all. He felt like an illicit lover or a thrilling stranger—someone who had stepped back into her life to remind her she was a woman.

You're losing it, Kate, the stiff-backed voice of reason reprimanded her as they slipped out the French doors and into the night. *Since when are you a romantic?* She was as practical as the day was long, a flannel-pajamas kind of woman who would rather curl up with a hot cup of tea than a hot hunk of man any night.

So why was it that all she could think about was standing beneath the stars with Tony?

Just one more time.

Manhattan seemed far away as he took her hand

and led her into the shadows. The new grass seemed springy and soft beneath her feet. If Walt Disney had designed the perfect setting for romance, this was what he would have come up with. The only thing wrong with the picture was the occasional snowflake drifting down from the milky night sky.

Tony put out his hand to catch some snow. "It's springtime, right?"

"It's springtime," she said. "Spring is always full of surprises."

He drew her into his arms and she laid her head against his chest.

"We always said we'd come to Tavern on the Green one day," he murmured, his lips brushing the side of her cheek. "Remember?"

"I remember," she whispered. "One day when we were rich and living in the suburbs with our two kids and our matching Saabs."

"I never wanted to be rich," he said, smoothing her hair back with a gentle touch.

"I know." Her smile was sad. "You didn't want the Saabs, either."

"I wanted the kids." He pressed his lips against the side of her throat and she shivered with pleasure. "You know I wanted the kids."

"So did I." They'd spent hours talking about the family they would have together. Deep, serious conversations that only the very young and very much in love could have. They'd picked out names, decorated the perfect nursery, discussed which college their brilliant sons and daughters would attend. But they'd been too young at the time—only kids themselves, with years more of college still ahead of them before they could even think about starting a family of their own. They'd contented themselves with dreaming about the wonderful future that waited for them out there.

"I wish it could have been different for us, Katie."

Once again her eyes burned with unshed tears. "I know," she managed. "So do I."

He dipped his head toward hers and she was powerless to do anything but look up at him. There was a world of regret in his expression—the same regret that tugged at her heart.

"For old times' sake?" he asked, the shadow of a grin tilting his mouth.

She looped her arms around his neck. "For old times' sake."

The air around them seemed charged with electricity. Kate wouldn't have been surprised if lightning bolts had sizzled to the ground all around them. He was going to kiss her...he had to kiss her. If he didn't kiss her, she'd—

"Uncle Tony!" A child's high-pitched voice broke the erotic stillness. "Gramma says get in here right now or else."

A spring blizzard couldn't have done a better job

of extinguishing the fire. Tony muttered something under his breath as Kate struggled to remember how to breathe.

"Uncle Tony, you better do what Gramma says."

Tony stepped out of the shadows. "C'mere, Ryan," he said. "You shouldn't be out here by yourself." He was giving Kate a chance to get her game face back on and she was grateful for it. Ryan Marino was Tony's brother Dom's child, a sharp little kid with an eye for gossip. Kate wasn't about to give him anything more to whisper about with the rest of the clan.

"Gramma wants you," Ryan said. "What're you doin' out here?"

"I was helping Kate look for her earring."

She heard Ryan rustling the rhodondendrons near the building. "I don't see Kate."

She knew a cue when she heard one. She unfastened her right earring, summoned up a big smile, then called out, "Success!" She moved toward them, her right hand extended. "My earring."

Tony winked at her over his nephew's head. She knew winking was as outdated as the Edsel but she couldn't keep from winking right back at him.

"Why are you winking?" Ryan asked as she put her earring back on.

"Because I felt like it," she said, rustling his hair with a gentle hand. "You don't like winking?"

"It's stupid," Ryan said. He looked up at her. "Were you kissing Uncle Tony?"

"Kissing Tony?" She didn't have to fake her shock. "Of course not!" Which, to her regret, was true enough. Another ten seconds, however, and it would have been a different story.

"Kissing's stupid," Ryan said, still looking at her the way a hawk watched a rabbit.

"You'll change your mind in another seven or eight years," Tony said with a laugh.

Ryan wrinkled up his face in an expression of utter disgust. "Will not."

"Will too," Tony said. "You can bet me on that one, Ry."

"We'd better go back inside," Kate said, feeling the pull of family curiosity tugging at her right through the restaurant's walls. "We've already given them enough to talk about as it is."

"They've been talking about us since the day we were born, Katie," he said as they followed Ryan toward the French doors. "A walk in the dark isn't going to change anything."

"I suppose you're right."

"I *am* right," he said. "So we danced a little and stepped outside for some fresh air."

"We danced close."

"So do my parents. What does that prove?"

She started to laugh. "In case you've forgotten, we have a history of not liking each other very much. They'll consider it significant if we don't come to blows."

"We've called a truce for the night. Our birthday gift to your dad."

"A truce?" she asked. "Is that what this is?"

"It's whatever we want it to be."

A moment out of time, she thought. That's what it really was. A chance to pretend a dreamer and a realist could find a way to be happy together.

TONY'S DAD CORNERED him between dinner and dessert. "So what's the story?"

Tony drained his second glass of champagne. "What story?"

Sal glanced around as if to make sure the coast was clear. "You and Kate O'Callaghan. You've been thicker than thieves tonight. What gives?"

"We buried the hatchet," Tony said. "Figured it was the least we could do for Matt's birthday party."

"You sure it's not more than that?"

"Get real, Pop." Tony forced a laugh. "I've known Kate all my life."

"So what?"

"So why would I start something with her now?"

"That's what I'm asking you."

"There's nothing," Tony said. "It's just time we quit acting like kids."

"You should've thought about that before she met that banker Mary Pat's always talking about."

"She's welcome to her banker, Pop," he said, ignoring the way his mouth seemed to fight his words. The banker was probably just what Katie needed. Someone solid and reliable. The kind of guy who put down roots in concrete and didn't go running off from jungle to jungle looking for something he couldn't quite define.

He found Kate a few minutes later and asked her to dance.

"I'm beginning to think we should stage a fight," Kate said as he settled his hand at the small of her back. "My mother's getting that look in her eye."

"My old man wanted to know the score."

"There is no score."

"That's what I told him."

"I tried to make my mother understand but I know she wasn't listening to a word I said." Kate sighed deeply. "She and Aunt Gina are probably picking out china patterns right now."

"Don't worry about it," he said as he spun her into a turn. "Tomorrow morning everything will be back to normal."

Katie would return to her banker and he would return to his jungle.

The way things were meant to be.

"THEY'RE NOT SMILING," Mary Pat observed as she and Gina watched their children dance together.

"You're right," Gina said. "They don't look very happy, do they?"

"I wonder what's wrong."

"Anthony's probably talking about the jungle," Gina said with a shake of her head.

"And my Kate's probably telling him all about her banker."

"Anthony leaves tomorrow afternoon for South America."

Mary Pat sighed. "Kate goes back to Boston in the evening."

"Then we have to do something."

"Do something?" Mary Pat asked. "What's the point, Gina? After tonight, it's all over."

"You're right." Gina's dark eyes glittered. "So let's pull out all the stops right now."

"IT'S SNOWING." Kate stood beneath the awning and shivered. "I knew it. I can't believe it, but I knew it."

The doorman chuckled. "Still March, ma'am. Plenty of time for a few more blizzards."

"Blizzards! Tell me you're joking."

"You never know." He smoothed the lapels of his black wool coat. "Can I get you a cab, miss?"

"Actually, I'm waiting for my ride." She peered down the snowy street. "I'm with the O'Callaghan-Marino party."

"The one with all the stretch limos?"

"That's the one."

An expression of concern darkened the doorman's pleasant features. "I'm sorry, miss, but they're long gone."

"They can't be. My mother said she'd wait."

"Which one was your mother?"

"A short redhead with delusions of grandeur, usually seen with an even shorter dark-haired woman with an attitude."

"They left about ten minutes ago."

"That's impossible. How am I supposed to get home?"

"I'd be happy to call you a cab."

"Don't bother."

Kate spun around to find Tony standing behind her. "I thought you left a half hour ago."

"I thought you left with your folks."

"They left me stranded."

Tony gestured toward the restaurant. "They said they lost my car. It took the valet forty-five minutes to track it down."

She shivered again as a cold gust of wind sliced through her clothing. "I think we've been set up."

"You've got to be kidding."

"Look at us," Kate said. "Your car was missing. My own parents left me standing here in the snow. We've been had by masters."

His expression shifted as reality sank in. "They figured this was their last chance to get us together."

"Bingo," said Kate.

"They're persistent."

"Deranged is more like it."

They turned at the sound of tires crunching through snow. A young parking attendant climbed out, then handed the receipt to Tony. "Your car, sir."

"How much did they pay you to lose it?" Tony asked as he reached for his wallet. The kid's cheeks burned bright red in response. "That much, huh?"

"Hey, I didn't say—"

Tony handed him a five-dollar bill. "I don't blame you, kid. I would've done it for less."

The attendant pocketed the money, then took off before Tony could change his mind.

"I'll take you home," Tony said, putting a hand under Kate's elbow.

"That's not necessary," she said, feeling suddenly more vulnerable than she had in a very long time. "I'll call a car service."

"I *am* a car service," he said, propelling her down the shoveled walkway. "At least tonight I am."

"I don't know. Maybe—"

"Maybe what? Maybe you'd rather get into a car with a stranger at midnight? I don't think so, Katie. Better the devil you know."

"No speeding," she said as he opened the pas-

senger door for her. "It must be years since you
drove the turnpike in snow."

He hurried around the back of the car, then slid
behind the wheel next to her. "I drove in a snowstorm last year," he said, adjusting the seat and the
mirror. "In the Alps."

A sigh escaped her lips. "The Alps. And here I
thought a skiing trip to the Berkshires was a big
deal."

He gave her a curious glance as he eased the car
down the driveway and toward the street. "I didn't
think you cared about things like the Alps, Katie."

"It's not that I care exactly," she said. "It's just
sometimes I wonder what I've been missing. That's
all." *Well, wasn't that a stupid thing to say, Kate
O'Callaghan. Why don't you just throw yourself at
his feet while you're at it?* It wasn't like she spent
any time thinking about the Alps or Switzerland or
nonsense like that. Where had that stupid statement
come from, anyway?

"Then we're even," he said as he merged carefully into traffic to avoid a skid. "Sometimes I wonder what it would be like to have a roof over my
head every night and clean water on demand."

"Your documentaries have been wonderful,
Tony." She sat primly in her seat, hands folded in
her lap like a schoolgirl.

He didn't turn to look at her but she sensed that

he wanted to. She knew that shouldn't matter to her but it did. "You've seen them."

"All of them." A wiser ex-wife would have pretended she'd missed at least a couple of them but Kate wasn't feeling particularly wise at the moment. Snow danced across the windshield, making lacy patterns as the wipers swept them away. The inside of the car was dark and warm, a haven against the stormy night, forging a sense of intimacy that, under different circumstances, she might have recognized as dangerous. "You really are wonderful, Tony."

He brought the car to a gliding stop at a traffic light, then turned at last to look at her. "I've waited a long time to hear you say that."

"You know I always thought you were wonderful. That was never the issue."

"Maybe not to you," he said. "This means a hell of a lot to me, Katie."

She forced a laugh. "You were nominated for two Emmys. How much could my opinion possibly matter?"

The light changed and the car moved slowly forward again, tires slipping gently against the accumulating snow.

"It was always your approval I was looking for, Katie," he said quietly as they approached the tunnel that would take them under the Hudson River to New Jersey.

"Don't." Her voice barely sounded above the

low rumble of traffic. "There's no point." She gasped as he swung the wheel to the right and slid toward the curb. "Tony, what on earth—"

The next thing she knew, he was kissing her. She had no idea how it was she'd found her way into his arms but there she was. The seat-belt alarm buzzed like a crazy swarm of bees, but it didn't matter. All that mattered was the feel of his mouth on hers, the smell of his skin as he held her closer than close. Could you faint from pleasure? Was it possible to take leave of your senses over a simple kiss? A moment ago she wouldn't have thought so at all, but then a moment ago she hadn't been kissing Tony.

"Ah, Katie..." Her name sounded beautiful when he said it, somehow soft and vulnerable and loved.

"Say it again," she whispered, pressing her mouth against the side of his throat where his pulse beat deep and fast.

"Sweet, sweet Katie."

She melted against him as his voice seemed to surround her heart in an embrace. Where were these thoughts coming from? She'd never felt this way with the banker—all heat and yearning. She'd never felt as if she would die if he didn't kiss her.

And he knew it. She didn't know how he knew it, but he did. He claimed her mouth again in a kiss so fiercely possessive that it made her cry out with joy.

The sound of her joy exploded inside Tony's head. She was the woman he loved, the girl he remembered. And he knew this wasn't enough.

"Let's go someplace," he said, his voice rough with desire.

"Tony, I don't think—"

"Don't think," he urged, cupping her lovely, serious face with his hands. "This one time, Katie, don't think at all."

CHAPTER FOUR

HOTEL ROOMS ON A SNOWY Manhattan night were usually in short supply.

But not for Kate and Tony. Not tonight.

"You're in luck," said the impeccably groomed desk clerk at the Plaza as he presented Tony with the guest book. "We have one suite left. I assume that's agreeable?"

Tony nodded. He signed his name and Kate's without saying a word.

"Bags?" asked the clerk.

"We'll manage," Tony said as Kate turned away to hide the look of guilty excitement she knew must be on her face. "Thanks."

He took her hand and they walked toward the bank of elevators. He looked so serious. Was it possible he was half as nervous as she was? Nothing had ever unnerved Tony. Certainly not the girl next door.

An elderly couple rode the elevator with them. They murmured to each other in that closed language that belonged to the long-married, and Kate found herself overcome with a longing so deep it took her breath away. That was all she'd wanted from life—that one simple gift. She'd wanted to grow old with Tony. Had she ever told him that? Had she ever found the words?

The elevator doors slid open on the fifteenth floor and they walked down the hall to their room.

"Second thoughts?" he asked as he slipped the key into the lock.

She nodded, unable to speak.

"Me, too," he said, then opened the door wide.

He motioned for her to step inside. She moved past him in a soft cloud of Shalimar and anticipation. He shut the door and locked it. The metallic click of the tumblers echoed in the stillness of the room.

They turned to each other and all of her fears vanished. This was Tony. The boy she'd known almost from the moment she drew her first breath. Her entire life was entwined with his—a braid of birthdays and first communions and family dinners.

But, more than that, he was her first love.

Soft kisses and even softer words. Touches with the promise of delights to come. He snaked the zipper of her dress down the length of her spine, trailing his tongue along the path. A shiver rippled through her at the paradox of cool air and moist warmth. He gently clasped her waist, then slid his hands slowly down until they rested low on her belly, his fingertips barely grazing the lacy trim of her bikini panties, the feathery edge of downy auburn curls.

It had been so long.... He would laugh if he knew

how long it had been since she'd been touched like that. Her head dropped forward and she moaned low as he pressed his mouth against the sensitive spot behind her right ear. He'd remembered. After all those years, he still remembered. That thought alone was almost enough to bring her to a climax. But there was more. There was the sweet weight of his body on hers as they fell to the bed in the other room. The smell of his skin, the slight scratchiness of his beard against her cheek, the unbearably erotic sound of his hand as he ran his fingers up her leg to the top of her stocking and that secret place between her thighs.

They were fierce with wanting each other. Too hungry to get naked. Too eager to wait another second. She murmured a protest when he stopped to protect them both, then sighed with pleasure as he found her and claimed her as his own. There was a second of awkward recognition as their bodies adjusted to each other, a swell of give-and-take that she felt from head to foot.

She met and matched his rhythm, then taught him a rhythm of her own. They rode the waves together until they crashed onto the shore where they lay together, speechless and breathless and amazed.

Then they took off their clothes—dress and shirt and pants flying—and did it again.

The night passed in an erotic blur of mouths and hands and tangled limbs, of whispered promises and

NO RISK, NO OBLIGATION TO BUY...NOW OR EVER!

GUARANTEED

PLAY "ROLL A DOUBLE" AND YOU GET FREE GIFTS! HERE'S HOW TO PLAY:

1. Peel off label from front cover. Place it in space provided at right. With a coin, carefully scratch off the silver dice. Then check the claim chart to see what we have for you – FOUR FREE BOOKS and a mystery gift – ALL YOURS! ALL FREE!

2. Send back this card and you'll receive brand-new Harlequin American Romance® novels. These books have a cover price of $3.75 each, but they are yours to keep absolutely free.

3. There's no catch. You're under no obligation to buy anything. We charge nothing – ZERO – for your first shipment. And you don't have to make any minimum number of purchases – not even one!

4. The fact is, thousands of readers enjoy receiving books by mail from the Harlequin Reader Service®. They like the convenience of home delivery...they like getting the best new novels BEFORE they're available in stores...and they love our discount prices!

5. We hope that after receiving your free books you'll want to remain a subscriber. But the choice is yours – to continue or cancel any time at all! So why not take us up on our invitation, with no risk of any kind. You'll be glad you did!

laughter. So much laughter. A lifetime of laughter in one too-short night. A connection had been made between them, a deep and real connection. They both knew it. It was in every word they murmured, every touch they shared. Just because it hadn't worked when they were teenagers didn't mean it wouldn't work now that they were older, more mature, more experienced in the ways of the world. This time, it would work.

They lay together in the old-fashioned sleigh bed and watched the light of the rising sun gild the tops of the trees beyond their window and sparkle against the snow that blanketed the park. If they could have stopped time, this was where and when they would stop it.

"We have to talk," Tony said, drawing the soft wool blanket up over her shoulders as he held her close.

"I know," she whispered, her lips soft against his chest. Their future was waiting right outside the door and they couldn't ignore it. Not after tonight.

"I'm supposed to leave for the Andes in five hours."

She leaned up on one elbow and toyed with the dark mat of hair on his chest. "And I'm supposed to go back to Boston later this afternoon."

"But not to The Banker."

She smiled at him. "Not to the banker."

"Good." He kissed her deeply. "You're mine now."

"And are you mine?" she asked, unable to pretend that it was a casual question.

"You don't know the answer to that?"

"I need to hear you say it."

"I'm yours," he said. "There's nobody but you."

"I'm glad to hear that."

"Did you doubt it?"

"It's been a long time," she said simply. "People change."

"It's always been you, Katie. Nothing can change that."

"We didn't do very well the first time around," she reminded him.

"We're not kids anymore. It'll be different this time."

They fell silent again for a moment as the sky outside grew brighter. Then Kate took a deep breath and said, "You like Boston, don't you?"

He didn't answer right away. She told herself that it didn't mean anything, but the sudden knot in her stomach said otherwise. "As much as I like any city."

That wasn't exactly the answer she'd been hoping for, but she was willing to try again. It didn't have to be Boston, she told herself. She could always transfer to the New York office. Or maybe even Philadelphia. Wherever he would be happiest.

"McKinley Publishing has four branches on the East Coast. I'm sure I could transfer to one of them."

Again that long beat of silence. "You haven't been listening, Katie." She heard caution in his tone. That wasn't a good sign. "I'm leaving for the Andes."

"Of course, I heard you." She sat up, clutching the blanket to her breasts. "But that was before we..." She let her words trail away.

"You're right," he said, sitting back against the headboard. "This changes everything."

Relief overwhelmed her. He understood! Maybe this wasn't going to be too difficult after all. "We'll work everything out," she said, her words tumbling out before she could think. "I mean, you're a brilliantly talented man. There must be thousands of TV stations looking for someone with your abilities."

"Come with me," he said.

His words shocked her into silence. "Where?" *Please don't say the Andes.*

"The Andes," he said.

"You're joking, right?"

"Do I look like I'm joking?"

He didn't. Not one little bit. She felt her happiness begin to slip away. "I can't go to the Andes."

"Why not?"

"Where would I work?"

"Work for me," he said, not pausing at all this time. "We could use you on our team."

"I'm a researcher, Tony." Her throat was tight. "I don't know anything about jungles."

"We could use you," he said. "There's more to putting together documentaries than hiking up a mountain."

"I thought you were in the jungle."

"Mountains, this time," he said, watching her carefully. "We could use your expertise."

"I couldn't possibly do my job in the middle of nowhere."

"We'll get you a laptop and a cell phone."

"And do my research on the Net?"

"Lots of people do."

"That's a great jumping-off place, Tony, but I need real libraries and magazines and interviews. I need to have access to people."

"Bull."

She stiffened. "I resent that."

"You're afraid, Katie. Admit it."

"I am not afraid," she said. "That's ridiculous."

"You don't want to let go of your nice safe life."

She scrambled to her knees, still clutching the blanket. "I resent that even more."

"Yeah, but you don't deny it."

"Of course, I deny it. You make me sound like a coward."

"You don't like change, Katie. You never did.

Moving to Boston was more than I ever expected you to do.''

She wasn't a redhead for nothing. Her temper flared dangerously. ''Take that back.''

''The hell I will. It's the truth.''

''It's your opinion, not the truth.''

''Then what is the truth, Katie? Why won't you come with me to the Andes?''

''Why won't you come to Boston?''

Their eyes locked. The silence was impenetrable. She saw the wall rise up between them and it came close to breaking her heart.

He was the first one to speak.

''Let me show you the world, Katie.'' He reached across the bed for her hand but she stayed just beyond reach.

''Let me show you Boston.''

''What are you afraid of?'' he asked.

''What are you running from?'' she countered.

''I can't live locked up in a city.''

''And I can't live on a mountaintop.''

His voice dropped to little more than a whisper. ''But you can live without me, Katie?''

She willed herself not to cry. Crying wouldn't change anything at all. The problem between them went too deep for tears. ''If you can live without *us*.''

And there it was—the one thing neither one of them had an answer for. If they couldn't find a way

to live together, then they would have to find a way
to live apart.

For good, this time.

Six weeks later

"THE PLANE, *SEÑOR*." The young man looked at
Tony with stern disapproval. "You must board
now."

"A second," Tony said, pressing the phone closer
to his ear. "The call's going through right now."

"*Señor*, your entire party has already boarded.
We are waiting for you."

"They won't leave without me," he said, cupping
his ear to block out the airport noise all around him.
"I'm the boss."

The young man's expression grew more serious.
"They will leave, *señor*, when they are given clear-
ance to leave." He paused for effect. "With you,
señor, or without you."

"Give me a break, will you?" he practically
growled at the poor guy. "This is an important
call." Hell, it was probably the last time he would
be able to contact the outside world until next
spring. This unexpected foray down into Santiago
had been a total waste of time except for this last-
chance opportunity to hear Kate's voice one more
time.

They'd parted in silence and anger. She wanted

no part of his life; he couldn't understand hers. They loved each other but couldn't live together.

So, damn it, why couldn't he accept that? Why couldn't he pack Katie away with the yearbooks and the rest of his memories? There was no future for them. Why not accept her as part of his past and get on with it?

If he had an answer for that he would be a hell of a lot happier man than the one who stood there in the middle of the Santiago airport waiting for his call to Boston to go through.

The phone rang once.

His heart accelerated in anticipation. What was he going to say to her? Damn it, he hadn't thought that far ahead. All he'd wanted was to hear the sweet sound of her voice.

The phone rang twice.

His mouth went dry. He would start with hello. That was a good opener. Would she recognize his voice? He wasn't sure. It had been years since they'd talked on the phone.

He heard a click as the call connected.

Okay. This was it. She would say hello. He would say hello. She would say, "Is that you, Tony?" He would say, "Listen, there's gotta be a way we can make this work, Katie. I can't stop thinking about you. Every time I close my eyes, I see your face. Maybe—"

"Hi. This is Kate. I can't come to the phone right now, but if you leave your name and number, I'll get back to you as soon as I can."

Beep.

He realized he hadn't pulled in any oxygen since he'd picked up the receiver. He inhaled deeply, then spoke. "Katie, it's me. If you're there, pick up the phone. You're not there? Damn it, Katie, I'm at the Santiago airport.... We leave for base camp in a few minutes and I won't have another chance to reach you until next year.... I wanted to— The thing is, I've been thinking, and—"

Click. The damn thing disconnected him.

He swore softly and slammed the receiver down.

"*Señor.*" The stern airlines attendant stepped into his line of sight. "The plane will leave now."

"Gimme five more minutes," he said. "One more phone call—"

The attendant turned on his heel and started for the gate. If the plane took off without him, fifteen people would be stranded on a mountaintop without direction or support. He would be letting the entire team down, and for what?

For a future that was as impossible now as it had been eight years ago.

The plane took off ten minutes later.

Tony was on board.

Boston

"SIT DOWN, KATE." Dr. Rhinebeck motioned her toward a chair.

Kate murmured her thanks, then perched stiffly on the edge of the swank leather wing chair. "I know it's nothing," she said, aware of the slight quaver in her voice. "I mean, I'm overworked and underslept. Of course I feel tired and dragged out. Who wouldn't? I need vitamins. Maybe some B12 or—"

"You're pregnant, Kate."

She stopped in mid-sentence. She felt as if someone had reached into her skull and removed her brain. There wasn't a single thought in her head. Just empty, whooshing silence.

"You're pregnant, Kate," the doctor said again, watching her eyes for signs of intelligence. "About six weeks along."

He continued talking while Kate nodded at what she hoped were the appropriate places. Poor Dr. Rhinebeck, she thought. He obviously wasn't a very good doctor. A good doctor would know she couldn't possibly be pregnant.

He was still talking. "I'd say you're due around December 23rd, give or take a day. We'll know more after the sonogram."

Suddenly she snapped back to life. "I don't need a sonogram," she said with conviction. "I need vitamins."

"Yes, you do need vitamins," the doctor said, an amused smile on his face. "Prenatal vitamins."

"That's impossible."

"It's not impossible," he said.

She felt her face burn hot with embarrassment. "We used a condom."

"Only abstinence is a hundred percent effective."

"Now you tell me," she murmured.

The doctor laughed. Kate didn't. This couldn't be happening. She lived such an orderly life. She alphabetized her spice shelf. Everything in her freezer was neatly wrapped and labeled with an expiration date. Her entire existence was planned out months in advance on the pages of her organizer. She was not the kind of woman who turned up pregnant after a one-night stand with her ex-husband.

Somehow she made her way back to her apartment. She had no memory of leaving the doctor's office and driving home. It was a miracle she arrived in one piece. All she remembered was the sound of the refrain *You're pregnant...you're pregnant... you're pregnant,* as it repeated itself inside her head.

Why didn't she feel anything besides utter disbelief? Shouldn't she be struck with wonder about the new life growing inside her?

She hung up her coat in the hall closet, then walked toward the bedroom to undress. She was on automatic pilot, going though the motions of unbuttoning her skirt, sliding down the zipper, slipping on her robe, without ever engaging her brain.

Maybe that was a good thing, she thought as she wandered toward the kitchen. Maybe the way to get through the next seven and a half months was in a fog. No worries about labor pains and delivery. No worries about colic and teething. Not a single worry about the child's future: SATs, college, marriage, grandchildren. She would just sail through the whole experience in a fog of total denial.

She glanced at the answering machine as she entered the kitchen. The red light was blinking and a jolt of excitement zapped through her. The doctor, she thought, pressing the Play button. They'd made a mistake, mixed up her test result with that of another woman. Those things happened all the time. No, she wasn't pregnant at all. It was just one big misunderstanding.

Tony's voice filled the room. "Katie, it's me. If you're there, pick up the phone.... You're not there? Damn it, Katie, I'm at the Santiago airport.... We leave for base camp in a few minutes and I won't have another chance to reach you until next year.... I wanted to— The thing is, I've been thinking and—"

Click.

She stood there alone in her kitchen for an eternity. He'd called her. After all these weeks of dreaming about him, he'd found a way to call on the night of her doctor's appointment. If that wasn't the biggest cosmic joke of all: She was pregnant and the father of her baby was en route to some desolate, dangerous spot on an Andean mountaintop. The next time she saw Tony, she would be holding their child in her arms.

The next time she saw Tony, she would be a mother.

If she saw Tony.

Tony courted danger the way other men courted beautiful girls. He was a risk taker, one of those men who couldn't be happy unless they were walking on the razor's edge. Seven and a half months was a long time. Anything could happen on a desolate mountaintop in the middle of nowhere. Even to a strong man like Tony Marino.

Even to the father of her child.

Kate lowered her head and began to cry.

CHAPTER FIVE

New Year's Eve—seven and a half months later

MARY PAT POURED TWO CUPS of coffee, then sat down at the kitchen table opposite Gina. "Are you as depressed as I am?"

Gina wrapped her fingers around the bright yellow cup and sighed. "More."

"I can't believe it's New Year's Eve and he isn't here." Their annual New Year's Eve/birthday bash was set to begin in eight hours and neither one of the women had so much as checked their nail polish. "It's their birthday today. I thought that would be the lucky charm."

"We both knew it was a long shot, Mary Pat. When Tony said he'd be out of reach, he meant it."

"But you sent a special guide up there to look for him."

"Right," said Gina. "And now we can't even find the special guide."

"It's a lost cause, isn't it?"

"I don't believe in lost causes," Gina said, straightening her shoulders. "Kate hasn't gone into labor yet. We didn't serve the birthday cake. We still have time.''

"She's—what?—eight or nine days late," Mary Pat reminded her friend. "It could happen any minute.''

"It won't happen before Tony gets here," Gina said.

Mary Pat rolled her eyes. "It'll happen when it happens and it won't be when we want it to happen.'' She gestured toward the living room with her coffee cup. "If Kate knew what we were up to—'' She stopped and faked a shudder.

"Like my Tony would be sending us roses?''

Mary Pat laughed. "We're about to be grandmothers. We did what we had to do.''

"It's going to work out," Gina said. "It isn't midnight yet. I just know tonight's the night. Just you wait and see.''

"CAN'T YOU DRIVE ANY faster?" Tony urged the cabbie as they barreled along Route 78 West.

"Not unless you wanna pay my fines, pal. The place is lousy with fuzz on New Year's Eve.''

Tony checked his wallet. Slim pickin's but he could pay a speeding ticket or two if he had to. "I'll pay your fines," he said. "Just get me down to Princeton before noon.''

"That's a tall order.''

Tony checked his wallet again. "There's an extra twenty in it for you."

"Now you're talking." The cab leaped forward like a racehorse at the Meadowlands.

Tony tried to sit back and relax but he was half-wired on adrenaline. In fact, he was so filled with the stuff he could have run the whole way from Newark Airport to Katie's house and made better time. Hell, he'd been running toward Katie his whole damn life.

The note she'd sent him was spread out on his left knee, scribbled in some American Express clerk's handwriting. "Come home," it read. "I need you. Katie." Six words. That's all it took. Six words and he knew exactly what he had to do.

After all the years of running, all the years of searching for answers, he knew. Without Katie he had nothing. Happiness wasn't hiding on some mountaintop or hidden deep in some faraway jungle. Happiness had always been right there within reach. It was Katie. Nothing else mattered a damn. He didn't care if it meant being a wage slave, strapped to a desk somewhere for the rest of his life. Not as long as he had Katie to love.

And she'd taken the first step. Cautious, careful Katie had tracked him down and declared herself. If he'd needed proof that this time it would be different, he had it right there in black and white.

KATE MUTED THE SOUND on the television and inclined her head in the general direction of the kitchen. Her mother and Aunt Gina had been whispering back there for a good fifteen minutes and Kate knew they weren't discussing cocktail meatballs for tonight's party.

They were talking about her.

So what else was new? They'd been talking about her for the past six weeks. They'd accompanied her to doctor's appointments. They'd watched her diet like twin hawks. It seemed to Kate that either her mother or Aunt Gina was watching her every single minute of the day. And if it wasn't her mother or Aunt Gina, it was her father or Uncle Sal or one of her five siblings or one of their spouses or any of a dozen assorted Marinos. She hadn't had a minute to herself since she'd moved back home.

Why on earth had that ever seemed like such a brilliant idea? She'd come down from Boston for Thanksgiving and they'd plied her with turkey and stuffing and pumpkin pie and before she knew it, she'd agreed to move back until the baby was born. "This is the time you need your family the most," her mother had said with conviction. "Come home, sweetie. Let your family take care of you."

It was the first and only time in her life that Kate had fallen for that line. She'd left home because she'd felt like she was drowning in family. She and Tony had eloped because they'd wanted to create their own idea of marriage, not recreate their parents' idea of wedded bliss. If she was honest with herself, she would admit that she'd taken a job in Boston for the same reason Tony traveled the world: She wanted to find out who she was away from scores of O'Callaghans and Marinos. She'd lived a productive and independent life in Beantown and she would still be living that life if Mother Nature hadn't had other ideas.

So there she was, back in the bosom of her family—and during the holidays, no less. She would have found more privacy in an airport terminal. Solitude was viewed with suspicion by her family. The O'Callaghan house was bursting with a steady stream of relatives, all of whom seemed intent upon staring at her belly and speculating on when she would "pop." They also seemed determined to speculate on the father's identity, but Kate refused to say a word.

Bad enough that she'd told her sister Erin. She hadn't intended to tell anyone at all, but when she'd burst into tears at the mention of Tony's name at Thanksgiving, explanations had been in order. She'd sworn Erin to secrecy and so far, so good. If the combined forces of the O'Callaghan and Marino families found out she was expecting their first collaborative grandchild, there would be no living with the lot of them. They would probably have her encased in cotton and seated on a throne.

Actually that didn't sound so bad. It had to be easier getting up from a throne than an easy chair. She'd rolled her eyes at all the sitcom pregnant women who made a production about getting up from a chair—but now she knew they had underplayed the situation. And that wasn't all. Taking a shower was a major undertaking. Getting dressed was even worse. Panty hose were a thing of the past. Shoes with laces, a forgotten dream. And, if she had any more time left over for worrying, there was always the question of whether the baby had decided to stay in there forever.

"I know you're talking about me," she called out to her mother and Aunt Gina. "Don't think you're fooling me, because you're not."

They fell silent for a good five seconds, then Mary Pat piped up with, "We have a couple hundred cocktail meatballs to make for the party tonight, honey. We don't have time to be gossiping about you."

"Sure, you don't," Kate yelled back. "You're just lucky I can't get out of this chair or I'd come back there and give you both a piece of my mind."

All they did was laugh.

Kate couldn't blame them. Between them, her mom and Aunt Gina had given birth to twelve children. They'd endured swollen ankles, heartburn, false labor and everything else under the sun, and had lived to tell the tale. No wonder they found Kate's situation so amusing.

Kate, however, wasn't laughing. All she wanted was to have her baby. She wanted to finally see that dear little face, count the fingers and toes, and forget the fact that Tony hadn't been there to share it all with her.

Because it mattered.

She didn't want it to matter, but it did. Tony was the first thing she thought about when she woke up in the morning and the last thing she thought about when she went to bed at night. She hadn't thought about him this much when she'd been married to him. She tried to blame it on hormones, on the stresses of pregnancy, but she knew there was much more to it than that, even if she didn't want to speculate exactly what that might be.

Maybe you're in love with him.

What a ridiculous thought. She refused to even consider the notion. He wasn't the kind of man you settled down with, and that was the kind of man she wanted.

Banker John wanted to settle down with you. Why didn't you say yes?

Because she was crazy, that was why. Because she had this crazy idea you should love the man you married, not just like him.

You loved Tony once.

And what if she had? She'd also loved her Barbie

doll and she'd gotten over that. It was no different with Tony.

Then why did you sleep with him nine months ago?

"Because I was an idiot," she muttered, brushing away her tears with an angry gesture. Because she'd let herself get swept away by lush music and champagne and the smell of his skin.

Because sometimes even smart women made stupid mistakes.

She shifted position in the lounge chair, which was no mean feat when you were the size of the Goodyear blimp. "Darn it," she muttered, reaching for one of the pillows on the floor next to her. She'd made a big production, telling her mother that she didn't need a pillow at the small of her back, but apparently Mother really did "know best." The nagging pain in her back had started not long after breakfast and so far it showed no sign of going away.

The pillow was two inches beyond her grasp. Nine months ago she could have done a back flip across the living room. Now she couldn't even bend over to pick up a throw pillow. Between the pain in her lower back and the gargantuan size of her belly, she was doomed. Why didn't they just put her on an ice floe and let her drift away?

That would be the best birthday present yet. At least she would have a little privacy on an ice floe.

The doorbell rang. Great, she thought. Probably a score of second cousins who had trouble telling twelve noon from twelve midnight on New Year's Eve.

"Ma!" she called out. "Someone's at the door."

"You get it," Mary Pat called back. "We're making meatballs."

Kate was stung. You would think a woman who'd carried six children would understand how hard it was to get up from a chair nine days past your due date.

The doorbell rang a second time.

"Keep your shirt on," Kate muttered as she pulled herself to her feet with all the grace of one of those elephants in Disney's *Fantasia*. Grumbling, she waddled to the door. Her hair was pinned loosely on top of her head. She wore the world's largest flannel nightgown and big fluffy slippers. Nine months ago she would have died a thousand deaths before she let anyone see her like that, but not anymore.

Her belly reached the front door a good two seconds before the rest of her did. "This has to come to an end soon," she said, placing a hand against the rock-hard expanse. "I refuse to go to college with you."

The doorbell rang a third time. That did it. The person on the other side was going to get a piece of her mind, holiday or no holiday.

She started talking as she opened the door a crack. "What on earth is your problem? Why can't you give a person time to—"

"Katie?"

She had a glimpse of thick black hair and big dark eyes and slammed the door shut. She leaned against it, her knees trembling. She had to be hallucinating. Tony couldn't possibly be standing there on the doorstep. He was on an Andes mountaintop. Last she'd heard, a man couldn't be two places at the same time. At least not in this universe.

"It's freezing out here, Katie. Let me in."

It sounded like Tony. Especially the way his voice slid over the *A* in Katie—like a soft caress.

"Go away!" she called out. "Why don't you go pound on your parents' door?"

"They're not home."

"Use your key."

"I don't have one."

"I don't care. Just go away, Tony." Her voice broke and she sucked in a deep breath. *"Now!"*

She waited for him to pound on the door again but he didn't. She pressed her ear against the door and listened. Not a sound. Since when did Tony Marino do what he was told? He was probably headed for the back door.

Moments later, her Aunt Gina's shriek of delight confirmed her worst suspicions.

After all the months of fantasizing about the moment he discovered he was about to become a father, she found she wasn't quite ready for it. In fact, there was a good chance she would never be ready for it. He had himself a nerve, showing up now just in time for the main event. Where had he been when she was throwing up and feeling weepy and scared and more alone than she would have imagined possible? If he thought he was going to waltz back into her life in time to take a bow as a brand-new daddy, he had another think coming.

The answer was clear. The thing to do now was retreat. With a little luck she would make it upstairs to her room before Aunt Gina was finished interrogating her prodigal son.

She'd made it halfway to the foot of the hall stairs when that persistent pain in her lower back stopped her in her tracks. She placed her hand just above the upper curve of her buttock and waited for it to pass. It must be all the sitting, she told herself. That and the extra forty pounds she was carrying. No wonder she had a backache. It was like carrying around a pair of fox terriers. Big ones.

"Kate!" Mary Pat's voice rang out. "Do we have a surprise for you!"

"I don't want any surprises!" she shouted back as the pain began to ease. She turned for the stairs again, praying she could waddle fast enough to gain some distance before Tony found her.

"Not exactly what I was expecting to hear, Katie." Tony's voice sounded too close for comfort.

She urged her *Queen Mary* girth to move faster. Why did they have such a long hallway? Nobody needed a hallway the length of an airport runway. If they'd had a shorter hallway she would have been halfway up the stairs by now.

"Where are you going, Katie?" It was Tony again. This time he sounded closer and slightly annoyed.

"You don't take a hint, do you, Marino?" she complained over her shoulder as she continued moving toward the staircase. "Tonight's New Year's Eve. We're busy. Go bother your own family, why don't you?"

"Katherine!" Mary Pat's voice rose in dismay. "What on earth's the matter with you? Tony's come back home!"

"And that's what's the matter with me," she said without turning around. "I want him to go away."

"Tony looks wonderful." Another county heard from, this time Aunt Gina. "Like he spent nine months at a spa."

Now that was exactly what a pregnant woman wanted to hear. She looked like a beached whale while he was buff and gorgeous. Yep, life wasn't fair. No doubt about it.

"Go back to your spa," she said to Tony as she

neared the foot of the stairs. ''Don't let me keep you.''

''You want me out of here?'' Tony sounded more than a little bit annoyed. Under normal circumstances she might have felt guilty. ''Why the hell did you—''

''She doesn't mean it, Anthony,'' Mary Pat piped up. ''She's not herself.''

''Don't you go apologizing for me, Ma,'' Kate retorted, still with her back to the meddlesome crowd. ''He's the one who came barging in uninvited.''

''Uninvited?'' Tony snapped. ''What do you mean—''

''Why don't we all have some hot chocolate,'' Aunt Gina said. ''Maybe some—''

''You owe me an explanation.'' Tony sounded a lot less friendly than he had a few seconds ago and she felt her temper begin to heat up.

''Don't you go telling me what to do, Anthony Joseph Marino. You're not my husband anymore—''

''Anymore?'' Mary Pat and Gina spoke in unison.

''A—a slip of the tongue,'' Kate said, grabbing for the banister. Her back was in an uproar again; she could feel the muscles drawing into a painful, throbbing knot. All she had to do was get to her bedroom and lock the door behind her. She would come out when the baby was ready to start school.

Maybe.

"She said 'anymore,' Gina!"

"I heard her!" Aunt Gina's voice was climbing toward the audible-to-dogs-only range. "What did she mean 'anymore'?"

"What do you mean 'anymore'?" her mother demanded. "Turn around this second, young woman, and tell us."

"Tell them, Katie." Tony sounded too close for comfort now. "It was a long time ago. Why keep secrets?"

Try as she might to control her temper, she wasn't a redhead for nothing. Her last shred of self-control vanished and she spun around to face him.

"Surprise, Tony," she said as back pain gripped her one more time. "How's this for keeping secrets?"

THE FIRST THING TONY noticed when Katie turned around was the fire in her eyes. He'd dreamed about those eyes for months now. It didn't matter that the O'Callaghan temper was responsible for the heat and fire in their green depths. The only thing that mattered was that he was there in the same room, breathing the same air, close enough to touch her beautiful—

Belly.

Her huge *pregnant* belly.

His jaw sagged open. He would probably need a forklift to close it again.

His mind went blank. Maybe his heart even stopped beating. He sure as hell had stopped breathing. In fact, he wondered if he might have stopped permanently.

"Quit staring," Kate snapped. "Haven't you ever seen a pregnant woman before?"

The only sound in the hallway was the soft ticking of the grandfather clock to the right of the staircase. He was dimly aware of Mary Pat and his mother slipping back into the kitchen and closing the door behind them. He wasn't born yesterday, though. He knew they were eavesdropping.

"Eloquent, aren't you? If you have nothing to say, I'll go upstairs and—" Kate's voice broke on the last word. She drew in a loud, shuddery breath. Her hand grabbed at a spot on her lower back.

"What's wrong?" He moved toward her.

"My back," she said through gritted teeth. "It's nothing."

"How do you know it's nothing?"

"Because I say it's nothing." She straightened and met his gaze. "You try carrying forty extra pounds in front of you and tell me how your back feels."

His hand hovered an inch above her belly, drawn to it by a combination of fear and wonder. He didn't touch her. She didn't ask him to. Suddenly he re-

membered The Banker, and a sick feeling settled in
the pit of his gut. He glanced at her left hand. She
wasn't wearing any rings, but the forty-pound
weight gain might be the reason for that. But why
the note? Nothing made one damn bit of sense.

He stepped back. "Congratulations," he managed. "When are you due?"

"Nine days ago," she said. Her eyes still flashed
fire but her tone of voice was carefully neutral.

He glanced around. Where was The Banker, anyway? "Why aren't you up in Boston?"

"I moved down here last month to have the
baby."

"You moved down here alone?" What the hell
was wrong with The Banker? Didn't he give a damn
that he was about to become a father?

"Of course I moved down here alone."

"So where's The Banker?"

"The banker?" She looked at him blankly for a
second. "You mean John? I haven't seen him since
Memorial Day."

"The bastard," Tony muttered.

"Actually, he's a very nice man," she said
evenly. "But how would you know? You've never
met him."

"I know his type." His gaze was drawn once
again to her enormous belly. "Hit-and-run. Take no
responsibility."

"Yes," she said, hands clasped across that wide

expanse of new life. "The kind of man who'd take off for an Andean mountaintop and never look back."

"It's not the same thing."

"Oh no?"

"Damn right, it's not." All of his emotions were suddenly engaged. She'd always had that effect on him. There was something about Katie that brought him to life the way nobody else could. "I didn't run off on the woman who was carrying my child."

Her eyes suddenly filled with tears. "Didn't you?"

Her words hit him with the force of a punch to the gut. "What did you say?"

"You heard me, Tony."

"I want to hear it again."

"You used to be good at math. Think about it. The party back in March. I'm nine days overdue. I'd say the clues were all there, Columbo."

He let his hand come to rest on the hard swell of her belly and a sense of wonder exploded inside his heart. Wonder and amazement and anger.

"Why the hell didn't you tell me?"

"How could I?" she countered. "You were up there on that godforsaken mountaintop without a phone or a fax machine or a mailbox. Did you want me to hire a helicopter to drop a letter on your head?"

"That's what you did, isn't it? That's why I'm here."

"I don't know what you're talking about."

"The letter you sent that guide to deliver," he said. "The one where you said 'I need you.'"

"I said I need you?"

"Without the question mark."

"Tony, I still don't know what you're talking about."

They locked eyes.

"*Mother!*" they cried simultaneously.

The kitchen door opened a crack and Mary Pat and Gina peeked out.

"You want some hot chocolate?" Mary Pat asked, all innocence.

"Or a cannoli?" Gina offered. "I made two hundred for the party tonight. We won't miss a couple."

"You actually hired a guide to climb up into the mountains and find Tony and blamed it on me?" Kate demanded. "How could you?"

"It wasn't easy," Mary Pat admitted. "Especially when you're in New Jersey and the guide is in South America."

"You had no right, Mother. This is my life, not yours."

"Somebody had to find him," Gina said. "Didn't you want him here for the birth of the baby?"

"You *knew* the baby was Tony's?" Kate shook

her head in disbelief. "I didn't tell anyone but Erin."

"Don't go blaming Erin," Mary Pat said. "I overheard the two of you talking on Thanksgiving."

"And then Mary Pat told me," said Gina, "but we haven't told anybody else."

"Well, except for Daddy," Mary Pat said. "I had to tell him."

"And I told Sal," Gina said. "I tell Sal everything."

"I can't believe this," Kate said. "They all knew. Every single one of them."

"Yeah," said Tony. "Every one of them but me."

"If you hadn't gone off to Chile, you would have known, too."

"That's what I do, Kate. That's how I earn my living—"

"I've heard it all before," Kate interrupted him. "You made your choice, Tony. Live with it."

"Live with it? I've known about the baby for less than five minutes. First I come home because I think you need me, then I find out you're about to have our baby. Gimme a break, will you, Katie?"

"Quit calling me Katie. My name is Kate. I wish you'd use it."

"You used to like for me to call you Katie."

"I used to like being married to you but that's ancient history."

The kitchen door opened wider.

"There you go again," Mary Pat said, stepping into the hallway. "What do you mean, 'married'?"

"You two are married?" Gina asked. "You mean I've been worrying myself into an early grave for nothing?"

"We're not married, Ma," Tony said.

"I know what I heard," Gina said. "You said *married.*"

"It was a long time ago," Kate said. He noticed her hand was once again resting at the small of her back. "Barely worth mentioning."

Their mothers swept down on them like avenging angels with attitude.

"When were you married?" Mary Pat demanded.

"And where?" Gina joined her friend. "How could you do that without your family with you?"

"We were in college," Tony said, looking over at Kate. She looked paler than usual and he noticed a faint sheen of perspiration on her forehead.

"First year," Kate said. "We got married in a little town in North Carolina on spring break."

Mary Pat burst into tears. "I can't believe this! You two were married and you didn't tell us."

"We would have helped you out," Gina said, dabbing at her own eyes with the sleeve of her dark green sweater. "You wouldn't have had to worry about a thing."

"That's why we didn't tell you," Katie said. Her

voice quivered slightly and he knew what that meant. Any second her temper would erupt and they would be reminded why she'd been born a redhead. "We wanted to sink or swim on our own."

"I can't believe this," Mary Pat said, shaking her head. "Daddy and Sal would've been happy to find you a nice town house and—"

Kate let out a shriek and looked over at Tony. "We didn't stand a chance against them, did we? We were doomed no matter how you look at it."

"Doomed?" His mother sounded downright outraged. "Because we want to help our children get a good start in life? If that's 'doomed,' then we should all be so lucky."

"Katie didn't mean it like that, Ma."

"I did so." Kate shot him a fierce look. "We would've been gobbled up by family."

"Well, that's nice talk for you." Mary Pat looked aggrieved. "We wish we could've helped you. So why don't you shoot us for it? Maybe you'd still be married."

"This is about the dumbest conversation I've ever had." Katie started toward the hall closet. "I can't take another second of this."

Tony stepped in front of her. "What're you doing?"

She placed her hands on his chest and pushed him away. "None of your damn business."

"She's going out in her nightgown," Mary Pat said.

"Do something, Tony," his mother said. "She's wearing bunny slippers."

"What do you want me to do?" he said. "Put her in a headlock?" Not that he hadn't thought about it many times over the years.

"You're her husband," Mary Pat said.

"Ex-husband," Katie snapped as she slipped into her coat. "Remember that."

"Kate!" Mary Pat sounded horrified. "You can't go outside in your nightgown and slippers."

"Oh, yes, I can," Kate said. To prove it, she opened the front door and marched out into the snow.

Mary Pat started to run after her but Tony stopped her. "I'll go," he said, then set out after his crazy pregnant ex-wife in the bunny slippers.

He started down the path after her.

"Don't talk to me," she called over her shoulder. "If I hear the sound of your voice, I'll scream."

"Fair enough," he said, catching up with her in three long strides. "I don't much feel like listening to you, either."

"Good," she said.

"Great," he said.

They walked another three steps, then she stopped.

"What's wrong?" he asked.

"N-nothing."

"Why did you stop?"

Her hand was pressed once again to the small of her back. "None of your business."

"Does your back hurt?"

She started walking again with that strange, side-to-side motion he'd noticed in other pregnant women.

"I asked you if your back hurts."

"I'm fine," she said.

"You didn't answer my question."

"That's right," she said, flashing him a phony smile.

"Let's go back into the house," he said. "They're watching us from the living-room window. We might as well answer the rest of their questions."

"I'd rather eat dirt."

"We need to talk."

"We needed to talk nine months ago but you weren't here, Tony."

"If you'd picked up the phone the night I called from Santiago, I would've come home."

An odd look flickered across her lovely face. "That was the night I found out I was pregnant. I'd just come home from Dr. Rhinebeck's office and there was your message waiting for me...." Her voice trailed away and he saw her, scared and alone.

"I would have given anything to have you here with me, Tony. Anything."

"I love you, Katie." He hadn't meant to say that—not yet—but the words tumbled out as if they had a life of their own. He couldn't have stopped them if he'd wanted to.

"Too late," she said, turning away from him. "I don't want to hear it."

"I realized how much I love you that night at the Plaza."

"How wonderful for you."

"That's why I came home."

"You came home because our mothers fooled you into it."

"I came home because I thought you needed me." Because he'd thought they had a chance.

He saw the look of recognition in her eyes and took heart. She knew what he was saying, even if she wasn't ready to admit it. He still had a chance.

"I don't need you at all," she said, but her tone had softened. "You might as well catch the next plane back to your mountaintop because I'm doing just fine without you."

"*I'm* not," he said. "I'm not doing fine without you at all, Katie." He wasn't going to let her slip away from him now. "Remember what you said that night? You wanted to know if I could live without us."

"You didn't answer," she said, her voice barely

above a whisper. "That told me everything I needed to know."

"There's only one answer, Katie, and neither one of us had the guts for it that night."

"I don't want to hear this." Tears ran down her cheeks. "I really wish you wouldn't—"

"I love you, Katie."

She cradled her belly with her hands in that ages-old gesture. "Please, don't," she whispered.

"I've always loved you. It's you, Katie. It's always been you." He tried to gather her into his arms but she was as stiff and unyielding as an ice sculpture. "If it takes a three-piece suit and a desk job to prove it, then that's what I'm going to do."

She met his gaze. "That's not funny."

"I'll do it for you, Katie." He didn't blink or look away. "I'll do it for us."

"I can't ask that of you."

"You didn't."

"You'd never be happy behind a desk."

"I'll be happier behind a desk than on a mountaintop without you. It's no contest, kid. No contest at all."

Hope was a sneaky emotion, Kate thought, as her heart pounded wildly against her breastbone. Just when you think you've convinced yourself that you're satisfied with what you have, that you can live without the things you used to dream about, hope rears its ugly head and makes a fool of you.

She wanted so much more than what she had. She wanted to spend her life with Tony and their child.

But not like this. She also wanted him to be happy. That was part of love, too. Maybe the biggest part of all. Tony had figured that out on his own. Why had it taken her so long?

"I've had a lot of time to think lately," she began as they stood there on the shoveled pathway with the sun glittering off the snow and neighbors hurrying past on last-minute New Year's Eve errands. "There's nothing so special about Boston."

His eyes narrowed as he watched her, but he said nothing.

She swallowed hard. "And there's nothing so special about working nine-to-five either."

He considered her for a moment. "So how do you feel about Manhattan?"

Her heart leaped. "I feel good about it." She paused, ignoring the stretching pain that wrapped itself around her hips. "How do you feel about fatherhood?"

"Scared," he said, then laughed. "And overwhelmed."

She laughed with him. "Welcome to the club."

"And lucky," he said. "Like I'm the luckiest man in the world."

Funny how words could heal even the loneliest heart.

"No regrets?" she asked as her eyes welled with

tears. "I won't turn around one day and find you've headed back to your mountaintop?"

"Only if you and the baby come with me."

She took a deep breath, then made a leap of faith. "I'd like to see your mountaintop and your jungle and anyplace else you want to show us." There was a whole big wide world out there and who better to show it to her than the man she'd always loved?

"I have an offer from the Nature Channel to oversee a series of documentaries about the natural history of New York City. It would keep me in town for three years. Think you can stand the stability?"

It seemed too good to be true. "How do you feel about that?" she asked cautiously.

"Good," he answered. "Damn good."

There it was again—that outrageous burst of hope that made all things seem possible.

"And how do you feel about us?" she whispered.

"I think we can make it work this time," he replied. "I think we know how to do it now."

She looked at his beautiful face and felt her heart open up wide. "So do I," she said.

"Tell me, Katie," he said, cupping her own face between his two hands. "I'm still waiting to hear it."

She hesitated, suddenly shy and embarrassed and overwhelmed by the greatest miracle of them all: love.

"I love you," she said, letting the power of those

words fill her soul with joy. "I think I've loved you since the day I was born."

Through childhood and high school, through the years when she could only dream about him, he'd always been there, inside her heart.

"This time it's for keeps," he said. "No matter what happens, Katie, we'll work it out together." He drew her into his arms, laughing at the barrier of her enormous, overdue belly. "As a family."

"Tony," she said as an odd sensation spread across her pelvis, "they're still watching us from the living-room window."

"I know," he said, as he bent down to kiss her. "Let's give 'em something to talk about."

"I think we already have," she said as his mouth met hers. "My water just broke. Looks like we're about to have a baby."

CHAPTER SIX

"I'VE NEVER MARRIED anyone in the labor room before," Father Campbell said as he took his position next to Kate's bed. "This is a first for me."

"I've never had a baby before," Kate said, hanging on to Tony's hand for dear life. "I'd say we're even."

"You both are entering into this marriage willingly?"

"We are," Tony replied as he watched Kate ride the wave of another monster contraction. Her grip was so strong, he thought she would break his fingers.

"Almost eight centimeters dilated," said the doctor from the foot of the bed. "Not too much longer."

Kate's breathing settled back down to normal. "Is it going to get a lot worse?" she asked nobody in particular. "It is, isn't it?"

"Nothing you can't take, honey." A nurse patted her shoulder. The woman grinned in Tony's direction. "She must love you a whole lot. Any woman who'd even think of getting married during transition..."

The room erupted in laughter. Even Father Campbell seemed to get the joke.

"If this wedding is going to precede the birth, you'd better get moving, people." Dr. Rhinebeck stripped off his gloves and tossed them in a trash pail. "We're moving along quite nicely here."

"Call in the family," Father Campbell said, "and let's have a wedding."

Tony bent down and kissed Katie lightly on the mouth. "No second thoughts?" he murmured.

"Only about childbirth," she said.

He grinned. "I'll be right back."

He stepped out into the hallway. The place was teeming with O'Callaghans and Marinos. Mary Pat was serving birthday cake to anyone who wanted a slice, while Gina had set up a hot and cold buffet for the New Year's Eve celebration. His dad and Matt O'Callaghan were holding court in the lounge at the other end of the hall, while assorted siblings, nieces and nephews claimed every sofa and chair and floor space.

He whispered something to his mother and to Aunt Pat, then rounded up Matt and his old man.

"This marriage isn't legal in New Jersey," his father reminded him as they filed into Katie's room.

"We know that, Pop. This one is for us," Tony said. "We'll have another one for the state after the baby's born."

"You'd better," Matt said, then laughed and clapped Tony on the back.

Mary Pat and Gina were too busy crying happy tears to say much of anything at all.

Kate was starting another contraction. He took his place next to her, held her hand, and whispered encouragement as she panted and huffed.

"It's almost show time, folks," Dr. Rhinebeck reminded them. "This baby is coming whether you're married or not."

Tony handed a pair of wedding rings to the priest.

"Wh-where did you get those?" Kate managed.

"They're from our first wedding," he said. "I held on to them."

Her beautiful eyes swam with tears. "I love you," she said. "I—"

Another contraction. She mumbled a few choice words that turned the men's cheeks red. The women in the room simply laughed.

"That's it," said the doctor. "Everybody out!"

"Not until they're married," Mary Pat said. "I'm not moving until I hear those two say 'I do.'"

"Amen, sister." Gina stood her ground next to her old friend. "We've waited twenty-seven years for this moment and we're not about to miss it."

Father Campbell cleared his throat. "Now you'll have to bear in mind that I'm doing this from memory," he said, eyeing Kate as if he expected her head to spin around like that character in *The Exorcist*. "Dearly beloved, we are gathered together—"

"Aaaaieeee." Kate's yelp split the air. "I think I'd better push." She arched her back, then sat up straight. She still had Tony's hand in a death grip.

"No pushing," Dr. Rhinebeck said from his position at the foot of the bed. "It's not time to push."

"It's time to push!" Kate's eyes were wild and feverishly bright.

"Hang on, Kate," said the doctor. "Not too much longer now."

Tony met Father Campbell's gaze across Katie's belly. "I think we'd better cut to the chase, Father."

Father Campbell nodded. "Do you, Katherine, take Anthony as your husband?"

"I...*pant, pant*...d-do...*puff, puff*..."

"And do you, Anthony, take Katherine as your wife?"

He squeezed her hand. "I do."

"I usually make a little speech here about the sanctity of marriage but, in the interests of time and nature, I'll skip to the part you've all been waiting for. By the power vested in me by the state of New Jersey, and even though no banns have been posted or marriage license filed, in the eyes of God I now pronounce you husband and wife."

Mary Pat and Gina burst into noisy tears while Matt and Sal wiped their eyes with their sleeves. Even the no-nonsense nurse sniffled audibly. Tony had the feeling Kate wasn't exactly in a kissing mood but he decided to take a chance. He leaned forward, prepared to veer back and run for his life, when she fixed him with a look of such happiness that he forgot everything but the sweet touch of her mouth beneath his.

Suddenly Kate spoke. "*Now* can I push?"

"It's time!" the doctor cried. "Everybody out except the father."

Father Campbell was the first one out the door. Matt and Sal were close behind. Mary Pat and Gina had to be forced out by the nurse.

Tony held Katie's shoulders the way he'd been shown to do it.

"If you faint, I'll kill you," she said fiercely.

"I won't faint." He hoped he wasn't lying.

"Push," said the doctor. "Come on, Kate... Now!"

"You can do it," Tony said.

"No, I can't."

"One more push, Katie," Tony said. "Just one more..."

Now he knew why they called it labor. He'd never seen anyone work harder than Katie was working to bring their baby into the world. Although she was trembling with exhaustion, somehow she found the strength to push again and again until the doctor called out, "It's a girl!"

Katie laughed and cried. "I love you," she told

Tony as they placed the baby against her chest. "I love you both so much— Tony?" She leaned up on one elbow. "Tony!"

He didn't answer.

Her new husband was out cold on the floor.

Just before midnight

MARY PAT AND GINA stood in front of the nursery window and admired the pink-wrapped bundle called Baby Girl Marino.

"She's beautiful," Mary Pat said, dabbing at her eyes with a Kleenex.

"A perfect little doll," Gina agreed, reaching for a tissue herself.

Mary Pat linked her arm through Gina's. "We did it, old friend."

Gina rested her head on Mary Pat's shoulder. "And that little darling is the proof." She grinned. "Even if my son did pass out during delivery."

Mary Pat laughed out loud. "That's why women give birth and men hand out cigars."

They exchanged grandmotherly high fives.

"Can you believe it's been twenty-seven years since we stood here, admiring our firstborns?" The memory was so clear to Mary Pat that it could have been just last week.

"It all goes by too fast," Gina said. "You blink and it's gone."

"But not family," Mary Pat said. "Family is forever."

"WILL YOU LOOK AT THEM?" Katie whispered to Tony as they watched their mothers admire baby Sarah. "You'd think they were responsible for everything."

"Maybe they were," Tony said, holding her close to his chest. "I mean, they had this planned from the day we were born."

"Don't tell them that," Katie said. "They're too smug right now as it is."

"It's been one hell of a day," he said.

Katie laughed. "Two birthdays, a wedding, and a new arrival. This might be one for the record books."

"I love you, Katie," he said. "And that's for the record, too."

"I'm glad to hear that," she said, "because now that we've united the O'Callaghans and Marinos, there's no turning back."

"Regrets?" he asked.

Her eyes filled with tears. "Only that we wasted so much time apart."

"Sounds like you love me, Katie."

"Sounds like," she agreed, laughing softly. "Sounds like I'll love you this New Year and next New Year and all the New Years of our lives."

And so Kate and Tony Marino welcomed in the New Year the same way they would welcome every new day from that moment on—as a family.

Leandra Logan

MOTHER FIGURE

CHAPTER ONE

"YOU'RE LATE."

Her small sleepy voice startled Nick as he tiptoed across the kitchen floor. He stumbled, bracing himself against the edge of the counter, reeling from the excesses of the evening. The last thing he wanted was to be caught in this condition.

"I hope you didn't drive."

"No, no. I left the Blazer downtown."

Nick set his keys and wallet on the kitchen counter, aware of the tension slicing through the dim stillness of the room. Everything always seemed so magnified in the middle of the night. And Heather, with her adolescent silhouette backlit by the hall light, her voice steeped with the confident indignation of a judge and jury, was indulging in deliberate high drama.

"You *said* you'd be home by eleven and it's way past midnight."

Nick drove a hand through his thick shag of blond hair, struggling to right the mild slur in his voice. "And you should be in bed. Asleep."

"Sleep?" His daughter's long blond hair flew as she tossed her head with a battle cry: "You come—and see something!"

She moved swiftly down the bungalow's main hallway, her bare feet picking up their slapping tempo on the worn pine, her slender body shimmying beneath her long peach nightgown. He lumbered behind her with a clop of boot heels, his broad shoulders accentuated by his bulky leather jacket.

Their home wasn't large, with two bedrooms at the back and combination living-dining room in front. Nick quickly got the score as Heather snapped on the floor lamp near the living-room sofa, her childish features coming into sharper focus in the harsh light. "How can we sleep with this kind of noise?"

Nick stared down at his business partner, Phil Mahoney, stretched out flat on his back on the brown velour couch, his arms flung over his head. His mouth was open, his nostrils flaring wide, and he was sputtering like a lawn mower.

"Take a good look, Dad, at the baby-sitter who's supposed to watch me!"

"Not bad for the last minute," he mumbled in apology.

Heather threw her arms in the air. "C'mon, get real. I'll be thirteen right after Christmas. I can take care of me and Cassie. I already do it after school. What's so different about the night?"

Nick smiled wanly, reaching out to her. "Oh, baby."

"Don't 'baby' me." She reeled back to escape

him. "That's the trouble. You're stuck in time. You can't see me getting older every day."

Very ironic observation, as Nick was feeling every bit of his own thirty-three years more and more by the hour. He unzipped his soft brown bomber jacket, shuddering as a trace of new-and-yet-familiar perfume from the collar reached his nose.

Traces of the delectable Jayne Ashland. *Oh, what a night...*

Common sense swiftly returned under his daughter's demanding glare. How could he have expected to lose himself in heaven for a brief sizzling encounter, and not catch hell for it in the end?

"At least tell me what happened here, Dad."

"Nothing." *Everything.* How could he explain? He shouldn't have to, of course. He was head of the house, with a right to some privacy, some what he called "hooky time." But his woman-child daughter's possessive attitude was his own doing. For much of Heather's young life he'd been home at five on the dot every night. She was in the habit of counting on him.

It had been aeons since Nick had allowed himself a secret or a selfish treat. Guilt warred inside him along with a sense of masculine satisfaction. He hung his jacket over the back of his favorite recliner, avoiding his daughter's gaze as provocative images danced through his head in a dizzying rush. Yeah,

Jayne Ashland certainly was a treat. He'd done more living tonight than he'd managed in the past eighteen months since Sharon had died.

"Earth to Dad!" Heather snapped fingers in his face. "What kept you?"

He covered his mouth, cleared his throat. "It was a business obligation. Phil and I flipped a coin over the choices. Heads was to come back here to play chef and big daddy, and tails had to stay behind at Paxton Limited and make nice at their office Christmas party."

"And you won."

"I lost, kiddo. You know Phil and I don't go out of our way to impress temporary bosses in fancy suits. We're carpenters, roving from one project to the next." Nick gestured to his friend and business partner with a measure of pity and disgust. "Heads. Huh! I've never seen him so smug, so triumphant. So relieved."

"Oh. Well..." Heather smiled, on the melt.

Nick drew her close, reveling in the way she burrowed her nose into the softness of his plaid flannel shirt. She was a small and supple willow shoot against the broad expanse of his chest. So completely dependent upon him despite her spunky bid for independence. "It was only polite that Minnesota Remodeling be represented at the bash," he murmured. "And so nice of Mr. Paxton to invite us, even though we're almost finished with the job."

Heather stole a peek up at him, her voice faint. "We just expected you, like always."

He gazed down lovingly, brushing corn-silk hair from her eyes. "Sure. But Phil is the best kind of substitute. He's a mighty fine cook, for one thing."

"That part was pretty cool. He made some pop-over things from scratch."

"Yum. What else did I miss out on?"

"A salad. Not the kind in a bag, either." Her soulful blue eyes grew in wonder. "He chopped up fresh vegetables himself!"

Nick smacked his lips. "Imagine that."

"And his steaks didn't come swimmin' in a tin pan of gravy. They were real red meat first. He broiled them in the oven the way Mom used to."

Nick lifted his golden brows in hope. "Any leftovers?"

Heather squinted guardedly. "You went to a party. The extra food belongs to me and Cassie."

"Okay," he grumbled, kissing her temple. "Guess all's well that ends well."

"But there's more." She reached up to brace his shoulders, pursing her lips as her late mother often did. "I think you'd better sit down for the rest."

"Huh?"

Heather sighed. "I got something to tell you. Something real important. Why you shoulda been here."

"Hang on." Nick turned to collapse in his favorite old orange velour recliner, the only secure place left for him on the face of the earth. Heather climbed into his lap and stroked his angular jawline—a ritual she'd all but given up with age. But Nick realized she was humoring him, plain and simple.

He touched his jaw. "C'mon, sock it to me."

"Grandpa called."

Nick's heart skipped. "Which grandpa?"

"Hubie."

Hubert Miller. Damn. Nick's head rolled to the side, his cheek grazing the jacket draped behind him. A mingling of perfume and cigarette smoke rose from the leather, attacked his senses again. Those pesky remnants of "the party." He didn't want to think about it and his father-in-law in the same frame. Hubie was Sharon's father, after all.

Heather was cupping his whiskered cheeks now. "They're coming back to St. Paul for Christmas, just like always."

"All the way from Miami? Ah, no, they can't want to anymore." He was as bleak as a lost boy. "Not after last year...being so difficult."

More precisely, it had been horrible. Sharon had been gone only six months then and they'd all still been in shock. After all, it wasn't easy to accept a woman so young—barely thirty—suddenly dying of a heart attack. Christmas had been more a duty, a drudge. They'd settled for a small plastic tree on the coffee table and had jammed token gifts under the table. They'd eaten with plastic forks and worn plastic smiles for a full week right through the New Year. Horrible. Simply horrible.

Raw human grief at the jolliest time of the year.

But in retrospect, Nick recognized it as a transition they'd had to make. A bitter taste of Christmas without their precious Shar. Their clumsy behavior had been a sort of protest against their loss, in direct contrast to all the genuinely merry Christmases she had put on for them. Lord, how he still missed her. She'd been the perfect wife—so happy to be a homemaker, willing to keep to an inventive budget to make their single income work.

Back then, his old orange chair had been the second most secure place on earth for him. Their marital bed had been number one. Soft, cozy, snug. Without Sharon, it was a vast, cool, deserted plain.

Heather was pushing hair from his eyes, staring at him intently. "I'm sorry, Dad. I wish I could've stopped them."

Nick knew full well that Heather had tremendous insight into the situation and he appreciated the support. He curved his huge hand around her chin, speaking hoarsely. "Oh, honey, it's not your fault."

"But we had our plans made. *No plans!* Just us. Peace."

"Well, it's tradition that they come."

"Grandma Doris was asking about our tree and presents and holly and cookies." She sniffed stubbornly, looking around the barren room with not a single sign of the impending holiday. "I dodged her the best I could. Okay?"

"A-okay. Now, leave the old man alone to think." Nick gave her a pat as she scooted off his lap. She paused to cover Phil with one of Doris's handmade afghans, then skipped off to bed.

There were homey touches, like the knit blanket, scattered all over the house, courtesy of the Millers. And they still called every other weekend on their own dime, all in the interests of keeping the bonds tight. Nick had been fine with it until recently, when slowly, subtly, he'd gotten the impression that they were ready to pick up some of the pieces and expected him to do the same. He was touched, offended, mortified, he'd glossed over their insinuations with platitudes and distractions.

Their last call had been the worst, more blunt and demanding.

Damned if they hadn't tried to wangle some sure action out of him in the form of a New Year's resolution: *Be a happy family again. Embrace life's wonders with enthusiasm and cheer.* It was what Sharon gloried in, they'd said. What she would want for the girls.

He strongly suspected they were coming for Christmas in order to check on his progress.

Nick's large mouth curved wryly. As assertive as they were, there was still one subject they fumbled over: his falling prey to a conniving female. They claimed to be concerned for the grandchildren, tried to soothe his ego with the compliment that he was quite a catch. Naturally, he suspected they simply weren't yet ready to see another woman take their late daughter's place.

They had nothing to worry about. Nick wasn't in the market for a real romance. He had a rich family life, good friends like Phil; and from a distance, there were his parents, too, who wintered in Arizona to escape the Minnesota cold. A new love would mean step-relationships, readjustments, the end of their comfortable circle as they knew it.

But Nick's contentment didn't stop his passions from flaring to life. And tonight...he'd given in. Heck, he'd let down his guard and exploded. Nick closed his eyes as visions of the party washed over all else for a brief, hot moment. Jayne Ashland, attorney-at-law, assistant to old man Paxton himself.

Sparks had flown between them right off. She'd supervised the remodeling of Paxton's private quarters for three weeks straight, marching around with a saucy smile, a wiggle to her curvy hips.

Alcohol tossed on those sparks tonight had made for one roaring fire. After dry champagne, blended with even drier wit, they found themselves inspecting the inside of one of his own newly constructed cabinets in Paxton's private office.

That inspection was only a pretense. In the time

allowed the average coffee break, they'd peeled and groped and stroked, coming as deliriously close to consummation as a man and woman could get.

He shuddered now as he relived the sensations—her softness against his hardness, her saltiness against his tongue, her moistness, her eagerness, her aggressiveness against every inhibition he possessed. He was a little rusty, having been out of the dating game since high school, and in the habit of leading everywhere, from the dance floor to the box spring.

But the world was different now, on the brink of the millennium. Jayne had not been the least bit shy about meeting him halfway, her lusty desperation every bit as potent as his own.

They were on the brink of taking their red-hot petting to a shattering release, when old Paxton entered his office to make a long-distance call. Instantly their shenanigans came to a halt, of course, replaced by pin-drop silence and absolute stillness in the stuffy, musky box. The jeopardy of their respective jobs was mutually understood.

Nick had always prided himself on being a gentleman, however. Given the chance, he would have said *something,* anything to make their parting a bit more civilized. But it all happened so fast! Paxton was off with the thump of an outer door. With a measure of numbness Nick had held the cupboard door open for her and she had barreled out, tugging at her basic black shift, struggling with the heel strap of her silver sandal.

Don't let the screen door hit you on your way out.

That was to be his unintentional send-off.

He was dead certain she'd expected nothing more of their chance encounter. Lubricated with booze, their sexual awareness had simply gotten the better of them. The ambitious female executive and the earthy carpenter. The lines drawn were clear enough: silk versus denim, art films versus Vikings games, city apartment versus suburban bungalow. Their interests and viewpoints were poles apart.

It was probably fate that they hadn't finished what they started. A sane-and-sober Nick couldn't abide making love with a woman he wasn't *in* love with. He would have felt lower than a snake the morning after.

He heaved a huge sigh. The incident was best forgotten. Still, it had been dynamite while it lasted. And he could have sworn he'd sensed a new vulnerability in Jayne's eyes in that lamplit room. Those huge hazel peepers... It did bother Nick that they hadn't made eye contact in the end. But it had been *her* choice not to look back.

How cruel the Fates were, having Hubert call on the very same night, when all he'd wanted to do was collapse in bed, numb from drink, blanketed in Jayne's sweet web of seduction. A woman taking a man on like that—for all he knew, it might be a once-in-a-lifetime deal.

But the Millers were family and took priority. They were on the move, preparing to launch their new Get Happy plan. A morbid repeat of last year wouldn't do at all. They would want to spin back the clock to all those holidays beforehand, recapture some of that lost spirit.

If not for the champagne he'd drunk, the pressure might have killed him.

CHAPTER TWO

NICK WOKE UP IN THE recliner to find sunshine streaming through the front room's picture window. He blinked and stiffened. Morning already? By the angle of the rays, it had to be nearly nine o'clock! He was an hour late. Langley Paxton would have a fit.

Then Nick remembered. It was Saturday. He eased back against the cushions with a new feeling of contentment. This was his idea of an enchanted kingdom. The chatter of cartoons coming from the television in the girls' bedroom. The furnace clicking downstairs as it belched out hot air through the floor vents. The smell of fresh pancakes—

Pancakes! Where the heck were the traditional Pop-Tarts? Nick grasped the lever at the side of the chair and lowered the footrest. In one fluid motion, he sprang to his feet and dashed to the kitchen.

Phil was at the old white stove, adjusting a square griddle over a blue gas flame. "Morning."

"Yeah." Nick sauntered closer, hungrily eyeing the circles of bubbling batter on the griddle. "May I say you look absolutely ravishing this fine day."

Phil grunted. He looked anything but—a wiry man of fifty, his hair more gray than brown, his skin leathery year-round from long days spent outside on one construction site or another. With a deft flick of his wrist he flipped the cakes on the griddle.

"Thanks for staying on last night."

"Sure didn't expect to," Phil admitted in confusion. "Not for some outfit's hoity-toity office party."

"Did it put you out?"

"Naw, not really. Had a fresh change of clothing in the gear bag I keep in my truck. Wouldn't have bothered with it, though, had I known you wear your clothes two days in row." Phil measured him with open curiosity.

"Well...the party was better than expected. I got back later than I'd planned."

"That's all you've got to say? I figured you'd be home by the ten o'clock news for sure. I dozed off between the weather and sports." He aimed the tip of the round black spatula at him. "The next thing I knew it was daybreak and you were snoozing in the chair beside me."

"It was way too late to send you out in the cold, so I let you snore on."

"So exactly what did I miss out on?"

Nick tasted a dot of batter from the griddle. "Some great appetizers, some very rich pastries, and some very fine champagne."

"Good bubbly is a favorite of yours, isn't it? Is

that why there were no tire tracks in the fresh snow on the driveway? Tell me it ain't so.''

Nick shuffled his stocking feet, shoved his hands into the pockets of his wrinkled jeans. ''I took a cab.''

''Aw, I hope you didn't sully our company name.''

Nick shrugged. ''Of course not.''

Phil rubbed the bony bridge of his nose on his denim shirtsleeve. ''I should've just gone to that damn party. I'm incorruptible.''

''Nothing went wrong, Phil.''

Phil rolled his dark eyes. ''I can't help but be jittery. Our two-man operation is my dream come true. After all those years working for somebody else, I don't want to blow it.''

''I'm in the same boat, you know.'' Nick lowered his voice. ''And I have two extra mouths to feed, besides. All you have to concern yourself with is your own hide.''

''I should've gone, all right,'' Phil fretted. ''I just wasn't sure I'd know what to say to that ritzy crowd.'' He paused, his bristly brows crunching. ''How'd you handle socializing in your sorry state?''

''Kept quiet. Mostly grinned.'' Nick demonstrated, baring his teeth.

''Okay, okay.'' Phil turned back to the griddle.

"So how did you do with my pair of blond cyclones?"

Phil's expression softened. "Dandy. I can't believe the effect a little good cooking has on them." He opened his palm. "Could've had 'em eating out of my palm—literally. Don't you feed 'em at all?"

Nick's smile thinned. "Gee whiz, I intend to, with Christmas right around the corner."

"They showed me your freezer downstairs, full of all that instant gunk."

"It's not as bad as you think."

"If ever a man needed a new wife—"

"Never mind," Nick interrupted sharply. He generally gave Phil a lot of rope, accepted that the old bachelor considered himself the Nolan family godfather. But Nick could hear the tap-tap scoot of slippers on the pine hallway, signaling an invasion on the rise. Sure enough, Heather and her little sister Cassie breezed into the kitchen in matching yellow fleece robes, a shade darker than their long shiny tresses.

Cassie, a tomboy at six, was more spontaneous than young lady Heather. She charged at Nick like a little linebacker, wrapping her small sturdy arms around his waist. "Daddy!"

Nick hoisted her up into the crook of his arm and kissed her button nose. "How's my rough 'n' tumble?"

"Real good." Cassie pushed her hair off her

round face and stared him down. "Why'd you sleep in the chair, Daddy?"

"I got home late, went to check on Phil, and sort of konked out."

Cassie's china-blue eyes grew wider. "Why'd you check on an old man like *that?*"

Nick reared back. "Because he was snoring so loud!"

Phil raised a mock protest to the insults being bandied in his name as he shifted pancakes to a platter.

"You snore, too, Dad," Heather reported, moving in to assist Phil.

"Naw, not me."

Cassie pinched his nose. "You."

Nick laughed. "Guess I'd better make it to my room next time."

"Or put a grocery bag on your head," Cassie chirped.

Nick set her down and turned to the refrigerator. "I'll pour the juice."

"Frozen from a can," Cassie reported, her small chest puffed with pride. "I showed Phil all our frozen foods. He never seen a thing like it."

Nick handed Cassie a bottle of syrup and the butter dish. "Make yourself useful, child."

Cassie skipped to the table with the items. "This is like a party! The napkin holder's filled up!"

Phil rolled his eyes, sliding more griddle cakes onto the platter in Heather's hands.

"Yes," Nick agreed, producing a carton of milk and orange drink before kicking the fridge door shut. "And Uncle Phil is the life of our party."

"Maybe he should stay with us for Christmas," Cassie suggested.

"I'd love to," Phil said, "but you're having your grandparents, like always. There wouldn't be room for me." He checked out Nick for shock value and found him wistful. "There's just no usurping you, is there?"

Jayne certainly had given it a shot. Nick ignored the heat growing in the pit of his belly, taking glassware to the table. "Heather already told me about the Millers. Believe me, I'm rattled."

"Seems a guy can't sleep a wink around here without missing out." Phil turned off the burner and sent Heather along with the pancakes. He followed with a carafe of coffee and two mugs. There was a measure of pandemonium as everyone crowded around the chrome dining set, sliding back cushioned chairs, getting positioned for the unexpected feast.

"There'd still be room for you, Uncle Phil," Heather said gently as the older man deftly moved around the table, pouring coffee for himself and Nick. "You'd understand...everything."

The Adam's apple in Phil's skinny throat bobbed.

"I'd love to join you, but there's a nice lady across from my apartment who's giving sort of a soirée."

Cassie sipped her milk, pursing her lips at Phil as he sank into his chair at her left. "What's a sworry? Is that like getting married?"

Phil nearly choked on his coffee. "No way, sweetie. You're looking at one natural-born bachelor." He snatched a paper napkin from the wooden holder beside the sugar bowl. "Fifty-three and there's only me."

"Fifty-four and kind of a bore," Nick drawled, reaching over to tuck a paper napkin into the neck of Cassie's nightie.

Cassie brightened at the game. "Fifty-five with a big beehive."

"Fifty-six and outta tricks. " Heather gave him a flutter of lashes.

Phil held up his hands. "You're supposed to honor the cook. Don't you people know anything?"

"We don't know anything about cooks," Heather retorted, dousing her stack of cakes in syrup.

Nick's eyes fell to his plate. At the moment he felt as if he knew least of all. Not that he minded being upstaged in front of his daughters by their loving Dutch uncle. It was worth the decent meal. His main concern was the impending visit from the Millers. They'd settled for a string of frozen entrées last year because life itself sort of tasted like cardboard. Now what?

Phil was watching him from across the table with sympathy. The men were extraordinarily close. Like Heather had said, he understood. ''If you're worried about the Millers expecting too much—''

''Of course, they will!'' Nick sighed, then apologized for his thunder. ''The hints are hot and heavy that we're supposed to be getting back on track. But how can I hope to supply all the bells and whistles Sharon did?''

Phil gazed at the girls, seated side by side, absorbing the gist of the conversation. Nick was so immersed in his misery, he wasn't thinking of how this would affect them. Cassie was still young enough to take all words literally, and Heather was at the age when a young lady needed a role model to emulate, to confide in.

''You need help, man,'' Phil said. ''If you hope to pull this off, you need help.''

Nick rarely argued with Phil. He *knew* things. He didn't spend much time yammering to people, but he had quick and wise answers for life's foibles just the same. Even his coffee was brewed to perfection. Wistful, Nick sipped from his mug. ''So how can we steal you away from the soirée?''

Phil slanted his eyes toward the girls. ''Only a woman will do. A friend, a mother figure.''

''That's fine in theory. But where am I going to get a—'' Nick mouthed the word *platonic* ''—friend like that?''

"Daddy doesn't want a girlfriend," Heather declared flatly. "And with his luck he would find one that couldn't cook, anyway."

Phil roared with lion-size laughter.

Nick sort of barked like a sick hound. "You'd look decent in a skirt, my friend. If it covered your knobby knees."

Phil strained to control his laughter. "Not my sort of fashion risk. But all's not lost. I think I may have a realistic solution for you. That holiday deal back at Paxton. The Friends Are Family program."

Nick had seen the flyers on desks, the posters on walls. The program had been in full swing during their remodeling gig. Nick had paid little attention.

Phil chewed happily on some pancake, swallowing quickly. "The idea is to reach out to all the small, incomplete family circles in the law firm, match them up to form bigger groups."

"Guess I've heard talk of it around the water coolers."

"Happy talk. Lots of excitement. I happen to think it's a great gesture, myself. Christmas can be so lonely for so many."

The girls hated the plan and were quick to offer whiny objections.

"A total stranger, Dad?"

"What if she's mean, Daddy, like a bad witch?"

Nick found himself caught in the middle. His heavy golden brows joined over his nose as he weighed the opportunity. The girls' eyes were anxiously trained on him, just daring him to rebel. The ever-subtle Phil was more merciful, busying himself in snagging a couple more pancakes from the platter and dousing them with syrup.

Of course it would be awkward, Nick realized; a strange female barging into their lives. But the element of control made the arrangement very appealing. She could be instructed to enter the scene just before the in-laws and breeze out shortly after them. As by the program's design, she would have no expectations beyond the holiday.

His mouth curved in hope. Where else could he find a no-strings-attached platonic mate on such short notice?

Phil cleared his throat, braving to add another two cents' worth of opinion under the girls' watchful gazes. "There's no time to lose—if you want to go ahead. We're just about finished with the Paxton job. And it seems to me there was a deadline for the program, too."

Nick's tired, whiskered face brightened suddenly. "I may as well look into it Monday morning."

Heather gasped, her fork clattered to her plate. "You can't be serious—"

Nick grew slightly stern. "Don't upset your baby sister over nothing," he cautioned, aware that little Cassie was on the alert, her eyes mirroring confusion. "I wouldn't pull in just anybody."

"Someone *you* like, though."

"And you," Nick assured. "I won't commit to anything without committee approval." He reached out to tweak Heather's cheek, then, remembering she didn't care for such gestures anymore, grasped his juice glass instead.

Phil nodded. "Can't hurt to inquire."

Nick winked at his pal, hoping to shift the crew into a lighter mood. "You're a wonder, Phil. When you're not cooking my bacon, you're saving it."

Phil took a half bow in his chair. "As long as you understand, I don't do windows and I don't do dishes."

"Me neither," Cassie piped up, tossing aside her napkin just as Phil did.

"Everything was so right before," Heather complained.

"For us," Nick clarified quietly. "But Grandma and Grandpa have to be considered now, too. The finest gift we can give them is a show of our contentment. They've obviously been worried, and that's not right."

"No, of course not! But to pretend—"

"What's 'pretend' about it, Heather? A new ladyfriend in the house, my daughters pleased to see their grandparents."

Heather rolled her eyes in an all too sophisticated gesture of "Liar, liar, pants on fire."

Nick squirmed a little in his chair, but didn't rise

to the bait. Much of it would be real. Most of it, really.

Cassie patted her sister's arm. "We'll just get one of those mommies who can do dishes. Right, Heather?"

Heather jumped to her feet, her complexion hot pink with anger. "This is really stupid, Dad. The worst!" With that, she flounced out of the room.

Cassie slipped off her chair and sidled up beside Nick, cuddling around his thick biceps. "Don't feel bad, Daddy. Heather cries too much. Don't help nothin'."

Nick gave the child a pat and a kiss before she dashed off. He sort of felt like crying himself. If only the world would let them alone. But this could work, with the right woman.

Visions of Jayne Ashland danced in his head all over again. He tried her on for size, imagined her flipping pancakes. In nothing but an apron.

Wrong! Oh, so very wrong.

He nervously took a slurp of coffee to cover his discomfort, nearly scalding his tongue. It seemed that sometime during his musings, Phil had given him a refill.

Phil was returning from the coffeemaker as Nick started to sputter and choke. "What's the matter with you?"

Nick pressed his burning tongue against the roof of his mouth. "Guess I was thinking of the most unsuitable woman on the planet there, for a minute.''

''Hmm, explains the red lipstick on your earlobe.''

Nick's hands quickly flew to his ears. ''Why didn't you say so before?''

Phil shrugged his shoulders as he sank back in his chair. ''Just noticed it under that shag you call a haircut.''

''Great.''

''So who was she?'' Phil demanded excitedly. ''Anybody I know?''

''Well...yeah.''

''That cute little receptionist at the front desk? Curly hair, high giggle.''

''No, not her.''

''Give me a hint.''

''I wish you'd just forget it, Phil.''

''No way. I deserve a sporting chance.'' Nick sat in stony silence. ''Maybe someone from the executive wing, where we've been working...'' Phil squinted as he studied the possibilities. ''The file clerk with the pouty lips?'' He pursed his own in mocking seduction.

Nick blew on his steamy coffee. ''Nope.''

''Well, most of 'em are married. But I guess that wouldn't stop 'em at a wild party.''

''Give it up!''

Phil ignored him. ''The only other single woman

I know of is that Jayne, the cool blonde with the steel panties and sharp tongue—'' Phil watched his buddy's expression mellow. ''Not her!''

Nick sighed in concession. ''On her behalf, I have to say both your observations are very unfair.''

Phil opened his mouth to speak, then reconsidered.

Nick watched him impatiently. ''What were you going to say?''

''Nothing that won't keep. So how'd it happen? The two of you have been at odds all along, trying to please Paxton on your own terms.''

Nick propped his elbows on the table and rubbed his hands over his face. ''I guess all that electricity sort of exploded on us.''

''Wow.''

''Wipe that gleam from your eye.''

''Don't think I can. It's like the old you is finally coming back to life.''

''You know I'm not shopping for a real mate,'' Nick said urgently with an eye on the door.

Phil squinted, wily and wise all at once. ''But you must have really felt something to get that close.''

''It was impetuous and irresponsible!''

''Maybe she likes you, too.''

''Too? I didn't say— Anyway, don't count on it. *She* walked out on *me* in the end.''

''Somebody had to leave first.''

''Look, for all I know, this might just be another

notch in her belt. I'm the rusty one, lost in my own troubles.''

''And vulnerable enough to fall with the slightest tap to the chin.''

''I resent that!'' Nick's roar had volume, but tore with anguish.

Phil leaned over the table earnestly. ''Maybe, on second thought, you should forget the Friends Are Family program. Better yet, forget about going back to the firm at all. I'll hire on some temp help for Monday and finish it off.''

Nick wouldn't hear of it. ''Why the change? Afraid I can't keep my hands to myself for one last day of work?''

''Just seems like you're in deep enough at that place.''

Too deep to back off. Nick liked the temporary-mother idea, and he had to see Jayne at least one more time to find some closure. As lovely as her backside was, it wasn't the way he wanted to remember her.

CHAPTER THREE

JAYNE ASHLAND GOT OFF to a rocky start on Monday morning. Her curling iron burned out, making a hasty blow-dry hairstyle necessary. Her car wouldn't start, which made a city bus her mode of transportation downtown. Tests of endurance to the generally optimistic attorney. But not one to ever say die, Jayne eased into her black wool coat, covered her head with a wraparound scarf and hustled down to the bus stop directly in front of her East St. Paul apartment building, where there was a downtown pickup every fifteen minutes.

She must have missed the last bus by exactly one minute, allowing just enough time for the wind to blow loose her bangs and send a whipping chill up beneath the hem of her tailored black coat.

But it was all right. After all, it was Christmas, the jolliest time of year.

She even managed a cheery greeting to the burly bus driver as she dropped coins into the fare box. He nodded, sparing her trim legs an approving glance before pulling back out into the heavy traffic along Minnehaha Avenue.

Jayne slipped into an empty bench seat near the

front, surrendering to the jerky twenty-minute stop-and-start ride ahead.

She was going to be late, for the first time in months. That and an especially sharp turn brought her yogurt-and-toast breakfast to a roil in her stomach. Ignoring the discomfort, she dipped a black-gloved hand into her briefcase, extracting a notepad and pen. Balancing the case on her knees, she used it as a writing table.

At the top of the paper she wrote: "Things to do today." Where to start? She tapped her ballpoint on the paper, then to her coral-glossed lips. She had an interview with a hit-and-run witness, a subpoena to request, not to mention the important client coming in first thing regarding the Bremer Trust account.

All in the name of Langley Paxton, the driving force behind the law firm of Paxton Limited. Jayne drew circles around the firm's letterhead topping the page. Langley Paxton seemed to be relying upon her more and more with each passing month, drawing her closer to his inner circle of associates. As it darn well should be. She was twenty-seven now, with a full two years at the firm under her belt. It was only right that bigger challenges came her way now. Hadn't she spent the bulk of her time making herself indispensable to the senior partner? Acting as his confidant, his gofer, his gal Friday—often through the weekend?

She forced herself not to dwell on what her hourly

wage would be if she broke down her salary in terms of hours worked. No, she never wanted to do that. Instead she viewed her efforts as an investment. There would come a day when Paxton would be looking to replace one of the associates and there she would be—the willing, able and qualified assistant. It was a little risky, but what in this world wasn't?

Risk. Another term that triggered uncomfortable memories of Nick Nolan, handyman extraordinaire. She traced the tip of her pen around her lips, the same territory he'd so thoroughly covered with his hard, delicious mouth. It was funny how so many small things had brought him to the forefront of her mind all day Saturday and Sunday. It had happened again first thing this morning, promptly at sunup, over her chipped nail. She'd cracked it stabbing at the snooze button on her alarm clock and had reached for the emery board on her nightstand. As she'd sat up to do some filing she'd quickly recalled Nolan's roughened fingertips, scraping the tender skin of her throat, of her thighs.

The all-important list was quickly forgotten as she floated off on a blissful recap of the sexiest encounter of her life. Nothing much had really happened. A cramped cupboard, clothes askew. Hot strokes, fevered kisses. Naughty whispers. It had lasted no more than ten minutes, tops.

Nevertheless, she was still in awe of his charisma.

Never before had she met a man who could make so much of so little so fast!

Her wind-chilled cheeks suddenly flamed, causing a strange icy burning sensation to travel from her face clear down to her toes. How could the lingering memories still cause such a tremor so many hours later? Accustomed to analyzing everything to death, Jayne reviewed the little she knew of her seducer.

Nolan was a golden-haired "daddy bear" of a man, several years older than she. A widower with children, a quiet, intent worker with a natural confidence in himself. She'd enjoyed bossing him around these past weeks, childishly hoping to make him squirm a bit under his tight jeans and flannel shirts. His blue eyes glittered coolly behind his polite, deliberate demeanor day after day. He'd never cracked, no matter how she'd needled him over nails and shelving and stain. Instead, he'd tossed back witty gibes of his own, proving to be a most worthy opponent.

She stared out the window as the bus roared down Sixth Street into the heart of St. Paul, self-consciously fearing her expression might be gooey. She'd finally managed to make Nick squirm. No quip or retort had done it. No, she'd been reduced to wedging her knee between his thighs. Boy, was she the clever one. Reduced to an adolescent trick like that.

The bus wheeled its way along Cedar Street, stopping before the World Trade Center, where the Paxton firm called a sizable space on the fourteenth floor home. Collecting her belongings, she joined the passengers exiting the back door.

Time to face the music. The real stuff. Not the mushy sounds of ''If I Were a Carpenter'' that had played background to all her visions of Nick Nolan; but a snappier rendition of ''Jingle Bell Rock,'' reflecting the office energy—work and play in harmonious tempo. Langley Paxton adored Christmas and expected everyone else to adore it, too, all while shouldering one's regular workload.

She deliberately hastened her steps on the snow-dusted sidewalk as she barreled into the tall imposing building in a wave of well-dressed professionals.

Time to grow up, Jayne. There is nothing sentimental between you and Nolan, no cherished memory to cling to. A quick squeeze, a few sweet murmurings in the dark. End of story.

Why had she given in to her desires in the first place? Why had she bothered with Nick, of all people? A little Christmas gift to herself, perhaps; an indulgence to wipe out the solitary blues of the season.

The timing did seem suspect. Nick showing up in early December, just as the office trimmings started to appear. Jayne struggling with her career-girl Christmas persona: *endure and it will pass.* Every Christmas eventually became a Christmas ''past.''

Other years, she'd thrown herself into a brief. This year, she'd nearly taken hers off. Did it matter as long as she survived?

She pressed a hand to her coat lapel, sure the hammering of her heart thundered through the airy lobby. It was all right. No one was hurt. Nick's last day was today. Any awkward moment would be fleeting.

She stepped inside the first elevator to open, careful of her newly filed nail as she jabbed the proper button. She would avoid him at all costs. Let him go without the awkward morning-after scene. Men liked that best, didn't they? Part of her wanted to explain that she simply wasn't herself during December, but that rang too much like an apology. No point in doing that, for she didn't feel wrong. She didn't feel right, either, for that matter. She just *felt*. In fact, she bubbled with uncontrollable emotion.

And darned if she would admit that to anybody.

"GOOD MORNING, JAYNE!" Miss Florence Belford, Langley Paxton's private secretary, greeted her with stern relief as the younger woman breezed into the senior partner's private suite.

"Florence." Jayne's voice and moves were modulated as she set her briefcase on one of the formal chairs set strategically around the sumptuous gray-and-burgundy reception area. She stripped off her gloves, studying the large-boned, fiftyish secretary.

There was no mistaking the disapproving note in Florence's greeting, or the glint of disapproval in her small gray eyes. Florence was indeed her subordinate, but she had the formal air of a bygone generation, never allowing her modest place in the Paxton pecking order to stop her from acting the superior.

Florence was in the process of taking down the posters announcing the Friends Are Family project and didn't bother to turn away from the wall as she spoke. "He's waiting."

She was referring to Mr. Paxton, of course, Jayne knew. There was no other "he" in the huge trade-center building as far as Florence was concerned. "How long, exactly?"

Florence turned then, glaring at the sight of Jayne unbuttoning her coat. "Too long to strip."

Was that the innocent remark it seemed, in reference to her coat, or something more snide about the party? But no one knew about that infraction— did they?

Jayne jammed her gloves into her pockets as she went, feeling like an awkward schoolgirl on her way to the principal's office.

With a single knock she barged inside Langley Paxton's office.

"Sorry, sir, I got held up." She skidded to a stop in the center of the richly paneled room.

As expected, Paxton was ensconced behind his huge desk, looking far more fit and youthful than most men approaching seventy. No false modesty prevented him from keeping the thin ring of gray hair above his ears trimmed close, or displaying his bifocals on the tip of his nose a good deal of the time.

It was his guest who caught Jayne short. For some indiscernible reason, Nick Nolan was seated in one of the deep wing chairs, a china cup and saucer riding piggyback on his knee!

He simply didn't belong in the picture. With carpentry tasks completed in here, all he and Phil Mahoney had left was some shelving in the law library.

It appeared that Nick hadn't started his final project yet, as his tool belt was set down beside the chair. Clearly he was here to work, though, dressed in his regulation jeans and plaid flannel shirt with hints of a white T-shirt peeping out at the open collar.

So what was the delay? Naturally her mind leaped to the worst scenario—that Paxton knew of their romp in the cupboard.

She didn't mean for it to happen, but her eyes surreptitiously slid to the walnut cabinet in question. She jumped a little when she realized Nick was watching her every move with masculine appreciation.

"Join us, Jayne." Paxton's invitation was an order delivered with silky impatience. "Help yourself to coffee if you like."

"Had my morning quota at home," she lied, not

trusting herself with a china cup and saucer under these shaky circumstances.

Circumstances that greatly puzzled Jayne. Coffee break with the hired help? It hardly seemed Paxton's style. But he had taken to Nick from the start, sharing his widowed status, showing an interest in his girls. And it was Christmas.

She quickly unbuttoned her coat all the way and hung it on a small rod near the door. She returned to the desk with her last shred of poise, smoothing her jade two-piece suit along the way. With a tight smile she sat in the chair flanking Nick's. "So sorry for the delay. I'm afraid my car wouldn't start, so I was pressed to catch the next available bus."

Paxton pressed the tips of his fingers together beneath his chin. "Should've taken a taxi."

She grimaced. Yes, probably. But she'd been too wound up to think of it. As a student back in Baltimore, she'd relied on the bus. "They can take forever at this hour, too," she managed with a breathless laugh. "Besides, I figured I'd be in time for the Bremer appointment either way." She pushed up the sleeve of her jacket to glance at her silver watch. "Yes, time to spare."

"Something else has come up, Jayne. We've been waiting for you."

"We?" Her long fingers dug into the chair's soft leather arms. Her stomach lurched forward and back, much like the city bus she'd ridden in on.

She thought Paxton knew about them. Nick made the deduction as she began to pale under her makeup. A rush of sympathy hit him hard and unexpectedly. He'd meant to be iron man, here. After all, she hadn't even looked back. Only a damn fool would brood over that detail under these new conditions, though. The worst kind of damn fool.

Nick cleared his throat, forcing a smile. "It's my understanding that you're behind the Friends Are Family program."

Jayne shifted in the huge chair, her voice a startled peep. "What?"

"Jayne. Miss Ashland." Paxton stared her down over the golden rims of his half glasses. "You're behaving very queerly today. Are you feeling well?"

She stiffened, patting her flyaway hairdo as Paxton's eyes centered on it. "I'm fine. Super!"

Paxton nevertheless continued to speak in the same imperious tone. "Nick Nolan wishes to inquire about Friends Are Family."

She looked from one male to the other. How dared he wish it? Was this some sort of game? She kept her chin dizzyingly high. "Have you explained that the program's over, sir?" She spoke to Nick's profile. "The deadline was Friday, before the party."

Nick slowly leaned forward in his chair, setting his delicate cup and saucer on the edge of Paxton's desk. He turned to her then, his handsome face shifting with a full range of emotion. He managed to keep his voice level, though, with the prowess of an experienced lawyer. "I didn't know—"

"There were posters hanging everywhere!"

"No, I mean I didn't know I'd be in need of the program before the party." He struck each word with forceful enunciation. "And I never dreamed you were the one in charge."

The last statement was delivered on a mere whisper, needing no extra effort to cross home plate. The way his blue eyes were shifting from shades of blue to black, very much like a stormy winter sky, she was inclined to believe him. Even inclined to believe he felt as trapped as she. Maybe.

In any case, they barely knew each other and were once again clamped together in a tight spot. This was bound to be less fun than the first time; they were both stone-cold sober and there was a witness.

"Nick has explained the circumstances between the two of you—"

"What circumstances, sir?" she squealed.

Nick raised his brows in astonishment, cracking a smile. "That we spar quite a bit, Jayne. Natural thing."

Paxton chuckled. "Jayne's full of spunk. Likes to challenge. Likes to win. Hope it hasn't caused irreparable waves, her being your overseer, Nick."

"We weren't distracted from our duties," she

clarified as breezily as she could manage through
gritted teeth. She needed to be taken seriously at all
times. She couldn't let Nolan shed doubt on her
drive or her abilities.

"My partner, Phil, has a way of making sure I
keep my nose to the grindstone," Nick added pleasantly. "But I wouldn't dream of selling Jayne short
on her dedication. She even took the time to make
a final inspection of my work." He gestured to the
cupboard of passion. "Inside out."

Nick offered her a mocking smile then—one that
she would gladly have slapped away. So that was
how it was. He was protecting their secret, but he
wasn't above finding humor in it. And why not?
This was her turf, her permanent job. His last day.
Whoever said chivalry was dead—

"Then you will gladly bail Nick out?" Paxton
queried. "Show him some of the Paxton teamwork
spirit?"

"Of course, sir. Teamwork's the inspiration that
ignited my Friends Are Family idea in the first
place," Jayne reminded him, sucking up in sheer
defense. If only she hadn't worn jade today. She
looked so much more no-nonsense in the navy blue
wool she'd been considering.

"Your talents are always noted and appreciated,
Jayne. As a matter of fact, I was just singing your
praises in your absence. Nick seemed mighty doubtful that we could pull a mother figure out of a hat

for his daughters at this final hour, but I told him my gal Friday, my Mrs. Claus herself, would come up with something."

He was serious in his request? The shadow crossing his eyes removed all doubt. "You're strictly looking for a mother figure for your girls...?" Her voice was soft, like a tissue floating on the wind.

"Yes," he said soberly. "If miracles happen."

Like it or not, the statement floored her, niggled at the secret child in her. "That is so very sweet."

He studied his large hands. "Intended to manage on my own. But things have evolved, and, well, I can use a boost."

Jayne swooned. A mother for Christmas, a female to round out the family circle. Sweet. Why hadn't he said so up front? She was desperately torn between moving in for the kill or a kiss. In deference to the company, she did neither.

A knock on the door brought Florence into the scene, Jayne's briefcase in hand. "Here you are. You forgot this out front. That's not like you."

Jayne took her brown leather attaché from the preening secretary and set it by the front right leg of her chair. The air was quiet, expectant. Jayne, for her part, was waiting for Florence to leave.

Florence mistook the silence for an opportunity. "Have you heard his story yet, Jayne?"

"Not really. Not yet."

"Well. Well!" With a blubbering sniff, Florence whisked a hankie out of the cuff of her beige linen dress. She sank into a chair by the door. "Never been a more touching New Year's resolution. So selfless, so thoughtful."

Paxton favored his secretary with a cluck of concern, then refocused on the couple with moistened eyes. "I'll leave you to it, then."

"This minute?" Jayne gasped. "With Bremer—"

"You still have some time."

"But—" She stopped short under Paxton's glare of dismissal. "I have to warn you both, there aren't many eligible women left."

"Work wonders," the older man directed.

Jayne was floored by her boss's fervor. What on earth was Nick's story? Paxton generally didn't bend like this for anyone or anything. As for Florence, she didn't shed tears over *people*. A sad old song, perhaps, a belly-up goldfish, definitely, but surely not a temporary carpenter's plight. Nick most definitely packed an enviable power.

It was a little scary to learn that he could work his magic in broad daylight, on the most seasoned kind of victims.

Nick watched her carefully, growing uncomfortable with Florence's teary background sounds, which greatly resembling a choking vaporizer. "I'll try and make this easy, Jayne—Miss Ashland."

She fumed over his solicitous approach. As if they

could go back to square one, not knowing much about much. Even then, he hadn't called her Miss anything!

"I'll tell you what I'm looking for and you can match me up with the best you have," he said in quiet clarification. "Won't take long."

The telephone rang on Paxton's vast desk. Florence came scurrying up to handle it. "Get on with it, Jayne," Paxton urged impatiently, shooing them off with an index finger. "Take him away and show him the grace and service we're known for around here."

CHAPTER FOUR

"DON'T EVEN SAY IT." Jayne sank against the heavy walnut door connecting her office with Langley Paxton's, all too aware that it was Nick's palm, braced above her fair head, that really shoved it firmly closed.

He was towering over her now, his body poised to crush. "Say what? Something clever about Paxton's directive concerning grace and service?"

Finding she could scarcely breathe, she eased out from under him, pulling a rueful grin. "You got it."

"Ah, but we always say clever things to each other."

Didn't they just? She regarded him in wonder, large as life, crowding her space. It seemed impossible, but he was every bit as appealing as she remembered. Every bit as tempting. How naive to think that, if faced with him again, she would feel some regret, make it easier to forget their cupboard clutch. Unfortunately, she couldn't quite muster the necessary indignation. And *he* was certainly miles from it, judging by that lazy grin of his.

Yep, she definitely should have worn the prim navy blue wool today.

"So-o-o." She rounded her smaller, more functional desk and sank into her chair. Minutes passed for hours as she slowly took dyed-to-match jade shoes out of her briefcase and exchanged them for the boots on her feet. Closing her case, she set it on the floor and began to rummage through her left bottom drawer. She produced a brown accordion envelope from its depths and smacked it with force atop her desk, making the nearby telephone jingle a little. "About that resolution of yours."

He leaned over her desk, placing his palms flat on either side of the envelope. "No need to be so frazzled."

She squinted in sheer self-defense. "Like you're not thoroughly pleased that I am!"

It pleased him only because it distracted from that resolution of his. Further intimacy between them, especially on an emotional level, would make it all the tougher to keep a distance. And he'd appeared so strong in her eyes till now. Needing a caregiver this way was a huge weakness in the old armor. Nobody in the building would believe the way his former in-laws and young innocent daughters tied him in knots.

"I humbly understand that your boss is the one you were tap-dancing for in there," he intoned. "Can't blame you to some degree, I guess—the up-and-coming mouthpiece."

She tipped her face to his, her glare promising candor. "Don't underestimate your unsettling influ-

ence, caused by...whatever it is that we have—
had— Whatever.''

He lowered his thick gold lashes. ''I humbly can't
explain our 'whatever,' either.''

Her lower lip trembled. ''Don't humble me, mis-
ter. Not after weeks of strutting around here like the
lion of the jungle.''

Poised over the desk, Nick frowned in thought.
''The lion and the...canary,'' he ultimately decided,
his eyes roving over her silky green suit and egg-
shell blouse. ''That's you—a chatty little birdie full
of bounce and color, who likes having her feathers
ruffled.'' He leaned even closer, blowing in her
fluffed tide of hair. ''Those tight knots and curls you
usually wear simply don't do your pretty face jus-
tice.''

She curled her fingers around a pencil, certain she
could snap it in two. ''This is how it all started,
Nick, how we got off track in the first place.''

''How?''

''Bantering this way.'' She squinted. ''You know
what I mean.''

Nick's low, satisfying sound took on a life of its
own as it crawled up his throat. ''And how....''

She sniffed in cool counterpoint. ''Naturally, I
didn't expect us to flare up so hot in the end. Into
such a compromising position.''

''Yeah, sure.''

His flat tone scalded her. "You know what I mean!"

He reared in disbelief. Theirs was not a case of spontaneous combustion. They'd been on a slow burn since hour one, on that day back in early December when he and Phil had come in to take some preliminary measurements in Langley Paxton's office.

How dare she lie this way!

Because she was as upset as he was? Because she was attempting to throw a bucket of cold water on the fire, too? His male ego had blinded him for a bit, there, but the haze was clearing fast. She wouldn't be any lingering trouble, after all.

He should be glad, damn glad.

So why was he still a fireball of longing and regret?

Further confidences would be a risk, but Nick was accustomed to speaking his mind. It usually worked. He heaved deeply, rapping his knuckles on the desk as he tried to find some truth in the middle ground. "What I see here are two desperate people trying to sort things out. Knowing they should be repentant about their encounter, but not quite making it stick."

She slid her pencil through her fingers, pensive. "The carpenter philosopher. I'm impressed."

"Majored in philosophy at the University of Minnesota," he returned, not caring much for her flippancy. "Completed my sophomore year before my elder daughter was born. I couldn't afford to finish, but the background does give me lots to think about during my more solitary jobs. Though I have to admit you've kept me more than distracted these past few weeks. I haven't had a spare minute to study world-shaking issues."

He sure knew how to shake Jayne's neat little world. Disturbed by his proximity, his breadth, she tossed the pencil aside with a clatter, rolled her chair clear of the desk and rose in a jerky motion. Folding her arms across her chest, she went and stood by the room's only window. The view was spectacular, the domed St. Paul state capitol building visible in the distance, set off in grand display against the bright morning sky. But all Jayne could see at the moment was a trace of Nick's reflection in the glass as he closed in on her. She flinched when his hands landed on her shoulders. The blue wool suit had bulky shoulder pads, but not this silky green one—another way she was dressed wrong. The pressure of his fingers seemed strong enough to leave prints on her skin.

So, who was she kidding? She'd ultimately decided on this softer suit just in case. If by happenstance she ran into Nolan for one last goodbye, this outfit would give him something to remember. Something chic, flouncy, the antithesis of her uptight reputation. She could be carefree without the bubbly cocktails. And she would have preferred to leave him with that suggestion—from a safe distance. It would have worked out, too, if not for his need of a mother figure.

She kept her eyes trained on the window. "No offense, Nick, but this belated request of yours makes you a pest I don't need right now. The program was wrapped up. A huge success, in Paxton's eyes."

"If I'd known you were in charge of it all, Jayne, I wouldn't even have considered it."

"Oh, really?" Her voice was dipped in sarcasm. "It's above you to put me on the spot? You're finding no joy in watching me squirm?"

His response was hot against her ear, liberally laced with cynicism. "Punishing you isn't my goal. It just seems like the more we talk, the more entangled we become in a single web. But on the other hand, it seems impossible not to talk things through because we're so close. A catch-22, for sure."

His logic made sense. "Oh, Nick. I know— I just didn't expect..." She allowed the half-formed confession to die on her lips.

"Hey, I understand that you did what you did— with me—because you thought this would be the end of the road. It was a fair assumption. Phil's in the library now, finishing up the last of the shelving." He gave her a mild shake from behind. "You saw my exit in your sights at the party and decided to indulge in a little no-strings pleasure. It's no crime."

Despite his claim, something in his tone made it sound like a felony. She turned around slowly, laboriously, as though encased in concrete shoes. "Did you expect more?" Her eyes searched every inch of his lean angular face. The working jaw was enough to give him away. "You did!"

"Nothing big," he said on the defense. "But a 'Goodbye, it's been swell' would've been nice."

Her fragile jaw sagged. *He* wanted that? She could scarcely believe it. "We didn't do much talking that night. The sentiments seemed obvious from start to finish. I mean, you didn't call out to me, either."

But all their foreplay had been verbal. Delightful banter that had made the season brighter. "You sure were in one hotfooted hurry," was all he could manage.

"Naturally! What if Mr. Paxton had returned to make another call? Once he gets going on something, there's no stopping him. Time was tight."

Nick sighed. "Yeah, that possibility occurred to me, too."

"All right, then, we both made a hasty getaway. We both acted on impulse," she added chidingly. "Equal down the line."

"You're right." He smoothed his hands down her collarbone, trying to calm himself over her up-front methods. Had he been out of circulation for fifteen years or fifteen hundred? He struggled to understand the differences between his shy childhood-sweetheart wife and this aggressive rising legal star.

"You look simply mortified," she stated.

"I'm grumpy because I'm confused, and I'm confused because I'm accustomed to behaving myself."

She gasped in affront. "Are you implying that *I'm* in the habit of pulling all the guys I meet into dark corners?"

Nick made a strangled sound. "No! I— No!"

He looked genuinely contrite, trying, unsuccessfully, to convey his thoughts. As if in acquiescence she sighed, and became aware that her whole body was aquiver. She wanted it all to end; she wanted it all to sizzle on—and on and on....

But he had a ready-made family of his own. Two girls. She would do well to remember that, for it would surely help her to forget.

Jayne wrung her hands. "I understand the closure you're after, here. Let's just say all that champagne sent two platonic sparring partners off the deep end for a brief space in time. And it was a very nice experience."

"Sure." Nick forced a phony half grin. The summation was perfect. Case closed. Couple dismissed.

It shouldn't bother him that she refused to admit the truth—that sparks had crackled wildly since the first time she'd caught him adjusting the tool belt

wedged against his hip. He'd recognized that
"look" she'd worn, full of lusty hope that with any
luck, gravity and the weight of the laden belt might
pull his jeans just a little lower than protocol allowed. It hadn't happened, of course—not the first
day, nor any time since. But how she waited him
out, hoping for a glimpse, thoroughly enjoying her
role as overseer. No, sirree, Jayne Ashland was no
quitter. Or so he'd thought till now. All she wanted
to see him do was vanish. And he couldn't believe
how it offended him!

She was searching his features for confirmation.
What she found was sorrow that matched her own.
"We can handle this like two friendly adults. I
mean, it's not like we truly...bonded," she ventured. "You haven't even made me cry yet—as you
did Mr. Paxton."

His mouth curled wryly. "Well, that was just a
guy thing, believe me."

"But Florence was teary eyed, too."

Nick shook his finger. "She's a lot like one of
the guys, though, isn't she? Sensible shoes, flat
voice, flaring nostrils."

Jayne's coral mouth cracked with amusement.
"Okay, she has a manly way about her. But we're
really drifting off course, here."

"Lost at sea sounds kind of fun."

She huffed in disgust. "You aren't helping, Nick,
with all your little puns and twists."

He nodded solemnly. "I'll watch it. But we aren't through. I'm still determined to find a match in your program before the day is through—which calls for some intensive teamwork."

"Do your eyes always twinkle madly when you're so determined?"

"Well, there is some humor involved here."

She snapped her fingers in sour triumph. "Ah, you mean the way you suddenly hold the stability of my job in your hands, when you yourself have only hours left at the firm?"

He was genuinely startled again by her conclusion-jumping. "No. I'm talking about the way the tables have turned between us. I've spent the past few weeks working to your specs, and now it's your turn to please me. I certainly don't believe your job is at stake," he was quick to add. "It's just a final twist to our little game. A surprise stocking-stuffer."

How could he propose that such an inconvenient turn could hold out the promise of delights? And how could she find herself tempted to feel downright delighted over the prospect? But it was no wonder, considering that Nick was the most interesting man she'd met in ages. Her thighs were nearly melting beneath her fluid skirt as she marched back to the desk with a visible wobble.

But he was wrong about the importance of her showing in this Christmas matchmaking project. He didn't completely understand her relationship with

Paxton, her wish to make this Friends Are Family really count in the old man's eyes.

The widowed status that had warmed Paxton to Nick in the first place was the angle she herself had used. She'd known when she originally pitched the program to him back in October that he would see the value of bringing lonely people together. She had to have some edge over the male bonding that went on between Pax and his men out on the golf course, at the poker games. Because she wasn't allowed in the boys' club, she plotted to get his attention with a unique humanitarian angle beyond the ken of her male associates. She'd pitched the program using a feminine common-sense rationale: If the workers weren't battling the holiday blues, they would perform better on the job.

Paxton had loved it! The program soared. It had all seemed in the bag. Until now.

Nick was like a loose cannon—with their secret tryst embedded in his brain, his alliance with Pax, his new emotional hold on her. He simply had too much power for her own good!

Keeping all this in mind, she patted the brown accordion envelope with authority. "Time to get down in the trenches."

He reared in distaste. "Might help the cause if you don't pitch me as a swamp monster."

She raised a hand in protest. "That's not what I

meant. You're no worse than a fly in the ointment. Really.''

"Oh, well." He tapped his chin. "Let's see, how to word it: Mother Figure Wanted. One Pesky Insect, With Own Ointment."

She stomped a pump on the plush gray carpet, feeling the pinch of her too-tight shoes—shoes she'd worn to match the suit that was supposed to leave him in pining agony from afar. If she had known he wasn't going away so neatly, she would have come to work barefoot and dressed in a burlap sack. *Anything to keep this situation from spinning out of control. Anything to keep the widower from drawing her into his suburban lair.*

"I want to do a good job for you, of course. It's just that the choices are more narrow, far from the original pool."

"At least let's try."

"You think it's about *trying?* Ha! If I fail with you, the whole program will be tarnished in Paxton's eyes."

He wished she would think of him first, but he must keep in mind that her career was probably all she had. "Oh, c'mon. He must know your value, Jayne."

"Things are highly competitive around here and chances to shine are few and far between." She jerkily removed papers from the expandable folder and slapped them on the desk.

"You're taking this too personally. I'd walk out right now, if I could save my family another way."

She leafed through a sheaf of applications, keeping her eyes lowered. "And I'd show you the door if I could save my professional hide any other way."

"So you are pretty much married to your job, then."

She glanced up. "Irrelevant territory, but yes, I am. And quite content, thank you very much."

This couldn't be the same woman who had melted in his arms the other night. The needy egomaniac in him wanted a glimpse of her again—something small; anything to justify the attraction. "But surely you must appreciate the need for familial ties to have created the program in the first place," he urged.

"I understand good business," she was quick to clarify. "I spied a weakness in the company structure and found a way to support it. We're talking practicalities here, Nick. There's an epidemic of lonely hearts in this huge firm. Employees who mope around for a solid six weeks at least, during the holidays. Giving them some cheer, some hope, seemed like a way to keep production levels up."

She watched his brows rise over her objective viewpoint. "It might further surprise you to know that many of the employees weren't difficult about the matchup process. They were just so grateful to have an option. If you want to participate, you'll have to settle for less than Mary Poppins. It isn't my fault. It's just the reality.''

All in all, it was more reality than he could stand this close to Christmas. Unfortunately, there was no getting around it: Jayne was one sorry workaholic using a sentimental vehicle to crash through the glass ceiling at Paxton Limited. What a waste of a great kisser...

Embarrassed by his own thought, he grew stern. ''Don't think I'm dopey enough to expect a perfect mate out of there,'' he retorted, hitching a hip on her desk and leaning toward her to jab a finger at the fat envelope. ''Been there, done that. But at least select some happy, family friendly candidate. Okay?''

She beamed like a television pitchwoman holding up a can of oven cleaner. ''Simplicity itself. I promise.''

He looked down at his feet and tugged at his flannel cuffs. ''Oh, guess I should ask. You have any personal experience with kids?''

''Again, irrelevant territory, Nolan.'' She turned the question over in her mind, her eyes flashing in fear. ''You aren't foolishly considering *me* for the job, are you?''

''No way! I just want you to know up front that my girls will want a say in the decision and I wondered if you had a way of handling that angle.

Should I go get them on my lunch hour? They're home on Christmas vacation—"

"I don't know!" She threw her hands in the air, obviously at wit's end. "Kids haven't been consulted till now. All through the program, employees managed that hitch without me."

"Hey, don't pass out," he said, pinching some color into her pale cheeks. "It wasn't my intention to consider you at all. Really."

"Good! I am the idea person, the mastermind at the throttle."

"Sure, sure." He paused, waiting for her sigh of relief before dropping the bomb. "Just for your information it was Pax who wondered whether you'd like the position—at my place."

"He did?"

"Yeah. I'm just telling you as a courtesy, so you're prepared."

"If he's letting you call him Pax, he's becoming extremely attached."

"A couple of widowers chewing the fat. So what?"

"Follow the trail, man. If I don't volunteer as your caregiver, he's bound to see me as incompetent for sure!"

"Don't worry," Nick soothed. "I'll take responsibility for my choice. Tell him you tried real hard to make the grade, but just couldn't."

"What? I don't like to fail—at anything!"

Amazing what a little distress could do for a girl. Jayne had never looked lovelier outside the confines of their cupboard space, her mouth pouting provocatively, her hazel eyes deepening in hue.

His voice was a husky murmur when he sought to make amends. "Don't know where Paxton got such a notion about us," he said apologetically. "Called our pairing a real humdinger."

"He'd never—"

"Pair us up?"

"Use a word like *humdinger*." She compressed her lips. "I hope he didn't realize we were in the cupboard together. Maybe this is my punishment...."

"I highly doubt he knows." Nick tried to soothe her with his reassurances. "All in all, I'm sure his suggestion was nothing serious."

"But it couldn't have been based on much."

"Well, there *was* some chemistry to pick up on," Nick couldn't help but insist. "He merely threw out the idea for discussion, saying that you never go back home to Cleveland at Christmas." He stared down at her desk. "Any reason you don't?"

"Maybe because I'm from Baltimore. Besides, he knows all about the brunchy buffet thing at my apartment every Christmas. I'm expected!" She took a deep breath. "So, how did you handle him, Nick?"

"Hemmed and hawed, acted as though you'd be all wrong in general terms."

She stomped her foot again, feeling the pinch everywhere.

"Does that make you mad, too?" he squawked.

"You shouldn't have said flat out I was wrong, Nick—not to Pax!"

"Everybody's wrong once in a while."

Jayne sighed hard and rubbed her temples. "Women in high places can't afford to be. Besides, for all you know, I could have handled the job."

"You aren't even enrolled in your own program."

"It's the principle of the thing. I don't like to be automatically dismissed as unqualified for anything—ever! And I'll have you know, Mr. Nolan, I can cook, sew, clean and handle anything domestic."

"But you wouldn't do this time, Jayne," Nick said with odd gentleness. "So move on, be successful in finding me the right kind of woman."

The right kind... He was going to make her cry, after all. He wasn't going to know it, but the beginnings of tears were stinging the backs of her eyelids. There was no single reason for the reaction, more a buildup of little inconveniences and insults, starting with the telephone that never rang all weekend long. How could a man touch her that way and not call?

But she wanted to be equal to men every possible

way, didn't she? She hadn't turned back as she'd tripped out of the cupboard, hadn't even said goodbye, just as he pointed out. Had the guts to point out. Her excuse was that she'd simply been too darn scared at the time. If she'd seen a triumphant glint in his eyes, even hinting that she was just a notch in his tool belt, she would have died on the spot.

But the picture was growing incredibly clear now. He was more than a sexy widower with more one-liners than Seinfeld. He was a sensitive man; a doting parent who cared a great deal about his kids— enough to beg Langley Paxton for some kind of temporary mother for the holidays.

It painted a very nice family portrait. Touching, but not her style.

Now, if he'd been a bachelor with a little of that sensitivity, things would have been different. That would have been a man to take right out of the closet and show off to the world!

"You all right?"

"Fine," she said breathlessly, swallowing hard. "I just think we're drowning in our feelings here. Time to get practical."

"I suppose."

His relief was tangible, drying her eyes like a blast of desert air. "Why don't you go ahead with your work," she suggested in businesslike dismissal. "I'll thumb through the files and see what I can find."

He nodded firmly. "Okay."

"If anybody looks good, I'll send them down to the library for a preliminary meet."

He backed up a couple of paces. "Again, sorry for the last-minute pressure."

"Sorry the pickin's are so slim." She inhaled sharply as he veered for the connecting office door rather than the corridor one.

"That's Paxton's office!"

Grasping the knob, he turned back slowly. "Yes."

"Did he ask for a report?"

Nick barked with laughter. "Lighten up. I left my tool belt in there."

She joined her fingers and flexed them. "Oh. Well."

He shook his shaggy blond head. "You really shouldn't let that guy push all your buttons."

"Like you didn't get this thing started by pushing all of his. That story you told him must've been a doozy."

"'Irrelevant territory,'" he gruffly quoted.

"But as the mastermind, hoping to pinpoint the most eligible—"

"Aha." He tapped his nose and pointed to her. "Keep your pretty little button to the paperwork. Just think *nice*. N-i-c-e."

Nick picked up his belt from Paxton's empty office and breezed through Florence's office, lifting a hand to recognize her breathless greeting.

"Everything all right, Nick?"

"Fine, Florence." Nick realized the old sourpuss of a secretary found him appealing. Luckily, her affection leaned toward the platonic versus the romantic. She would be perfect for the caregiver job, if he half liked her.

Florence's thin lips pruned. "Jayne didn't upset you, did she?"

"No, of course not."

"I should've been in charge of Friends Are Family. I told Pax as much."

Nick gritted his teeth behind a false smile. He'd known all along there was some bad blood between the women, but he hadn't realized until this moment how nasty Florence could be. Why, the program was Jayne's from start to finish. "Jayne's got things well in hand," he assured. "She'll be sending candidates down to the library."

The older woman tipped her long head like a woodpecker sizing up a fine tree trunk. "Is she really?"

He made his escape down the corridor then, bracing himself against the blur of cheery faces and holiday decorations. Damn that petty Florence. It seemed now he could add righteous indignation to his list of feelings for Jayne. The last thing he wanted to do was get her in trouble with Pax, or anybody else. A part of him had also wanted to confide the whole story to her. Big mistake! She might have weakened enough to accept the job!

So she was qualified, after all. Too bad she wouldn't do. But he simply couldn't imagine keeping his hands off her if she were within easy reach under his roof. What a fine picture that would sketch out for the Millers!

Best to keep the Millers in the forefront of his mind every second, as their New Year's resolution for him was the whole reason for this fiasco.

He hitched his belt around his hip as he stepped into the law library, aware of every major muscle group knotting in sexual frustration.

CHAPTER FIVE

"WHERE HAVE YOU BEEN?" Phil glowered at Nick as he rounded the law-library door. The small, wiry man, dressed in khaki twills, was in the midst of measuring richly stained planks of shelving. "You know I can't assemble this stuff myself."

"You could."

"Not when you have my good hammer on that belt of yours." Phil made a clicking sound with his tongue as he marched up to take the tool from the loop over his partner's left hip.

Nick pulled a sheepish expression. "Sorry. Guess I can't stop making an ass of myself."

Phil's leathery face softened. "I send you on a woman hunt and you come back looking like a fox with its tail chewed off."

"Broadcast it to the world, why don't you!" Nick spun around on his heavy work boots, scanning the high stacks and wooden tables for any signs of life.

"We're alone," Phil assured. "Relax."

"As if I can, with Jayne Ashland in charge of the program. You knew it, too, didn't you?"

Phil exhaled, rubbing a hand through his salt-and-pepper hair. "Yeah. But I thought it would be worth your while to take that dose of medicine in one swallow and just lay out your request.'' His gaze flicked over the younger man's length. "By the looks of it, I'd say she laid you out. All over again.''

"It would've helped to have some advance notice about her, Phil. How could you keep quiet about this, in the center of all that Nolan hospitality?''

"It was because of your lovely girls that I kept my trap shut. I figured you'd run the other way if you knew the score. And Friends Are Family really did seem your only chance to fill that mother-figure slot. Wade through and get results—yeah, I figured that was best.''

"I did. I did just that.''

Phil brightened with hope. "You've got a line on someone?''

"Jayne's sending candidates down here.''

His brows rose. "Thought she might volunteer herself, in the name of convenience, I mean.''

"I want someone *in*convenient,'' Nick insisted. "Someone new who will not upset the Nolan harmony, who will vanish afterward without a squeak.'' With that he got to work.

A single but firm knock on the door interrupted them some twenty minutes later. Jayne entered, carrying a thin file folder in her hand. The men, in the midst of drilling screws into a massive floor-to-ceiling case, greeted her with gruff hellos.

Nick couldn't miss the way Phil paused to skim her length with appreciation. She was a knockout, after all, with a tide of rich blond hair swinging at her shoulders, sweetly rounded facial features, and the kind of willowy body that could carry the slimmest-cut suit with grace. He had no business feeling any pride or territorial urges, he chided himself.

"Sounds kind of noisy in the corridor," Nick observed. "I can't hear much through the thick walls with the drill running."

Jayne sidled closer. "I know. Florence is scurrying from office to office in a babble. It's connected to some punch-and-cookie break she's got going today." Jayne lifted her shoulders, as though summoning resolve. She opened her folder for a sober perusal. "I've come up with three possibilities."

"Wonderful," Phil observed, digging into his utility apron for some screws. "Go ahead, Nick, take a good look."

Nick set his drill on the floor at the foot of the bookcase and steered Jayne to the nearest table. She set the folder flat, tapping the top application with a coral-polished nail. "First off, there's Cybil Mullen. Twenty-three years old. Divorced—"

"At twenty-three?" Phil interrupted. "How could she have had time to make a mistake?"

"Hey, I'm not her analyst or her fairy godmother," Jayne said over her shoulder. "Anyway, Nick, she has a five-year-old daughter—"

Nick shook his head with force. "Oh, no, Jayne.

I can't have another child involved. Two's all I can handle right now."

"Okay." She slapped the application aside, tracing a finger over the second one. "There's Loretta Fretter. She's single. Childless—"

"And sixty!" Nick's eyes left the paper and rolled into the back of his head. "She won't do, either."

"I know you're fussy, which is understandable to a point. But you said find somebody nice, remember? You tapped your nose and told me to keep my button on the sniff for n-i-c-e."

From several yards away, Phil cleared his throat and aimed his drill toward the ceiling. "Didn't you tell her about the resolution, Nick?"

Nick glared at his partner. "Not everything."

"Not anything!" She was clearly exasperated, shifting uncomfortably, glancing from Phil to her watch.

Nick reddened when she homed in on him. "I'd rather not get into it."

The drill buzzed in three intermittent spurts. "It would make it easier on her, buddy."

Nick ignored his partner and forged ahead. "Who's the third candidate?" he asked above the din.

"Suzanne Detrich—"

"That vamp from billing?" he thundered. "Like

my girls need to watch her giggle and wiggle around the house in those low-cut dresses!''

"She is a little on the daffy side, but—"

Nick's glare shut her up. "She's no example for the girls. Nothing like my Sharon was."

"Is that what you're after?" she asked quietly. "A woman like your late wife?" Silence followed, punctuated by the spurts of drilling and the leaps in her pulse rate. Would he insist she herself was the closest thing the firm had to offer? How should she respond? *I can't come and save the day 'cause I've got troubles of my own?*

When he finally spoke, his voice was flat. "No. There's no one like Sharon around here. No one."

Jayne forced a faint smile. Problem solved. No regrets necessary. "Well, then. Where do we go from here?"

"I suggest you go back to your files. Narrow your focus."

"Narrow it to what? June Cleaver? Snow White?"

Humor skittered across his eyes. "Bingo."

She gasped in surprise. "If only you'd tell me that blasted story of yours, Nick. Help me understand!"

"Unnecessary, really."

In a burst of temper she collected the sparse total of paperwork, then tossed it into the air. She whooped in a fit of temper as the sheets billowed to the maroon carpet. "Go ahead, just shoot me." She pointed between her temples. "Right here, Nick. With the drill. One screw will do."

"Oh, Jayne." He said her name in a scoff, loaded with the kind of emotion worthy of ancient intimacy. She fought the tingle it sent through her body.

"Do you think Pax is going to take this well? Do you think he's going to appreciate the fact that you're impossible? He won't, I tell you! He'll blame me!"

"This can work," Nick insisted, carefully moving around the table and chairs to pick up the applications. "Listen to what I'm saying here." He held up the first sheet. "Cybil's too young and too complicated, with a child included." He slapped the paper down on the table and held up the second one. "Loretta's too old." He exchanged number two for three. "Suzanne's too much. Period."

"Fine. I know who you don't want. But I still have no reasonable picture of what you need."

A near facsimile of you without the sex appeal. Nick paused, measuring his response as he would a dose of cough medicine. "Look, about the resolution. What it amounts to is that my late wife's parents, Hubert and Doris Miller, would like to see the girls and me content again, going on...with things."

"Aren't you doing that?"

"We're perfectly fine!" Cringing at his own thunder, he made an effort for control. "They just expect too much too soon, and we hope to bluff our way through it, make a jolly holiday with a minimum amount of stress.''

"Fat chance. You're about to blow."

White-hot light flashed behind his eyes as she filled her cheeks with air, then let them explode. "Others around here are shedding tears in my honor."

Having shed her clothes, Jayne felt she'd already done her share. She smiled perkily. "Your rejection—of me for the job—has toughened me, I suppose."

"But you— You don't— C'mon, Jayne!"

He was confused by her unpredictable behavior, and rightly so. Deep inside she sympathized, empathized, and was dang near hypnotized. She desperately wanted the job. She wanted to get closer to him for a long luxurious nesting period. But there were obstacles to deal with, issues too fragile to confide.

She dipped into her jacket pocket and produced a slim gold pen. "I'll try again, if you'd supply a few more facts to go on. Ones that shouldn't invade your precious privacy too much," she quickly added as he prepared to snap. "Now where'd that folder get to?" Nick was the first to spot it under a chair and gallantly picked it up, setting it on the table before her.

Jayne poised her pen over its cover. "Give me an age group."

Nick tapped his chin. "I'm looking for someone between forty and fifty-five."

She wrinkled her nose in confusion. "Huh?"

Nick couldn't help but notice that Phil's drill had ceased to run at all. "That range seems best to avoid misunderstandings all around." He was thinking of no temptation to himself and no threat to Doris's grandmother status, but such confidences were unnecessary to someone so unmoved. "The homelier the better, too," he added.

"Ug-ly." She dashed it out in bold letters.

"Don't forget 'nice.'"

"Golly, no." She aimed the pen at him. "I even remember how you spelled it."

He rubbed the back of his corded neck, mental anguish tightening his jaw. "She has to be near perfect for the role."

"Perfect, Nick? That seems..."

"Impossible? I sure hope not. They've already lost their only daughter. The idea that their granddaughters aren't well cared for would do them in. This isn't some kind of game to me, Jayne. I truly love these people."

She closed her eyes briefly, thinking how nice it would be to be loved by Nick in that way. He was as nutty as a Christmas fruitcake, but the passion was real. Breathless. Irresistible. It was a wonder that he hadn't come across a real romance in a huge law firm like this one. Or were the women around here too snooty to appreciate a blue-collar worker?

Feeling illogical, possessive, impulsive, she rejoiced over the secrets that she did know about him. How unfortunate that his family life was exactly what was scaring her off. Suddenly she needed to escape his space, the scent of him, the powerful fallout of his emotions. With a promise for action, she glided toward the door.

"So I'll be hearing from you soon?" he asked.

Jayne paused at the door, forcing a jaunty smile. "No promises, Nolan. I may just have to fly to the Magic Kingdom to make this match."

Nick tromped back to the bookcase, waiting for the door to thump closed upon her exit before addressing Phil. "Thanks again, buddy, for involving me in this fiasco."

"You're welcome, pal." Phil didn't even register the sarcasm.

Nick picked up his drill, making it whir with the push of a button. "At least I didn't have to tell her all my secrets to get some results."

"Sure, buddy, sure." What had he left out? Phil wondered.

"THINK YOU HAVE everything straight, Jayne?"

Jayne uncrossed her legs, recrossed them, and adjusted the steno pad on her knee. "Certainly, Mr. Paxton." She smiled at her boss, who was suddenly leaning heavily across his desk, uncertainty hardening his brown eyes. It was understandable. Harold Bremer, seated in the guest chair to her left, represented one of the firm's largest accounts. She turned to Bremer with a broad, efficient smile. "I have all the changes you've ordered. I'll put Florence on the paperwork immediately."

Harold Bremer, a tall regal old gent who greatly resembled Pax, stood with a fluid grace. Jayne and Pax followed suit, stepping up for farewell handshakes. "Thanks to both of you," Bremer intoned. "Give my best to Florence."

Pax escorted his client to the connecting door leading to his personal secretary's office, opening it to find Florence still was not back at her post. "Can't imagine where that woman has gotten to."

Bremer took his leave and Pax steered Jayne back into his office. "Sorry you had to pinch-hit with the note-taking."

"I was going to be here anyway."

"Still, we all have our positions. Even if it is Christmas."

"Florence did call from someplace in the building and politely asked me to," Jayne explained, setting the spiral notebook on his desk. "Said she was unavoidably held up."

"Still…"

"I think she was in the copy center. I could hear the machines humming."

Pax wandered over to the window, staring down at the traffic congesting the street below. Jayne joined him, pausing to watch fluffy white flakes tumble from the sky, coating the dirty snowbanks and sidewalks. Unbelievably, it was nearly noon. It was unusual for her to lose track of time, or weather conditions. But it had been one of those mornings.

"How did things go with young Nolan?"

"Still working on it." Jayne went on to relate what had transpired, struggling to state the facts without revealing her growing case of severe subjectivity.

"His story was a dandy. What a fine man, caring for his in-laws that way. Sort of a poster boy for your project, I'd say. The very epitome of what family means."

"I guess."

"Such a delightful fellow, so immersed in his daughters' lives, so happy in his work, so well-rounded. Don't know many carpenters who can quote Keats, do you?"

She smiled noncommittally, her body tensing. "Don't know many carpenters, sir."

"Hate to see him left high and dry."

Was he going to do it? Suggest her for the job, as he'd done during his conversation with Nick himself?

Pax turned to openly size her up—thoroughly, as though measuring her for a suit of clothes. "I wonder...after all this fuss...if he's ready to settle for you.''

Set-tle? Jayne turned the two-syllable insult over in her mind. How could such an accomplished orator be so awkward in private moments like these? "I told you, sir, he's requested a middle-aged ugly woman.''

Pax backed down a bit. "Oh, my, I'm not implying you fit the bill, Jayne. I just thought, who better than a bright professional woman to impress these worried parents? And you two have hit it off. They'd be fooled into believing you're a real friend of the family, if that's what he wants.''

He sighed. "Actually, ironically, the job description better fits our Florence. She—'' Pax wheeled around as his secretary hustled into the room on sensible shoes, the hem of her linen dress billowing.

"Back at last," she said breathlessly, patting her high, swooping hairdo.

Pax showed some displeasure—a rarity in Florence's case. "Harold Bremer hoped to extend season's greetings.''

"Oh, dear, but it couldn't be helped.'' She seemed truly contrite, although her long face was twitching with mischief just the same. Her eyes gleamed in open triumph as they rested upon Jayne. "You'll be sure to forgive, sir, being that I've been on the hunt for Nick Nolan.''

Pax brightened immediately. "Makes our news

all the more amusing, Florence. Seems that you, of all people, are very close to what Nick ordered.''

Except for the ''nice'' streak, Jayne thought with a tight smile.

Florence, in the meantime, was making all sorts of purry sounds in modest protest. ''Me? Really? Lands, why didn't I volunteer!''

Jayne wryly noted that Paxton didn't expound on the strange qualities Nick had outlined for her in the library. ''What have you done on behalf of *my* program, Florence?'' she asked with strained politeness.

Florence stared down at the stack of bright pink flyers tucked in her arm. She peeled off the top one and handed it over for their perusal. Jayne's hand shook as she scanned the sheet along with Pax. It was an advertisement, similar in format to the ones Jayne had done for Friends Are Family. The major difference was that it was advertising Nick as a needy latecomer to the program, with the headline: Saved the Best for Last.

Florence was gleeful. ''That should capture some attention.''

''But what kind!'' Jayne advanced a step, only to feel Paxton's hand on her arm.

''You should've cleared this with Jayne first.''

''Perhaps, sir.''

Jayne curled a fist. ''Well, I'll nix it right now!''

Florence's face crumpled somewhere between regret and impishness. "I'm afraid it's a teensy bit too late for that, Jayne."

Jayne gasped in affront. "Why? You have the flyers in hand!"

"The ones for this department, yes. But these babies have been circulating throughout the firm for a good half hour."

"YOU DON'T WANT TO GO out there, man."

Nick was on bended knee, closing the lid on their toolbox, when Phil scooted back into the library seconds after leaving. He was a comical sight, his spare, wiry body flung against the massive carved door.

"What's the matter with you? It's lunchtime. I'm starved."

Phil reached into his pocket and produced a crumpled piece of pink paper, which he tossed at his buddy's foot. Still balanced on one knee, Nick took the wad and smoothed it flat on the carpet. "Huh?" His gold brows jumped to his hairline. "This is Jayne Ashland's way of helping?"

"I didn't get a good look at it, just couldn't catch my breath." Feeling no pressure on the door, Phil slowly eased away from it. "There's a wall of women out there, man." He shook his head in disbelief. *"A wall of women."*

Nick rose slowly to his feet and together they examined the flyer. He stalked over to a table holding a telephone, checked its console panel for Jayne's listing and jabbed the two-digit number. "Yeah, you. It's me. I'm still in the library. And there's a wall of women—" He listened, then stared down at the receiver. "She hung up on me!"

Phil's dark eyes shifted in fear. "How are we ever gonna get out of here?"

Nick stormed to the door and peered out into the corridor. Amazingly, there was a row of babbling female employees lining the holly-trimmed wall, each holding tight to a pink flyer. He quietly slid the door back in place.

"Psst!" Both men jumped as Jayne appeared in the stacks, looking equally as frazzled. "Sorry to startle you. I came in from through Pax's private entrance."

Nick advanced, his hands clenched at his sides. "What are you trying to do to me?"

"Nothing. This fiasco was Florence's idea."

"That's true." Paxton appeared behind Jayne, nervously tugging at the lapels of his dark woolen suit.

Nick made a choking sound. "Why, people, why?"

Pax shrugged. "Florence is a little competitive with Jayne and was trying to upstage her, I suppose."

Jayne turned to her employer. "She has no right to feel that way. I am an attorney. She is a legal secretary. Hardly common ground for any kind of one-upmanship.''

''Let's stick to my problem, if you don't mind!'' Nick interjected.

''Your problem, Nick,'' Jayne sputtered, ''is that every woman in this firm suddenly wants a muscle-bound hunk in her stocking!''

''Hmm... Guess I'm more popular than you first thought,'' Nick taunted with some satisfaction, sauntering closer to her. She was looking mighty jealous and he found himself liking it. ''Odd, the skinny folder you brought in here is nothing in comparison to this turnout.''

''Well... I—'' She broke off in a tizzy. ''You have to know they're not really serious. At least not the majority.''

''I do know that,'' he said quietly. ''Under other circumstances I might be more flattered, but not now. Not at this time.''

Jayne nodded vigorously at Pax. ''It certainly is a waste of time.''

Nick tapped the large face of his silver Timex, his voice a silky threat. ''Definitely a waste of mine.''

Paxton frowned. ''What do you mean, exactly?''

''There's no way I'm hanging around this afternoon, with all those females hovering, ready to strike. I might drill a screw through my hand—or something!''

''Are you quitting?'' Pax demanded.

"No, sir, I'm giving you the afternoon to get rid of the women. If the coast is clear, Phil and I will be back tomorrow. Right, Phil?"

Phil nodded, quickly going to gather up their belongings. Within seconds they were on their way out, through the stacks, in the direction of Paxton's entrance.

"What about the program, Nick?"

He turned back to find Jayne in hot pursuit. He suddenly looked tired, frazzled and old beyond his years. "Enough is enough. Let's just forget it." With a final nod, the pair was gone.

Jayne returned to the center of the room to find Paxton inspecting the unfinished bookcases. "They were going to finish today."

Jayne bit her lip. "I know, Pax."

"It was all going to be over."

All was right. "I was looking forward to that, too, believe me. Shall I go and disperse the crowd?"

"Splendid idea. Do it one at a time."

She gulped, leaning against a table. "What do you mean, sir?"

The old man thrust a gnarled finger in her face. "We are not giving up on our promise to help that carpenter. You dig up every possible candidate out there and get yourself right over to his place with the findings."

"Today?"

"I'd make it yesterday if I could put you in a time machine. Now get going!"

CHAPTER SIX

JAYNE LEFT WORK IN midafternoon, urged on by Langley Paxton, with enough cab fare in her pocket to get her back and forth from Nick's suburban Eagan home.

It was snowing harder now. Huge wet flakes flew against the windshield of the taxi as it roared down the freeway. It was close to three-thirty and traffic was getting heavier with the impending rush hour.

The young male driver was friendly; a student at Hamline University, he said. Jayne asked him some polite questions about his major, to which he gave her full and colorful answers. He was a classic flirt in tone and manner, intermittently peering at her through the rearview mirror as she shifted position on the back seat. Normally she would have been annoyed, insisting his complete attention be fastened on the road.

But that was life before Nick—before he'd tugged her passionate side back to the surface, making *her* feel like a college student again. She'd been so focused on her career for the past couple of years, she'd lost track of the full social life she'd known back in Baltimore. The Paxton firm had recruited her right out of law school, and she'd left everyone behind on very short notice. It had been necessary, the right thing to do. From the start she was determined to make a go of her law career.

She'd made a few friends around the Twin Cities thus far—connections through social events, surface relationships that complemented her all-important job. But real romance had never blossomed. Not that she'd ever met anyone charismatic enough to sweep her off her feet, volatile enough to rattle her senses. In short, no one had come close to sidetracking her from ambitious career goals.

Until now. Until Nick.

She stared blankly out her window at the whizzing traffic. After today's tango, there was no way she could imagine settling for her original plan to wave goodbye to Nick from some distant hallway. The bachelor father was all so wrong for her, but she still couldn't imagine letting go. Pax's errand gave her an excuse to chase him down, but she would have found something to keep the pursuit alive. Jayne barely recognized herself.

Naturally he would be intolerable now that he had that wall of women for leverage. Something basic and immature niggled at her about Nick's sudden stardom at the office. Hunk Widower in Need? It was more like Delicious Catnip to the Average Feline. He knew it was a lark, but he'd been as flattered as he'd been put off.

Her discomfort was the real problem. She'd come

to consider him her property around the office. No one had paid much attention to him before, save for admiring his sexy walk and mysterious smile. He was a blue-collar worker, so they hadn't bothered with his personality. Now, with everything out in the open, he was dynamite. The office poster boy for 1998. Happy New Year!

She recrossed her legs in the cramped back seat as the driver began to change lanes in anticipation of the Yankee Doodle Road exit. Almost there.

Jayne took a shaky breath, wishing she could curl up like a sex kitten and pull Nick back into the cupboard for more mindless communing. This whole situation was growing more complex by the second! Nick wanted nothing to do with her and here she was, rushing to his house. What would he think? What would he do...?

The driver rolled down busy Yankee Doodle Road through a patch of Eagan's business district. He eventually took a left at a stoplight, weaving his way into a residential area full of modest homes, many decorated with Nativity scenes and Santa figures.

"We're on Teaberry, miss. You know the house?"

Jayne was startled by the question, lost in her own worries. "No, I'm afraid I don't. But I believe it's a white stucco bungalow on a corner," she suddenly recalled. "With a stout oak out front with a tire swing. Dark shutters. Chain-link fence in back and—'' She stopped dead in mid-sentence as he pulled into the driveway of 4133 Teaberry Way. ''Ah, you found it.''

The student was staring at her strangely as he opened the car door for her. He had to think her daffy, or psychic. What she was, in fact, was a good listener, who had absorbed every single word the irresistible Nick Nolan had tossed at her during the past few weeks. Along the way he'd described his Eagan ''castle,'' right down to his daughters' cluttered bedroom.

Jayne laughed, feeling sheepish. ''Guess I knew more than I thought, didn't I?''

''Enough.''

Perhaps too much to remain objective in this family situation.

Jayne handed the young man her briefcase as she edged across the seat, then traded it for the fare as they stood on the snowy driveway. He nodded, touched the bill of his cap and dipped back in behind the wheel. She took a hesitant breath as the taxi backed out onto the street, brake lights flashing as a boy in a blue snowsuit scampered across with a red plastic sled in tow.

Should she use the delay to hail the taxi driver? Ask him to wait in case she was turned away? But all too soon he picked up speed and made the first corner. She trudged up to the front door and pressed the doorbell once, wiping her feet on a mat bearing a picture of an eagle. This was it. In for a pound.

She resisted the temptation to peer inside the square window at her left. That was probably for the best, as she would have startled the small cherub face that had appeared in the pane. Moments later, a lock turned and the door opened halfway. "Hello," the young voice squeaked. "Do we know you?"

Jayne smiled at the pert little blonde dressed in pink sweats, and she crouched a bit to make eye contact. "You don't know me, but you're Cassie, right?"

"How can you know me, if I don't know you?"

"Is your daddy home?"

"Nope." She tipped her head from side to side with curious innocence. "You know my daddy?"

"Yes, I—" Jayne broke off with some surprise as an older girl wedged her way into view. "Oh, hello. Are you Heather?"

"Yeah." A foot taller, a lot thinner, in the throes of adolescent challenges, Heather had already lost her girlish sweetness.

Funny how her proud papa spoke of his daughters as cut from the same childlike cloth. But Heather was a young lady—one who must be tempted at times to belt him over the head with that fact, Jayne decided wryly.

"Dad's not here," Heather said in blunt dismissal.

"Do you know when he'll be back?"

"Soon, I guess. Exactly who are you?"

"Sorry." She gave a breathless laugh, shivering as icy air swept under the hem of her coat. "I'm Jayne Ashland, from Paxton Limited. Your father's been doing some remodeling at my firm."

Heather's delicate face crunched in suspicion. "Are you the mother he was going to get? 'Cause if you are—"

"No!" Jayne exclaimed defensively, realizing the door was beginning to close. She patted the briefcase at her side. "I am in charge of the program, though." The door did swing harder then, but Jayne quickly braced her hand on it. "Hang on a second. I don't even have transportation. Can I please come in for a minute?"

Heather sighed to Grand Canyon depths. "I suppose it's okay."

"I didn't realize you're so mature," Jayne remarked, setting her briefcase on the tiles of the small square entryway. She looked around, curious about the lair behind the man. The place was small, the entry flowing right into the square carpeted living room on the right. He'd obviously used his talents wherever possible. All the woodwork gleamed and fine cabinets and shelving made the most of the limited space.

"Sounds like you do know Dad pretty well."
Heather was watching her perusal, a clever glint in
her blue eyes that reminded Jayne of her father. "He
loves to make me sound like a toddler."

"I hardly know him at all." Jayne smiled blandly,
fighting images of Nick's shadowed face in the cupboard, the sensation of his fingertips grazing her
breasts, the spicy scent of his aftershave. She closed
her eyes briefly, then snapped them open to find
Heather, arms folded across the front of her blue-
striped turtleneck sweater, studying her like a car-
nival soothsayer.

"Dad doesn't date."

Jayne feigned polite interest, even though her
pulse jumped like lightning through her system.
"Really?"

"Just thought you'd like to know."

Message received. Nick was off the market, much
to his daughter's pleasure. "Well, thank goodness
for the Friends Are Family program, then!" Jayne
lilted. "Just the thing for the busy single."

"You want a cookie?" Cassie chirped shyly,
shuffling her slippers on the tiles.

Heather sent her sister a scathing look. "Does she
look like a lady who eats Oreos?"

Cassie's chin dropped to her chest, her fluffy
blond hair clouding her face. "We don't got any
gingerbread men or frosty sugar trees."

Jayne's heart squeezed in sympathy. They had no

Christmas cookies, but knew the joy of having had them sometime in the past.

When their mother was alive.

Suddenly Jayne noticed that the bungalow was bare of all signs of Christmas. No wonder Nick was so desperate for help. The in-laws due and there was no one equipped to make this house a wonderland for the occasion. How frightened Nick must be right now. Out of options...no one to lean on.

Had Sharon Nolan been a professional home-maker? Nick had implied as much in conversation, relating small stories about his daughters' upbringing. Nothing solid; just vague remarks that added up. He'd been much more direct today in his fit of temper, stating beyond doubt that there was no replacement for Sharon in the Paxton firm. As if she would ever try!

But the longing in little Cassie's eyes for some attention was enough to melt Jayne's most chilly resolve for the moment. "I love Oreos," she confided. "Especially dipped in milk."

"You can't—" Heather halted in midsputter as Cassie made a whimpering sound. "You can't wear boots in the hallway," she went on to say. "Dad hates any tracks on his hardwood floors."

Jayne laughed, easing off her overshoes. "Your dad is a man of strong opinions."

Cassie giggled, grasping Jayne's hand in her

chubby one. "Daddy's strong everyplace. He has lots of muscles. C'mon!"

The kitchen was cozy and cluttered, with freshly painted white walls and hand-stitched floral curtains on the back-door and sink windows. The table was a chrome-framed one, with a speckled green top. This was definitely a household where corners were cut, Jayne decided, although not to sacrifice comfort. She sat in one of the yellow-cushioned chairs, while Cassie scampered around the room, standing on tiptoe to collect the package of Oreos from the bread-box and a jug of milk from the fridge. Heather sauntered in in her own time, fetching three drinking glasses from a cupboard near the stove.

They sat together in a clubby intimacy, twisting open their chocolate cookies, nibbling at the creamy white centers. Jayne couldn't help but think how much the girls happened to resemble her. Especially Heather, when she tossed her long fair hair back over her shoulders with a defiant air. And by no stroke of luck did the gesture happen to knock the chip off her shoulder. While Cassie handled her needs with bubbly puppy affection, Heather was determined to hide behind a stiff barrier of spunk. Jayne understood only too well.

"What do you do, Jayne?" Heather asked.

Jayne wondered if it was a trap, then felt some shame. It was a polite enough question. "I'm an attorney. Originally from Baltimore," she added conversationally.

Cassie's blue eyes widened. "You moved away? All by yourself?"

Jayne patted the child's hand. "Yes. I have an apartment all my own."

"What about your mom and dad?" Cassie peeped. "They just let you?"

Jayne suppressed a chuckle. "I was twenty-five at the time, had just finished law school. My father didn't mind. As for my mother...she died young, like yours."

Cassie's lower lip curled. "That's very bad."

No argument there. Jayne was rarely called upon to console anyone, but as with Nick, she couldn't help but be swept away with feeling for his daughters. "You have a wonderful daddy to take care of you, though."

"Sure, but it's been only a year and a half since Mom—" Heather suddenly stopped. "It's hard not to miss her the most now, at Christmas."

"Extremely hard." Jayne's own voice grew husky as she turned her glass around and around on the table. "Seems like it just happened yesterday, doesn't it?"

"Yeah," Heather agreed, eyeing Jayne with some respect. "A lot of people don't understand that."

Jayne lifted her shoulders. "I suppose not."

"We like being alone, especially at Christmas."

Heather was putting her to the test, Jayne knew. But she found it unnecessary to fake any of her feelings. She met the girl's flashing eyes with serenity. "Sure. Me, too. Alone can be better than other things."

"Do you get the message, then?" Heather huffed. "We don't want to be part of your company's program. And nobody can make us. Nobody!"

"I wouldn't even try," Jayne quickly assured, absorbing the new angle. Nick had said his request was mainly for the Millers, but it didn't seem right to Jayne if it was going to upset his daughters. The buffoon!

"So you can see you're wasting your time coming here."

"Probably so."

Heather paused, confused. "Is this a trick?"

"Nope." Jayne rested her forearms on the table and leaned closer. "I'm going to tell you girls the whole truth. Even your dad has changed his mind about wanting a mother figure." Loud whoops of glee sent her reeling back in her chair.

"So why'd you come?" Cassie asked. "If even Daddy don't want you."

The inadvertent crack stung deep, but Jayne kept her features even. "Because my boss, Mr. Paxton, thinks he knows what's best for everyone. He sent me over here with a long list of applicants. He insisted."

Both girls were astonished and intrigued by this new, unknown force called Paxton.

"So you see, I'm kind of stuck. I have to show the papers to your dad. It's part of my job. Even if he gets mad, I have to show him."

Heather relaxed, sinking into her chair. "We won't let Dad give you any trouble, will we, Cass?"

"No way." Cassie enunciated her words around her cookie. "Jayne hasta do it for that Paxton!"

NICK'S GIRLS WERE IN their bedroom.

The volume of their laughter made it a safe bet. It was the dinner hour and Nick had just tromped through the kitchen door. He stripped down to his flannel shirt and denims, savoring the feminine noise. It seemed they had company, judging by the cheerful chorus and the extra milk glass on the table. Just what this house needed—some gaiety from the outside, someone to snap the girls into the spirit before the Millers arrived. A pint-size pal seemed the perfect distraction.

"Honeys, I'm home!" he hollered, ruffling his damp shag of hair as he tromped through the house in stocking feet. "And whose little girl do we have for a visit?" He wheeled into their kingdom of pastel frills and white furniture, stopping short at the closest bureau. "You!"

"Hi, Nick."

Jayne. Here. Now. Talk about a distraction! She

had unbuttoned her jade jacket, opened the collar of her blouse. Her golden hair was in fluffy disarray, no doubt subject to a Cassie comb-out. She looked soft, approachable; like one of the girls. Catching their group reflection in a large wall mirror, he couldn't help but think that she appeared to round off the family circle.

A lovely mirage.

"Just getting the grand tour," Jayne ventured brightly, setting a Barbie doll back in its pink plastic dream car atop the window ledge.

Her casual greeting was an obvious signal to go with the flow. His ferocious frown might not reflect as much, but still, he knew that. But what a shock! Fight it as he'd tried, he had been envisioning her under this roof, in a bedroom.

But in *his* room, across the hall. And she'd been the swingin'-single Barbie with all those jazzy out-fits.

"Don't be mad, Daddy," Cassie said with a wag of her chunky finger.

His brows arched. "Mad about what?"

"About Paxton," Heather huffed in exasperation. "Making her come here about the mother thing."

He wrinkled his forehead in perplexity. "Oh, that."

"Pax was concerned," Jayne hastily explained. "He insisted on this house call. I've got a briefcase full of applicants from the 'wall.'"

Cassie stared up at him in wonder. "What wall?"

Nick reached out to tweak her cheek. "'A wall of women,' your Uncle Phil called them."

Heather made a disgusted sound. "You always have to stand out, don't you, Dad? Always have to look so—so great! Why can't you act like the other fathers?"

"What's the difference?" he roared. "What do they do differently?"

"They watch TV all the time, suck in their stomachs. Hire people to cut their grass, fix their cars— Regular stuff!"

"Heather," Jayne interceded, recognizing the hurt in Nick's eyes. "It's wonderful that your dad's so capable. And the more physically fit he is, the longer he'll be around."

"See," she said shrilly, "even you're attracted to him!"

Telltale heat splashed Jayne's cheeks crimson.

Nick was amused by Heather's powers to rattle Jayne, and touched, as well. So the savvy attorney did have weak spots away from Paxton's keen eye. He gallantly came to her rescue, sliding an arm around Jayne's shoulders in the wake of Heather's gasp of dismay. "Look, I'm sorry for the trouble you've gone to," he said gently. "But I feel more than ever that it's best we Nolans forget about the program."

She drooped a little, her suit seeming a size too

big all of a sudden. "Believe it or not, I have to agree."

He bent slightly to search her face. "No fight left?"

She dropped her voice to a whisper, even though there was no escaping their captive audience. "Realizing that the girls don't want anyone here, I'm sure it would do more harm than good." She poked him in the chest. "As for you, how could you even have considered it despite their strong objections?"

Nick grimaced, aware that his awestruck daughters were clued in. He saw the chance to niggle their consciences again. "I gave it a shot because Christmas means goodwill. And I thought they were old enough to understand how much older the Millers are, how much they need to see us happily settled."

"We care about them, Dad," Heather replied, her hands at her hips, tears a sure threat. "We're just not good at pretending something this big."

"Yeah," Cassie agreed, her chin thrust out a mile.

Jayne's fingers strayed to his flannel collar. "Such a shame you can't make everyone happy somehow."

Nick released Jayne in a surrendering motion. "We'll manage."

"I'm sure you will," she said evenly, hoping she didn't look as frazzled as she felt. It had been years since she'd been so involved in family conflict, and she didn't miss it. "As for Pax, I'll think of something."

"Thanks." He'd turned away from her, but then quickly wheeled back, finding the loss almost painful. The light in her green-blue eyes was like a beacon that drew him, energized him. Right now the light was dull with secret disappointment.

What did *she* want here? he wondered. Surely not the job. His daughters aside, they each claimed to have their own personal reasons against it. Although he couldn't imagine exactly what her reasons were. As for him, it was a man thing—a lust so deep that it vibrated all the way down to his toenails. He couldn't possibly sell the Millers a chaste picture if Jayne was within reach.

"Right." Jayne smiled awkwardly at the girls. "I think I'll be going now. It was nice meeting both of you."

Cassie flung herself on the double bed. "Don't make her go, Daddy!"

Nick gasped, mortified. "I'm not!"

Cassie buried her face in a yellow eyelet pillow sham. Nick rushed to the bedside and rubbed his baby girl's back.

Heather sighed hard, tapping a shoe on the pine flooring. "She could stay on. I mean, she understands us. She won't make trouble or anything."

Nick, his hip wedged on the mattress, slowly twisted around to Jayne standing behind the white footboard. Her lips were slightly parted, her eyes glazed, as though trapped in the glare of someone's headlights. How dared she look so doggone innocent when she'd just done the impossible—reached his stubborn daughters!

Cassie peeped her round face out of its downy cocoon. "I think we better feed her, Daddy. She doesn't have a mommy, or a car to drive, or anything."

CHAPTER SEVEN

"YOU'LL BE THE RUIN OF me yet, Counselor."

Jayne caught her breath as Nick sidled up behind her at the kitchen sink, drawing her against his length and placing some kisses on the back of her neck. He was so sturdy, strong. And aroused! She could scarcely believe how little it took. Or believe that she'd actually stayed to dinner to find out.

She dried the last cookie sheet with her dish towel and set it on top of the stove. "Nick, what are you doing?"

He gazed past her into the soapy water with appreciation. "Thanking you for cleaning up this messy kitchen, for starters. Heather was supposed to work on it this afternoon. I don't know what she does with all her time."

"That's because you've never been a starry-eyed girl."

"So true."

"Anyway, we made an even bigger mess with the baking," she said, "so it seemed the perfect time to get everything back in order."

"I want to thank you for that, too." He smiled at the array of freshly baked cookies on the table. "Nothing like homemade."

"It's just a simple sugar-cookie recipe of my grandmother's. One of the few I've memorized. A sprinkle of colored sugar on top and voilà!" Jayne looked with pride at the plates heaped with cookies in all different Christmas shapes. "The girls had a good time helping me."

"I know they did. Now they're planted in front of the TV."

"They did their share. You're the only one slacking off, Nolan, falling asleep in your chair." She smirked, folding the dish towel in half and hanging it on a rack.

"Yeah. I often doze off after supper, just to bank some rest."

Her soft forehead furrowed. "It must be hard, coping on your own."

"I'm not complaining. I'm luckier than a lot of guys. I'm loved."

And he loved back. Jayne couldn't stop thinking of how glorious it would be to live nestled in his warmth.

His face softened. "Funny how the girls say they're so set against a mother figure, but have nearly adopted you."

"You can't blame them for their protest, Nick. As much as they adore the Millers, they feel they can't adjust to the scheme."

"It's impossible to force-feed them anything. I found that out a long time ago. I appreciate you not hauling out that briefcase full of applicants for dessert. It would've been disastrous.'' He cracked a sly smile. ''But exactly how did you manage to win them over?''

''By promptly assuring them that I wasn't applying for the position. That threw them off guard. As for the rest, it was chemistry. Call it a kinship among daughters.''

''They said your mother died young, too.''

She turned her back on him in a pretense of tightening the faucet. ''Yes. I'd rather not talk about it.''

Suddenly he wanted to drive her melancholy away. Pushing aside the tide of hair at her collarbone, he dipped to plant a trail of small kisses along her throat.

Jayne's golden lashes fluttered to her cheekbones. It was happening all over again—the sizzling electricity, the surging desire brought on by the briefest contact. She trembled, grasping the edge of the sink. ''Where are we going with this?''

The query jolted him. Where, indeed? ''Nowhere, I suppose.''

His message was delivered in husky apology, but it stung Jayne like a resounding slap.

''I'm not ready for a relationship, Jayne. Looking for someone new has never entered my mind. But here we are, thrown together again, and I can't seem to resist temptation.''

His anxiety was real, defusing her anger. ''I wish

I understood you better, Nick—the way you kiss me, then kiss me off.''

"As if you're less complicated, woman! You show no interest in being a mother, but still you've come in here and behaved like one!''

"That's not what I said—that I have no interest in motherhood!''

"Then why don't you explain what you said?''

She was slow to respond. "Let's just drop it. People who share confidences are going someplace in a relationship.''

He made a surprising move by reaching for her hand and giving it a squeeze. "Care for a stab at friendship?''

About as much as I'd care for tooth decay. She sighed in resignation. "I suppose I should be getting home.''

"I'll drive you. It's only right, after we spent your company-allotted carfare on the Domino's pizza delivery.''

"You don't have to—''

"I want to.'' His bedroom eyes skimmed over her. "I've never delivered a steam machine before.''

"That's fine talk from a supposed *friend.*'' She tsked, a new gleam in her eye. "I think *you're* the one who needs to cool off.'' With a quick whirl she dipped into the sink for a handful of soapy suds and mashed it on his face. "There. Something for the bubble machine.''

"Why, you little lawyer, you..." With a bear-size growl he captured her face in his hands and brought his lips down on hers. Jayne could taste the soap on his tongue as it entered her mouth, sharing the bubbles. All she could react to, though, was the feel of his kiss. But as much as she wanted to give in to that feeling, to lead his kiss from playful to passionate, she couldn't. Instead, she blindly reached into the sink for more "ammo" when the telephone rang. Nick reluctantly tore himself away, moving for the yellow wall phone clamped beside the refrigerator. "Hello?" He gripped the receiver with a grim look, forcing cheer into his tone. "Hubie! Good to hear from you."

Jayne noticed that he was frantically swiping the soap from his face, while studying the magnets on the fridge door. All he was managing to do was spread the soap bubbles around. To add to the stress, the girls were barreling into the room, full of curiosity. The phone had summoned them, but it was the sudsy faces that held their rapt attention.

"Yes, the girls gave me your message. So, you still on for Christmas? Oh, you are." Nick braced himself against the doorframe, and the girls braced themselves against him, joining hands around his waist, tilting their heads into his ribs. The trio was so tensely alert, Jayne couldn't help but feel a wave of sympathy for them. "No, everything's fine. We were just having a little washing-up party here.

Sharon's reindeer ornaments? Can't say I've had a chance to look at them yet. The...ah...tree? You'll sure be surprised.''

Jayne found it hard to swallow. He was trying so hard not to lie, but the scene he was selling was so far from the lily-white truth he no doubt preached as a parent. The last of her objectivity dissipated as a gray cloud of desperation moved in through the whole kitchen. A woman of action, she wanted to snatch the phone from his hands, gaily tell Hubert Miller that everything was tip-top, or would be by the time they arrived. But she wouldn't. She couldn't. Nick had all but given her the final brush-off. *See ya 'round, when I'm not scared to love again.*

Having her own fears, Jayne knew she had no right to criticize.

He eventually hung up with a huge sigh. ''That was rough.''

''Tomorrow's Christmas Eve, too,'' Jayne said softly.

''I know that! Christmas morning in thirty-six hours. I get it.''

''Don't yell at her, Dad,'' Heather chided, flicking some soap from his nose. ''She's only trying to help.''

''But you don't want a mother figure.'' Nick looked at his daughters, then lifted his eyes to Jayne. ''And she doesn't want to be one.''

"It's not that. I—I just don't think I'm up to the job," Jayne corrected hotly. "There's a difference."

Heather blinked rapidly, fighting off tears. "This is too awful, Dad. It's wrong to hurt Doris and Hubie. We've got to do something."

"But what?" Nick stared up at the plaster ceiling, absently stroking Cassie's hair.

"One thing I can do is help you put on a Christmas," Jayne offered. The trio eyed her suspiciously and she ignored the painful pinch it caused. "It wouldn't take much to spruce up this place. Then I can disappear, long before the Millers arrive."

Nick's voice was hoarse. "I can't imagine digging out all those memories from the attic. Not this year. Not yet."

"So, we'll buy new. Nothing fancy. Just enough for minimal effect."

"That seems the best solution," he admitted. "But it seems too late now. I've lost half a day of work because of Florence's female stampede. I have to make that up tomorrow morning."

"It'll work if we plan it right," Jayne insisted thoughtfully. "I know. You bring the girls downtown and I'll keep them entertained until you finish. Things will be quiet. Most of the staff will be on vacation." She could see a seed of hope growing in his expression. "I can take the bus again and we can carpool for the day, tear up St. Paul with mad shopping."

"Yes, Daddy!" Cassie squealed, uncharacteristically making a call before Heather did.

"Trust me to think more clearly because I am on the outside, Nick. This is your last-ditch chance, but it's a good one."

Nick smiled sheepishly. What kind of woman turned around to help a guy who couldn't stop telling her they were through, once and for all? "You got a deal, Jayne, and thanks."

"Group-hug time," Heather lilted, opening an inviting arm to Jayne.

"Exactly." Nick gazed upon his eldest with such transparent approval that Jayne found her thighs on the melt again. She gratefully snuggled in to join them, only to have Cassie duck out of the circle. The child met their stares with an impish grin. "Be right back. We forgot the soap!"

"Arrg," Nick growled in frustration. "Family."

"Ahh," Jayne murmured in newfound wonder. "Family."

"NOW, WHO ARE THESE beautiful young ladies?" Florence was the first at the firm to greet Nick and his daughters the next morning. "Movie stars from Hollywood?"

"We're the Nolans from Eagan," Cassie corrected soberly.

Florence whinnied, pushing a dish of hard candy to the corner of her desk.

"Have you seen Phil yet?" Nick asked her politely.

"I have. He rode up in the elevator with me about forty-five minutes ago. He was lucky I was here to help him get in before opening time."

Nick smiled, thinking how power was ugly at times.

"Jayne was just telling Pax about your plans. He was delighted, of course." She stood, and briskly moved toward the girls, crouching over them with glee. "Did your dad tell you I was his first choice as your mother figure?"

Heather turned toward her father as she popped a mint in her mouth. If looks could kill, he would be a dead man for sure.

"Hello!" A wry-faced Jayne dressed casually in a pleated navy skirt and red angora sweater stood in the connecting doorway.

Cassie whooped with joy. "Hey, we're with her!" She charged forward as fast as her sturdy legs could pump.

Jayne stepped up to meet the child with welcoming arms, thrilled when Heather joined in. She'd had plenty of doubts in bed last night, but they seemed silly now. The girls liked her. That was of utmost importance, even taking precedence over her tussling with Nick.

Langley Paxton sauntered in on Jayne's wake, looking especially elegant in a pinstripe suit with a red carnation in his lapel. Jayne introduced him to the girls. He shook their hands with grave formality, commenting on their charms.

Nick cleared his throat as he strapped his tool belt on his hips. "Sorry I took off yesterday, Pax. Guess I've been under a lot of strain."

"Perfectly understandable." Pax frowned at Florence. "My secretary went overboard in her efforts to make you the happiest man on earth." His gaze softened upon Jayne. "Wires got crossed, and it is I who should apologize."

Jayne blushed, wondering exactly what her boss meant.

Nick didn't show any such interest in Pax's cryptic message; instead, he inched toward the corridor. "I appreciate you watching the girls. I'll make this as quick as I can."

"We'll take fine care of them, Nick," Paxton assured with a regal wave.

Cassie slipped her hand in Jayne's. "What you gonna do to us, Mr. Pax?"

His wrinkled face softened. "I've been talking to Jayne about that, and it seems fitting that Nick get a nice bonus for coming in on Christmas Eve."

"What kind of bonus?" Heather found the courage to ask.

Pax stroked his chin. "Well, I was thinking about two hairstyles at the Style Plus Beauty Salon on the floor below us. Then some new clothes from Dayton's, and some gift shopping—all on a company credit card, of course.''

"Daddy would hate those things," Heather decided, slanting a sly look at her little sister. "But we could use them for him, right, Cass?"

NICK FOUND PHIL HARD AT work in the law library, smoothing the bottom of a bookcase with a block plane. "Ah, my illusive partner."

"Sorry I'm late, Phil. Things have been really spinning. I brought the girls along."

Phil straightened, giving Nick his full attention. "Why? Don't tell me you're hiding from the Millers now."

"Of course not. They're not due until tomorrow."

"Look, I was thinking, maybe Sonia—my neighbor—and I could just pop in later with some decorations, some treats."

"Sorry, but—"

"It's not right, greeting the Millers with the stark, cold truth."

Nick stretched his torso, feeling the truth being ripped from the pit of his stomach. "Jayne's volunteered to help us get a face on the place."

Phil chuckled.

"It's not like that."

"Sure, sure, it ain't."

"She isn't staying on and I deeply appreciate it."

"But moping—" Phil cut himself short under Nick's glare.

"We'll fake it for the old folks when the time comes. Period."

NICK BARELY RECOGNIZED the girls, who greeted him back in Jayne's office at noon. "Where are my babies?" Heather and Cassie beamed, patting their elegantly upswept hairdos. Nick patted his own cheeks in dismay. "Heather, is that makeup you're wearing?"

"Courtesy of Dayton's Ultima II counter," Jayne confirmed spunkily, recognizing the disapproval shifting through his vivid blue eyes.

"I like it, Dad," Heather announced. "Makes me look the way I feel inside, for a change."

Nick swallowed hard. "Like a beautiful goddess on the brink of college?"

"Just a holiday lark," Pax interceded easily. "How's the job coming?"

Nick strained to refocus. "All finished. Phil's just collecting our tools."

Pax pushed aside his crisp white cuff to check his Rolex. "Good. Your reservation for lunch at the Radisson is for twelve-thirty."

"You heard the man," Jayne said gaily, bending to zip Cassie's pink ski jacket. "Everybody grab some stuff and head for the Blazer."

"Stuff?" Nick pointed to all the sacks and garment bags covering the chairs. ''That's Nolan stuff?''

''It's your bonus, Dad,'' Heather explained in a huff, pushing her shoulder bag higher on her shoulder, primed for a blowout.

Nick just shook his shaggy head in a daze.

Jayne sidled up to him, squeezing his arm. ''Aren't they happy? Have you seen them this way lately?''

''No. But I didn't know...this was what they'd want.''

''That's because you're not a girl,'' she retorted, pinching his cheek.

But neither was Pax—and he seemed to know. Nick was surging with feelings of gratitude, failure, and confusion. They'd had it all figured out, solitary time with no distractions. What happened to the pact?

''C'mon, Dad!'' Heather urged. ''You're holding up the show!''

''Coming, honey. Just bringing up the rear.''

''THAT MR. PAX ISN'T A BAD guy like I thought,'' Cassie said later on that day as they sat around the Nolan living room trying to assemble the artificial tree they'd purchased from the Eagan K mart. ''But you, Daddy...'' She wagged a chunky finger at him. ''You did a bad thing.''

''Me? What?''

Heather pulled a box of silver ornaments out of a sack. "You picked out Florence for us!"

"I did not!" he said hotly, gripping the modest tree as he jammed the last branch into its proper hole.

"She said so."

"Well, that's tough. Pax is the one who said she fit the bill. Though I've yet to figure out why."

"We like Pax," Heather announced, handing Cassie a silver ball to hang on the tree.

"We sure do," Cass agreed.

"Have mercy on your old dad. My butt is still cold from sitting in the truck while you ran back into that discount store to buy me a present."

"We couldn't find you nothin' at Dayton's," Cassie chided.

He expelled a lungful of air. "Okay, never mind. We all like Pax and we all know Jayne's a much better helper than Florence would've been."

Jayne reared in affront. "Gee, thanks a lot!"

Nick ruffled Jayne's hair. "That's a compliment, Nolan-style."

Jayne smiled prettily. "In that case, I thank you very much."

They got the tree in order by four o'clock, and quickly disposed of all the sacks and boxes littering the living room. The girls charged off to their bedroom to wrap their gifts in privacy, and Nick led Jayne into the kitchen for that same purpose. Or so she'd thought. She caught her breath when he gathered her into his arms for a kiss.

She looped her arms around his neck, responding to his mouth, to the hands gliding down her length. She was attempting to stow every nuance in her memory, for tonight and tomorrow, when she would be back on her own, enduring Christmas in her own protective cocoon.

She eyed the brimming grocery bags they'd left on the table, thinking that the stuff should be put away soon. Sometime soon...

It was with great reluctance that Nick eventually released her, giving her angora sweater a tug. ''I suppose we should keep on track, here.''

''To get rid of me all the faster?'' She probably shouldn't have challenged him, but things were going so well. And a part of her wanted appreciation and approval.

''No, Jayne, no.'' He paused, summoning courage. ''As a matter of fact, I wish you'd stay on this evening. You wouldn't mind missing that brunchy thing back at your apartment, would you?''

''That's tomorrow anyway,'' she said softly. ''Yes, I'd love to stay. I'll cook us a decent dinner while you wrap your gifts.''

''Gifts are all taken care of.'' He crossed the room to the cupboard over the refrigerator. He opened the door to reveal a shelf full of small wrapped boxes.

"It's not toyland, or anything. Just a few trinkets I picked up here and there."

Jayne opened her hands. "Shall we put them under the tree? Unless Cassie still believes in Santa." Her forehead creased. "I hadn't even thought of that! Hope I didn't slip."

"No, she no longer believes," he confided in disappointment. "With all the trauma of last year, the truth oozed out. But on the bright side, she does feel rather superior about the knowledge."

"There are bright sides out there, Nick. Lots of them."

"Oh, yeah?"

Her fingers grazed his jaw. "Show me where to put these groceries and I'll tell you all about them."

Nick and Jayne were just shuffling gifts under the tree when the doorbell rang. The girls raced in to answer it before either of the adults could make a move.

"Grandpa! Grandma!" the youngsters chorused, pulling the Millers and their luggage over the threshold.

"Hubie. Doris." Nick rose from his knees, tugging at his creased jeans. "You're early." Twelve hours, give or take.

Doris allowed her son-in-law to take her bulky green car coat, whisking off her woolen scarf, which she stuffed in a coat pocket. "We were concerned, dear,'' she whispered, standing on tiptoe to kiss his cheek.

"About nothing," Hubert boomed in delight as he stepped up to shake Jayne's hand. "Merry Christmas, and a Happy New Year."

"This is Jayne Ashland," Nick said in tense introduction. "Friends are family. I mean, a friend of the family." His pulse jumped in his throat as he backed away, gathering up Hubie's coat. Jayne could not believe the change in him—back to his old cautious self, facing the holiday with timid uncertainty.

She wanted to resent the new intrusion, but she quickly found it impossible. The Millers, short and plump, and merry by nature, were the fun Mr. and Mrs. Claus sort—parents she would love to claim. She readjusted some of the silver ornaments with a fortifying breath. If she didn't watch out, she would be acting as nutty as Nick.

And he was proving as nutty as a holiday fruitcake, explaining in strained detail how Jayne was a new friend he'd met on the job, and how that job had made time tight, hence the new decorations. The Millers were staring dumbly into space and Jayne didn't blame them. Nick wasn't a babbler, so why now, of all times, didn't he just shut up?

The doorbell rang again just as the girls were manhandling the Millers' brightly wrapped contributions to the tree. Jayne was closest to the door, so she answered. A familiar man in a dark topcoat and fedora was standing on the stoop, a huge deli tray in his arms. "Pax!"

"Or Santa's helper, if you prefer."

"It's Mr. Pax, Daddy!" The girls rushed up to meet him. Jayne took the food tray as they tugged the regal attorney inside like a sack of laundry. Judging by the twinkle in his eye, Jayne knew he was loving it.

"Wait for me!" a reedy voice echoed in the cold.

Jayne cringed with her hand on the doorknob as Florence scurried up the front walk, her frumpy plaid coat flapping, three bottles of champagne clenched in her hands. "Room for one more?" she greeted with forced gaiety.

"Make that three and four!"

Hearing another visitor, Jayne moved out to the stoop and peered into the street to find a truck similar to Nick's at the curb. Car doors slammed and Phil, along with a slender middle-aged woman, trotted up the walk.

Nick joined Jayne at the front-hall closet to hang up all the extra coats. "Looks like a bona-fide party," he said tensely.

"So run with it, Nick," she scolded softly. "Even if it's not the right tonic for you, take a look at your daughters."

Nick turned stiffly toward the scene in the living room, the girls with their guests, ogling the snacks on the coffee table. "You're right. But...does Florence have to sit in my big orange chair?"

Jayne had put hamburgers on the original menu and everyone heartily agreed they would be just fine. The girls had purchased some holiday CDs at Dayton's, so they brought out their boom box and got the music playing.

Nick joined Jayne in the kitchen just as she was pulling out a huge frying pan. She was sure he was going to touch her as he passed, then was painfully aware that he'd thought better of it.

"What's the matter with you, Nick?"

"Huh?"

"Suddenly you're treating me like a sister."

"Oh, that."

"Yes!" Her spatula clattered on the stovetop. "I probably have no right to ask for more, considering our agreement here, but dammit, I want more! Lots more!"

"I've been thinking the same, Jayne. It's just that...it would be simpler to wait until after the holidays—" He broke off uncomfortably.

"Why?" she cried out anxiously.

"Because of the Millers. What they'd think."

Jayne gasped as Doris appeared in the doorway. "Pax is wondering if you have glasses for the champagne— Oh, I didn't mean to interrupt anything."

"You weren't," Nick automatically said.

"Well, that's too bad, dear." Doris patted her

tight gray curls. "I thought maybe you were smart enough to see what a gem Jayne is and what a miracle to find a woman the girls like so much."

Nick stared mutely. "But— I thought—"

She made an exasperated sound. "Lands, boy, we were encouraging some dating caution for the girls' sake, not complete monkhood!"

"The girls are my foremost concern, too," Jayne assured.

Pax appeared next, carrying the bottles of bubbly. "Are we butting in?"

"Who knows?" Doris lamented.

"I certainly hope so," Pax grumbled, setting the bottles on the table with a thump. "After all the trouble I've gone to..."

"You, Pax?" Jayne moved away from the stove, homing in on her mentor.

"You think it was easy, making sure Nick and Phil saw all those posters for your program? Then, once Nick was hooked, getting him to confide his troubles? Then you had the nerve to balk over the opportunity, Jayne! So I had to strike again, feed you all that guff about Florence being the better candidate for the job, just to get your competitive juices flowing. Then the 'wall of women' came and I had to order you over here!"

Jayne pressed her hand against her chest, extremely touched. "You did all that for me? Not just to help a fellow widower?"

Pax gestured at the couple. "It was for both your sakes. Never seen such a perfect match in all my days."

Doris sighed happily and set off to tell Hubie the news.

Pax rubbed his hands together. "Now let's uncork this bubbly and have some fun. Not as much fun as you had in my cupboard, of course," he murmured dryly. "There are minors at this shindig."

Nick and Jayne flushed to a very merry crimson.

IT WAS NEARLY ONE o'clock by the time the party broke up, and half an hour after that before Nick was escorting Jayne home in his Blazer.

"Darn that Pax for all his tricks!"

Nick's eyes strayed from the freeway for the briefest moment. "I'm really grateful to him, Jayne. If it weren't for him, and you, the girls and I would be downright miserable right now. Even if we had made an attempt to celebrate, it wouldn't have been nearly as fun. A crowd is what we needed. What Sharon would've wanted."

Jayne sighed as Nick said his late wife's name with an enviable reverence. But he said her name with a new gentleness these days, too. As impossible as it seemed, they were falling in love in this whole crazy circus of circumstances. It had to be real? Didn't it?

Nick remembered every turn from his trip last

night, taking Minnehaha to Vale, making a left from Vale to the alley behind her two-story brick apartment building. He pulled into a turnabout near the garages, shielded from the glare of the streetlights by two large evergreens.

Jayne chuckled as he killed the engine. "Kids from the building park here all the time to neck."

"Anybody stop 'em?"

"I don't think anybody can *see* them. I just hear the rumors."

Nick unhooked his seat belt with a distinctive clink, then tugged off his gloves with erotic intent.

"You want to come up to my place?"

"Sounds dull." He edged across the seat, away from the steering wheel. "I think I've been dull long enough."

"Oh?"

He unbuckled her belt, and pushed her lower on the seat. Jayne rested gently beneath him, sighing as his body bore down on hers and his hand touched her knee. He began to kiss her, deeply, hungrily. She melted, giving in to the burning passions mounting in her belly. His hands were busy, the right one unbuttoning her coat, the left sliding beneath her skirt, stroking her skin through her silken hosiery. Her breath came in short bursts against his mouth. "There won't be any turning back this time."

"I love a woman who knows her mind."

The next moments were spent on buttons and zippers, and whispered endearments. She gasped as he opened her blouse wide, reaching around to unhook her bra. The truck was cooling down fast and the air chilled her skin. He pushed her bra up out of his way and took her nipple in his mouth, making it sting with hot-cold contact. She reeled from the intense new sensations, as he pressed his head to her chest. He luxuriated in her softness, kissing and kneading the tender flesh of her breasts.

Jayne massaged his back, then dipped her hands into his loosened jeans. Encouraged by his delight, she slid her thumbs beneath the waistband of his briefs. The butterfly-light movements brought him to a full, solid arousal.

"It was so much warmer in the cupboard," she teased.

"But not hotter." Near a shattering point, Nick grasped her bottom in his hands and lifted her off the car seat. Quickly he stripped away her intimate apparel. She peeled back his briefs.

It couldn't have been more awkward, bound at the knees, shivering from the Minnesota cold. It couldn't have been more exciting, stealing a naughty moment in the crisp, silent night.

Jayne made a wild needy sound when Nick touched her moist, sensitive spot, and loosed a moan of ecstasy as he moved inside her. Bracing his shoulder against the headrest and supporting her hips with his hands, he entered her over and over again in a trembling rhythm. He shivered from the cold, the risk, this insane new love.

Tensions mounted and peaked, until with heavy breaths, they sank against the passenger door. Nick rested his head on her chest, counting her heartbeats, counting his blessings.

It was Jayne who finally nudged them both back to reality, wiggling back into her underwear. Nick sat up, readjusting his clothing with a brisk shudder. "Damn cold. Oh, yes."

She leaned over to kiss his jaw as she buttoned up her blouse. "You care to come in now?"

He grasped her shoulders for one last kiss. "I love you so much," he confessed in wonder. "And I can't tell you how much I appreciate everything you did to make tonight happen."

She grinned mischievously. "Which part did you like best? The bump or the grind?"

He sobered. "I mean the holiday arrangements, getting the girls out on the town, all dolled up. It was a brilliant scheme, right down to the fake tree and trimmings."

She absorbed his words warily. "'Scheme' is hardly the right word, Nick."

"Hey, I don't mind," he marveled. "I needed to be tricked, led around by the nose. I was drowning in my own misery and I couldn't see straight."

Jayne sat up taller, pulling her coat closed in a

defensive gesture. "I still don't see what you mean by 'scheme.'"

"Call it manipulation if you will. Lucky thing the Millers showed up when they did." He paused in thought. "Or I suppose you'd have had to come back tomorrow with the same crew." He tapped her nose. "You'd have done it somehow, though. There was no other way to prove that 'friends are family' than to arrange for the brood to descend all at once. You are one savvy operator."

"Nick Nolan," she squealed. "I did not manipulate you!"

"I don't mind."

"I didn't do it!"

"Okay, if you say so. But does it matter? You're the smart one, Jayne. You realized we could work long before I did. I'm the dimwit."

"Oh, yes, you are that." Her voice was high and tight, and it finally sank in that he was in big trouble.

He reared back in shock. "What am I doing wrong here?"

She clenched her hands in her lap. "Nick, it's important that you understand I played no tricks on you—from the start."

"C'mon, Jayne."

"I did everything with your daughters' welfare at heart, tonight in particular. I had no intention of staying on. It follows that I did not invite any of those other people to join us."

"But Pax—"

"Pax dropped in on his own. He might have insisted you call me back had I left, but I didn't invite him and I didn't scheme with him. My guess is that Pax invited Phil. They even arrived together!"

"Jayne, this is nothing to fight about—"

"It's something big to me."

"Why?"

She sniffed in the darkness of the truck. "Because I had a stepmother forced on me." She turned to face him, raw with fury. "Never, ever, would I force myself on your girls. I would've left after we set things up tonight." Her voice filled with tears. "Or at any other point that I felt unwanted."

"I wish you had told me sooner. I blamed your career drive for your attitude. You seemed so savvy, so confident, that I never would have suspected."

"I wanted to tell you, but I was afraid. All along you've treated me like a forceful career woman. I didn't want to risk your not believing or understanding. Don't you see? My past is my weakest flank. To share it takes so much out of me. Believe me, Nick, I'm a caring woman first, just like your Sharon was. A woman who would like the chance to mother, who would like to shed her armor along with her business suit every night. I am not some snappy operator trying to fill a man's shoes. Why, half my own shoes are too tight for me."

"Oh, Jayne, it's amazing we've managed to come

this far." Nick reached out for her, but she sidled toward the door.

She went on, as if on a tirade. "Furthermore, it really hurt me that you didn't want to claim me in front of the Millers. What was that talk about caution between you and Doris? I'm not cheap or a gold digger."

Nick rubbed his eyes, aware of a stinging sensation behind his lids. "I simply had their message all screwed up. They had warned me about harming the girls with the wrong kind of dates and I jumped to the conclusion that they secretly couldn't bear to see me with any woman."

An awful fear lodged in her throat, but she forced the words out. "Look, maybe this isn't the kind of real love your family needs. We've had fun, but we've also been slow to trust, kept important things from each other that should've been aired."

"What do you mean, exactly?" he asked hoarsely.

"Maybe it's just best we slow down...see if this is all holiday glitter—or something deeper."

He rubbed his face with his hands, almost afraid to ask. "You aren't coming tomorrow, are you?"

"No," she said on a sob. "I think it's best that I...do my brunch thing like always. Tell the Millers that we decided you needed some bonding time." With that, she lunged out of the truck and ran to the back door of her building.

Nick got out and rushed after her. "Jayne, wait. How long do we need?"

"Quit treating me like the troubleshooter!" Jamming her readied key into the lock, she burst inside and shut the door right in his face.

"But you are trouble with a capital *T*." Turning up the collar of his jacket against the chill, he walked down the alley. Once in the truck, he inhaled the lingering scent of Jayne's passion—and wished he could go back and inhale all his mistakes just as easily.

"YOU'RE LATE."

Heather, junior head of the house, was waiting up for him again, dressed in her peach gown. Nick was glad he'd stopped in the garage to make sure he was properly put back together.

"Merry Christmas, baby. Officially." He kissed her forehead.

"You've made it the best it can be, Dad."

Nick arched his brows. "Yeah." *Right.* He studied his daughter closely for the first time. "Isn't that toilet paper wrapped around your hair?"

She patted her head. "Grandma said it helps keep the 'do' fresh."

"Oh." Nick sat at the table and unlaced his boots.

Heather sidled closer. "When I grow up, I want to be like Jayne."

"Really?"

"I mean, she's just perfect, isn't she? Efficient at work, soft at home."

"You noticed that, eh?"

"Why, sure. An hour in her office and any dope would see it."

Any dope but him.

She rubbed her hands together. "Tomorrow should be great. Everybody's in the spirit."

Nick decided to test the waters with his bad news. "Jayne's not coming tomorrow. We decided we need quality time with the Millers."

Heather sighed wistfully. "Isn't she the smartest, Dad? Understanding that our hurts are so personal to us? That we still need some space?"

Nick bared his teeth. Even when the woman was being damn difficult, she was getting credit. "I expect she'll give us the whole week to heal."

Heather yawned. "There's always New Year's Eve to make up for it. Doris and Hubie will be leaving that morning, probably sick and tired of us."

He stared at his drab gray socks. "We'll see."

"Oh, Jayne will see to it, silly." With a flutter of fingers, she was off in a peach swirl.

Nick banged his head on the table. Twice.

CHAPTER EIGHT

THE NOLANS DEPOSITED the Millers on a plane New Year's Eve morning amid teary eyes, frantic hugs and promises of a return trip this summer. Nick noticed the way Doris and Hubert were glancing around the terminal before boarding, no doubt hoping to catch a glimpse of Jayne, charging up to wish them well.

He'd explained in his own clumsy way over and over during the week, that Jayne thought it best they have some private family time. Oddly, though, it didn't discourage them from speaking of her nonstop, referring to her place in their family's future.

The in-laws were just too smart for his own peace of mind. They sensed the urgency of the relationship, and not only accepted it, but encouraged it. How ironic, that he first tried to conceal his romantic euphoria for their sake, and now was having to conceal the breakup from them, as well.

As much as he loved the Millers, he was ready to hand-carry each of them to their seats by the time boarding began.

NICK AND THE GIRLS arrived home to the smell of bacon cooking in the kitchen. Unfortunately, Phil was the "mother figure" on hand.

Phil easily read Nick's mind as the latter slammed the back door closed. "Who were you expecting? Betty Crocker?"

"A real live girl would've been nice."

"Yeah," Cassie peeped. "Like Jayne."

Phil suggested the girls wash up and change into play clothes as he whisked a platter of pancakes from the warm oven.

Nick unlaced his boots on the rug and crossed the kitchen to slap his pal on the back. "Happy New Year."

"It could be." Phil glared at him and delivered the platter to the table.

"Look, this is mostly Jayne's fault. She shouldn't have gotten so mad just because I suggested she's aggressive."

"The word was *manipulative*," Phil gladly corrected. "And I think she pretty much explained why it upset her. No woman I've ever met wants to be romanced in powerhouse terms. You been in a cave for half your life?"

"Yes!" he seethed. "I was happily married, romancing a mild-mannered woman. I don't mean to be a drag, but this whole thing seems more doomed with every passing day. I keep making tactical mistakes. First not claiming her as a love interest backfired in front of the Millers. Then the fight over my intended compliment, and finally my decision to try the deep freeze on her this week.''

"Romeo, Romeo.'' Phil rolled his eyes, and headed for the coffeemaker. He poured two steaming mugs and handed one to Nick. "The deep freeze? Jeez.''

"I thought she might miss us enough to come back. As unsure as I am about my charms, it seemed the safest bet. I did it for her, too,'' he added defensively at Phil's groan. "It didn't seem right to pressure a woman into accepting a brood like mine. Lots of women don't want stepchildren, and she had a bad experience as one herself.''

"So you told me. But she's crazy about the girls. Any fool can see that.''

"But she didn't miss them—us—enough to check in.''

The snap of Heather's bubble gum startled the men. She'd changed into some tattered corduroys and a white sweatshirt, and was focused on the appetizing food. "Cassie's coming.'' She slipped into her chair and took a sip of juice. "You aren't mad at Jayne, are you, Dad? I mean, Cassie would be upset to hear it.''

Nick's heart squeezed. Cassie wasn't the only one. Big sister had a major case of hero worship and was openly concerned. He felt helpless, as usual. "I was just telling Phil that Jayne hasn't checked in...lately.''

"Why should she?" Heather hooted, tossing her blond hair back.

Nick stared mutely. *Why? Because the deep freeze was supposed to tear her heart out and send her running back. Make his life worth living.*

"I mean," Heather went on, breaking a bacon slice in half, "Cassie calls her three or four times a day, as it is."

"What!"

"Brrr, the deep freeze." Phil folded his arms with a fake shiver.

Heather stared at the men as though they were a couple of morons. "She's like family now, Dad, she cares so much about us. Say, you aren't jealous that we've been going to her for advice, are you?"

Nick sank into his chair, sloshing coffee on his sleeve. "Maybe you should tell me about some of these conversations."

NICK WAS FRUSTRATED to find that Jayne's apartment building had a security system at each entrance. He couldn't bear to be rejected through a squawk box. He stood outside on the sidewalk in the early-evening chill, staring at the string of headlights along Minnehaha Avenue, wondering what to do next. He hadn't planned this trip out very well. He'd just grabbed a plastic horn and some paper hats from the New Year's stash and shot off in his Blazer.

He had a stroke of luck moments later when an elderly woman approached with a sack of groceries. He shouldn't have even considered taking advantage of the situation, but he couldn't resist. He waited for her to buzz her husband, then followed her inside, remarking that he was visiting Jayne. The woman knew Jayne and gratefully allowed him to carry her sack up the flight of stairs.

Jayne answered her door on the second knock. Dressed in black leggings and an aqua blouse that did wild things to her blue-green eyes, Nick vehemently cursed himself for wasting a whole week brooding about their differences.

"Happy New Year," she greeted in crisp attorney tones. If it hadn't been for the quiver in her hand, he might have bailed out then. Instead he stepped inside without invitation, closing the door for her. Fluffing her hair, she sauntered over to her small cluster of beige chairs. "So, how are things?"

"You know exactly how things are."

She turned to him in profile, her mouth twitching. "Do I?"

"Quit answering my questions with questions!"

She backed down a little, facing him. "Ah, so you've discovered the in-house stoolie, have you?"

"Oh, Jayne..." He trailed off in hoarse lament.

Her chin quivered as she watched his giant presence take over her small space, just like back at the office. "Cassie called first thing Christmas Day, just to wish me a merry one. I didn't know how long it would be until you revealed our breakup, but I invited her to call anytime. I took one day at a time after that, trying not to get my hopes high." She smiled tentatively. "But she just kept on calling."

"Over and over again, for advice on everything from making my good tie clip into a hair barrette, to spreading Cool Whip on cookies, to bleaching her bedspread, to putting a mudpack on Doris—with real mud!"

"Mistakes?"

"The Cool Whip was pretty good. But the other stuff..." He grimaced. "Dug a mighty deep hole in the frozen ground for that mud."

"It's tough making judgment calls over the telephone."

"Then why weren't you there? Where you belong, dammit!" Startled by his own admission, he took a ragged breath. "I mean, if a woman's going to give advice, she should be held accountable...." He nodded vigorously. "Yeah, that's right. Accountable."

Jayne rubbed her temples, blinking back the tears. "Look, I found I still desperately wanted to be a part of things, and this seemed the only way."

He ran his hands through his thick mass of hair, bewildered, furious. "I've been tortured over losing you, and here you are, with your thumb on the pulse of my household all the time, playing the mother figure behind my back!" He pinned her with a wild glare. "Why didn't you just come over? In the worst scenario, the family would've closed their wagons around you." *As if that would have been necessary!*

She answered matter-of-factly, amazed that he didn't understand. "Because you originally accused me of being heavy-handed, Nick. Naturally, I didn't want to make that mistake again."

"Oh. I see." And he really did, finally. The move had been his. He owed it to her.

She sauntered closer, seeking his wandering eyes. "So what's your excuse? Why didn't you come here?"

He was slower to respond. "Because it seemed so much to ask of a young single woman—to take on all the Nolan baggage."

"I suppose I didn't make my delight very clear during that rampage, did I?" She smiled contritely. "I just poured out my sad stepparent experience and dashed away. But I do adore those girls. And I like the Millers." Her shoulders sagged in defeat. "What's the use? Maybe in the long run I'm just not cut out for commitment. Every move I make is wrong."

"Same here."

She gave a sad laugh.

Nick noticed for the first time that not only was Jayne dressed up, but she was wearing full makeup. "So you have plans for tonight?"

Her soft forehead wrinkled warily. "Why?"

"Because you're all...beautiful."

"Even now you can't spill out an invitation!" she cried out in disgust.

"Huh?"

"My door has a peephole, Nick. Do you think if I had plans with anybody else, I would've let you in for this kind of emotional scene?" She grasped his sinewy arms and gave him a shake. "My stoolie called and said you were coming. Half an hour ago, I was hanging around here in a ratty robe, looking at *TV Guide*." She threw her hands in the air and turned her back on him. "You just leave me no dignity at all. How can I love a man every bit as clumsy as I am?"

"Would this be a good time to propose marriage?" he asked bleakly.

She spun back around prepared to throttle him, only to find he was wearing a pointy paper hat on his head, a tender gleam in his eye. Wrapping his lips around a little toy horn, he gave it a toot. "I mean, it, honey. I've come to accept that I've been in love with you since our first round of words. After this week, I can't imagine losing you ever again."

"You came over to propose? Really?"

He raised a hand solemnly. "Carpenter union's honor."

Her heart squeezed with joy. He did mean business. "Well, I guess if you ditch the crazy hat, we may have a chance."

"No way." He reached into his pocket and pulled out another one. "Put yours on and we'll go crazy together."

She inched her arms around her neck, easing her body close against his leather jacket. "So what do you have in mind for tonight?"

"A little family thing at my place, some talk about a marriage resolution for the New Year."

Jayne beamed. "I can't wait to tell the girls."

He worked open the top button of her blouse, moving his mouth over hers. "We'll make it. One resolution at a time..."

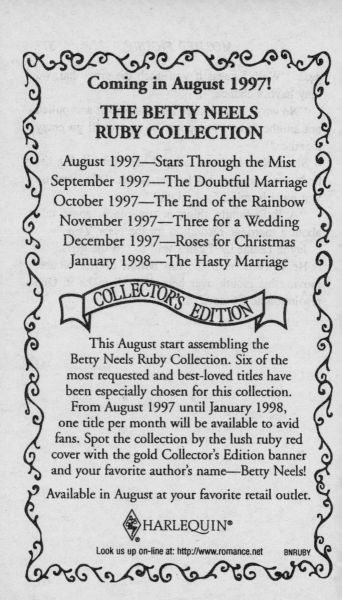

Coming in August 1997!

THE BETTY NEELS RUBY COLLECTION

August 1997—Stars Through the Mist

September 1997—The Doubtful Marriage

October 1997—The End of the Rainbow

November 1997—Three for a Wedding

December 1997—Roses for Christmas

January 1998—The Hasty Marriage

COLLECTOR'S EDITION

This August start assembling the
Betty Neels Ruby Collection. Six of the
most requested and best-loved titles have
been especially chosen for this collection.
From August 1997 until January 1998,
one title per month will be available to avid
fans. Spot the collection by the lush ruby red
cover with the gold Collector's Edition banner
and your favorite author's name—Betty Neels!

Available in August at your favorite retail outlet.

HARLEQUIN®

Take 4 bestselling love stories FREE

Plus get a FREE surprise gift!

Special Limited-time Offer

Mail to Harlequin Reader Service®

3010 Walden Avenue
P.O. Box 1867
Buffalo, N.Y. 14240-1867

YES! Please send me 4 free Harlequin American Romance® novels and my free surprise gift. Then send me 4 brand-new novels every month, which I will receive months before they appear in bookstores. Bill me at the low price of $3.12 each plus 25¢ delivery and applicable sales tax, if any.* That's the complete price and a savings of over 10% off the cover prices—quite a bargain! I understand that accepting the books and gift places me under no obligation ever to buy any books. I can always return a shipment and cancel at any time. Even if I never buy another book from Harlequin, the 4 free books and the surprise gift are mine to keep forever.

154 BPA A3UM

Name	(PLEASE PRINT)	
Address	Apt. No.	
City	State	Zip

This offer is limited to one order per household and not valid to present Harlequin American Romance® subscribers. *Terms and prices are subject to change without notice. Sales tax applicable in N.Y.

UAM-696   ©1990 Harlequin Enterprises Limited

LOOK FOR OUR FOUR FABULOUS MEN!

Each month some of today's bestselling authors bring
four new fabulous men to Harlequin American Romance.
Whether they're rebel ranchers, millionaire power brokers
or sexy single dads, they're all gallant princes—and
they're all ready to sweep you into lighthearted fantasies
and contemporary fairy tales where anything is possible
and where all your dreams come true!

You don't even have to make a wish...
Harlequin American Romance will grant your every desire!

Look for Harlequin American Romance
wherever Harlequin books are sold!

LI198

**Look for these titles—
available at your favorite retail outlet!**

January 1998
Renegade Son **by Lisa Jackson**
Danielle Summers had problems: a rebellious child
and unscrupulous enemies. In addition, her Montana
ranch was slowly being sabotaged. And then there was
Chase McEnroe—who admired her land and desired her
body. But Danielle feared he would invade more than just
her property—he'd trespass on her heart.

February 1998
The Heart's Yearning **by Ginna Gray**
Fourteen years ago Laura gave her baby up for adoption,
and not one day had passed that she didn't think about
him and agonize over her choice—so she finally followed
her heart to Texas to see her child. But the plan to watch
her son from afar doesn't quite happen that way, once the
boy's sexy—*single*—father takes a decided interest in *her*.

March 1998
First Things Last **by Dixie Browning**
One look into Chandler Harrington's dark eyes and
Belinda Massey could refuse the Virginia millionaire nothing.
So how could the no-nonsense nanny believe the rumors that
he had kidnapped his nephew—an adorable, healthy little boy
who crawled as easily into her heart as he did into her lap?

**BORN IN THE USA: Love, marriage—
and the pursuit of family!**

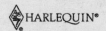 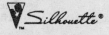

KEY ♡ TO MY HEART

Unlock the secrets of romance just in time for the most romantic day of the year— Valentine's Day!

Key to My Heart
features three of your favorite authors,

**Kasey Michaels,
Rebecca York
and Muriel Jensen,**

to bring you wonderful tales of romance and Valentine's Day dreams come true.

As an added bonus you can receive Harlequin's special Valentine's Day necklace. FREE with the purchase of every *Key to My Heart* collection.

Available in January,
wherever Harlequin books are sold.

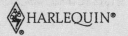

HARLEQUIN®

PHKEY349

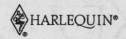

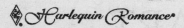

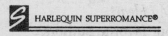

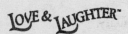